Neala stopped cold and looked at the devastating man. "I do not like in the least what you are doing."

Winterton paused and turned to face her. In the moonlight, she thought his dark gaze seemed unusually intent. "What *am* I doing, Miss Abercorn?"

Neala fought for control. On the one hand, she wished to slap his face for making sport of her; on the other hand, she . . . well, the thought crossed her mind to . . . oh! if she weren't so angry, she would . . .

Winterton moved a step closer to her. She felt his hand slip round her waist, and the pressure of that warm clasp on her back moved her gently, urged her close to him, and then even closer. When they were standing toe to toe, and his eyes fixed on her mouth, she knew that he meant to . . .

Trying to ignore the tingling shivers that quivered through her, Neala parted her lips to protest, but instead, the gentleman lowered his head and lightly, ever so lightly, brushed her mouth with his.

It was heavenly.

"Lord Winterton," she gasped. "I don't feel at all like myself."

"On the contrary, Miss Abercorn." His voice was hoarse. "You feel . . . magical!"

ZEBRA'S REGENCY ROMANCES
DAZZLE AND DELIGHT

A BEGUILING INTRIGUE (4441, $3.99)
by Olivia Sumner

Pretty as a picture Justine Riggs cared nothing for propriety. She dressed as a boy, sat on her horse like a jockey, and pondered the stars like a scientist. But when she tried to best the handsome Quenton Fletcher, Marquess of Devon, by proving that she was the better equestrian, he would try to prove Justine's antics were pure folly. The game he had in mind was seduction—never imagining that he might lose his heart in the process!

AN INCONVENIENT ENGAGEMENT (4442, $3.99)
by Joy Reed

Rebecca Wentworth was furious when she saw her betrothed waltzing with another. So she decides to make him jealous by flirting with the handsomest man at the ball, John Collinwood, Earl of Stanford. The "wicked" nobleman knew exactly what the enticing miss was up to—and he was only too happy to play along. But as Rebecca gazed into his magnificent eyes, her errant fiancé was soon utterly forgotten!

SCANDAL'S LADY (4472, $3.99)
by Mary Kingsley

Cassandra was shocked to learn that the new Earl of Lynton was her childhood friend, Nicholas St. John. After years at sea and mixed feelings Nicholas had come home to take the family title. And although Cassandra knew her place as a governess, she could not help the thrill that went through her each time he was near. Nicholas was pleased to find that his old friend Cassandra was his new next door neighbor, but after being near her, he wondered if mere friendship would be enough . . .

HIS LORDSHIP'S REWARD (4473, $3.99)
by Carola Dunn

As the daughter of a seasoned soldier, Fanny Ingram was accustomed to the vagaries of military life and cared not a whit about matters of rank and social standing. So she certainly never foresaw her *tendre* for handsome Viscount Roworth of Kent with whom she was forced to share lodgings, while he carried out his clandestine activities on behalf of the British Army. And though good sense told Roworth to keep his distance, he couldn't stop from taking Fanny in his arms for a kiss that made all hearts equal!

Available wherever paperbacks are sold, or order direct from the Publisher. Send cover price plus 50¢ per copy for mailing and handling to Penguin USA, P.O. Box 999, c/o Dept. 17109, Bergenfield, NJ 07621. Residents of New York and Tennessee must include sales tax. DO NOT SEND CASH.

Marilyn Clay

Bewitching Lord Winterton

ZEBRA BOOKS
KENSINGTON PUBLISHING CORP.

ZEBRA BOOKS are published by

Kensington Publishing Corp.
850 Third Avenue
New York, NY 10022

First Printing: September, 1995

Printed in the United States of America

This book is dedicated to . . .

Emily Braswell, my first critique partner—
thanks for all the great talks, lady.
To Kathryn Young, who believed in me more than anybody;
and whose encouragement and enthusiasm
for my efforts never once wavered.
To Paul and Freeda Botelho.
Thanks for all your great help with
The Regency Plume, *and for* wanting *to read*
my books as I wrote them. Your help and support
have meant so very much to me.
To my family—Bert, Mary, Freida and Linda—who
each in their own way have been helpful and inspiring.

And, lastly to Denise Little, my wonderful editor at Zebra,
who offered *to read my book . . . and*
then made my dream come true.

Thank you all!

One

"What a good 'un 'ye are, Nealie girl," said Miss Neala Abercorn's grandmother, as Neala helped Grandma O'Grady into a comfortable chair near the fire. Grandma, close on seventy years of age had just traveled by stage from Ireland to London, and Neala was certain she must be feeling quite fatigued from the long journey.

"There, now," said Grandma, sinking into the cushions with a sigh, then glancing toward sixteen-year-old Lilibet, who had followed her older sister and grandmother into the small parlor. With her blond curls and blue eyes, Lilibet did not look the least like her older sister, brown-haired Neala. "And here's me other gran'daughter, the birthday girl."

"Did you bring my present, Grandma?" Lilibet asked, her blue eyes round as she perched prettily on the faded mulberry silk sofa across from the elderly woman. "I declare I cannot wait another minute to see what i'tis!"

"Lilibet," Neala scolded, "Grandma O'Grady only just got here. We must see to her comfort first. Are you warm enough, Grandma? Perhaps I could fetch your shawl?"

"T'would be lovely of you, Nealie girl. What a good 'un 'ye are," she murmured again.

Neala managed a feeble smile. It had been five years since she had seen Grandma O'Grady and she was delighted to see her, but constantly being referred to as the 'good 'un' already felt a bit wearying. Though she supposed she should be accustomed to it by now. Mama had called her the 'good 'un' almost since birth, just above two decades ago.

Neala headed across the tiny parlor which the girl's mother, Lady Abercorn, persisted in calling the 'drawing room'. Passing Lilibet, she caught sight of the mocking gaze in her younger sister's bright blue eyes.

"Fetch my present, too, Nealie," Lilibet ordered, then turned again to Grandma. "Mama says you were bringing me a wonderful surprise, Grandma!"

"Sure, 'an I am, Miss Lilibet. 'Ye may as well bring the girl her package, Nealie, dear," Grandma called after Neala, the musical sound of her Irish lilt stirring something deep inside Nealie. " 'Ye'll find it nestled just inside me trunk. A pretty parcel, it is, too," she said to Lilibet, "all tied up with a pink satin ribbon."

On her way down the bare corridor toward the small guest bedchamber at the back of the house, Neala wondered why she was feeling so downcast today? Since Grandma had just arrived and since it was Lilibet's birthday, she should be feeling quite the thing. But she wasn't.

Perhaps it was because this was the first special occasion the Abercorns had celebrated since Papa died. Not that they were doing this one up proper, not by a long chalk. Sure, she and Mama had managed small gifts for Lilibet, but linen handkerchiefs and a new bonnet were a far cry from the manner in which Papa used to shower them all with finery; and not just on birthdays, but at Christmas and sometimes for no reason at all.

When Neala's lower lip began to tremble, she bit it to keep from crying. How *very* much she missed Papa, though she knew Mama didn't. She pushed down a pang of irritation. Papa *was* a good father and a very generous man. True, he may have enjoyed his drink a bit too much, and he might have lingered at the gaming table a trifle too long, but he was a good man none the less, and he did not deserve to be . . . She could not finish the thought.

Reaching the darkish little bedchamber at the back of the apartment, which Neala had tried to brighten up earlier with a bouquet of yellow daisies and purplish sweet William, she sank to her knees to open Grandma O'Grady's leather trunk. After pulling out the knitted green wool shawl and the birthday gift, a rather large parcel, she thought, she also took the liberty of laying out a few of Grandma's things—her warm nightrail, a wooly robe and a thick eiderdown quilt.

On her way back to the parlor, Neala heard the front door of the tiny flat open and close. Mama was home. A part of Nealie's mind wondered if Mama had been successful this afternoon in selling Lady Feathergill the design Nealie had sketched last evening for Lady Feathergill's new ball gown. If Mama had secured the commission to fashion the gown, it would mean food on the table for another month.

Hearing the joyful cries of Lady Abercorn's reunion with her mother, Neala smiled ruefully. She hadn't heard Mama laugh since the day news reached them of Papa's death. But Mama's delight then had been short-lived, for in less than a fortnight Mama had learned that her husband had gone through every last penny of the vast Abercorn fortune he had inherited upon reaching his majority.

Neala forced a bright smile to her lips as she reentered the parlor. "Here you are, Grandma," she said, as she handed the elderly woman the warm shawl.

"Thank 'ye, girl. What a good 'un, 'ye are."

"Nealie," her mother glanced up, impatience in her voice, "where's the tea? And the lemon cake? I declare," she exclaimed to Grandma O'Grady, "I cannot think what has got into Nealie today, she's always such a good 'un!"

"Never mind scolding her, Fiona, i'twas meself who sent the gel fetchin'." Grandma draped the shawl across her shoulders, then turned to Lilibet. "Now, let's have a look at Miss Lilibet's birthday present." Her watery grey eyes indicated the package Nealie still carried under one arm.

"Oh, Mama, can I open it now?" Lilibet snatched the parcel from Nealie and pressed it to her own bosom.

"Not yet, dear. Nealie, get the tea things, will you?" Lady Abercorn pulled up a chair and sat down while Neala headed obediently for the kitchen.

Though it had been a twelvemonth since they had moved from their lovely home in Mayfair; it still seemed odd not to ring for the servants when they desired tea, or when they desired anything, for that matter. All they could afford now was old Mrs. Montcreif, the elderly lady who lived in the next building. Twice a week, Mrs. Montcreif came in and did the cleaning and the shopping, since Mama's pride still refused to let her set foot in any of the shops. "Wouldn't do to let the servants of my dearest friends see me at the market buying potatoes and fish, now would it?" she had said.

Mrs. Montcreif also did the baking. She had come in this morning, and consequently the larder was now full of meat, fresh produce, delicious smelling bread and two pans of Lilibet's favorite lemon cake.

As soon as Neala had brought in the tea things and everyone had been handed steaming hot cups of it and a slice of the iced lemon cake, Lady Abercorn gazed fondly round at the small gathering.

"This is indeed a special occasion," she said solemnly. Neala glanced up from her plate, detecting a hint of something *odd* in Mama's tone. "Not only are we honored to have Grandma O'Grady here with us," Lady Abercorn went on, "but I've something of great import to share with you girls."

Neala's curiosity was fully aroused now.

Lilibet had also looked up. "Have we inherited another fortune?" she asked. "Because if we have, I should like to—"

"Hush, Lilibet!" Lady Abercorn said, her tone sounding more like it usually did. Stern. "What I have to say is *very* important. It is not to be repeated to anyone. *Anyone,* do you understand?" Fierce Irish eyes pinned both her daughters in turn. When they had both nodded obediently, Lady Abercorn continued. "Now then. As you girls know, my life with your Papa was . . . less than amicable; but, now that your Grandma O'Grady is here . . ." Lady Abercorn's voice trailed off. "W-Why don't you tell them, Mother."

"Nonsense, Fiona! The *Faie* spell is meant to be handed down from *mother to daughter.* Though I do recall it once went to a cousin, and it worked equally as well. But, 'tisn't my place to tell them. You must."

What on earth was Mama trying to say, Neala wondered.

"Oh, do tell us, Mama!" Lilibet cried impatiently. "I want to open my present!" She reached again for the package which Lady Abercorn had insisted she put aside while they had tea and cake.

"Do be still, Lilibet!" Lilibet fell silent and Lady Abercorn began afresh. "What I have to say concerns something that happened a long time ago, but now it affects all of us, especially you, Lilibet." A nervous smile flitted across Lady Abercorn's face and again she glanced toward her own mother.

"For pity's sake, Fiona," the elderly woman sputtered, "let the child open the gift! Sure, an' she sees what i'tis, it will be that much easier to explain."

"Very well," Lady Abercorn said. "You may open your present now, Lilibet."

With a squeal of delight, Lilibet tore into the wrapping, flinging aside the pretty pink ribbon and sending tissue paper wafting to the floor.

"Do be careful, Lilibet," her mother admonished, " 'Tis . . . quite old."

When Lilibet turned back the last layer of tissue paper, her brows drew together in a frown. As she held the soft folds of ivory fabric up before her, a dejected sounding, "Oh-h," escaped her pink rosebud lips.

Having vacated her chair, Lady Abercorn was now hovering over her golden-haired daughter. "'Tis more beautiful than I remembered," she breathed.

Lilibet turned a blank stare upon her mother. "But, what is it, Mama?"

"Why, it's your wedding gown, my darling."

"My . . . wedding gown? But I am not to be married!"

Neala was staring at the rather ancient-looking garment. With its low waist, full skirt, and puffed and banded sleeves, it was an outdated style.

"But of course, you are, my pet." Gingerly, Lady Abercorn reached for the garment and pressed it to her own cheek. "Once upon a time, I was to wear this lovely gown," her tone was near-reverent, "and now I am presenting it to you, Lilibet."

"Sure, an' I wore it, too," chimed in Grandma O'Grady's gravelly voice, pride evident in her thick Irish brogue.

Glancing Grandma's way, Neala noted moisture welling up in that faded pair of grey eyes. She stole across the room to drop a kiss on the old woman's weathered cheek. Unlike Mama and Papa, Grandma and Grandpa O'Grady had been *very* happily wed.

"I still don't see why you want to give this old thing to me?" Lilibet whined. "I don't want to be married. And if I do, I shall want a *new* gown. I *hate* old things!"

"Hush, Lilibet!" Her mother had slipped onto the sofa beside her willful daughter, the musty-smelling garment still clasped in her hands. "Neala, be a good 'un and sit down," she said absently.

At once, Neala obeyed, drawing up a low stool to sit near her grandmother's feet.

A far-away look crept into Lady Abercorn's eyes. "Many years ago," she began, "before I was born, even before Grandma O'Grady was born, Great-Great-Grandmother Drummond was betrothed to a very wicked man. He was quite a wealthy man, a powerful Irish lord, but Great-Grandmother Drummond did not wish to marry him. She did not love him. In truth, she feared him. But, she had no choice. She had been betrothed to the man since birth and was destined to marry him.

"On the day of her wedding, the young bride put on this very gown," one hand lovingly stroked the ivory silk, "but minutes before her parents were to carry her to the chapel, Great-Grand-mother Drummond decided to go for one last walk in the beautiful meadow she loved. Hours passed, and when she did not return, her parents began to search for her. At length, they found her, sound asleep in a meadow, lying on a bed of pale pink rose petals."

Lady Abercorn glanced toward her own mother, as if for assurance that she had indeed got the facts right. When the old woman nodded, she went on. "There, forming a circle about the bride, watching over her while she slept, was a band of little people."

Both Neala and Lilibet gasped.

"'Tis true," Lady Abercorn said. "The wee people were watching over Great-Grandmother Drummond. That night, her parents carried the sleeping girl back to her own bed and the next morning, they learned that the man she was set to marry had died in his bed."

This brought another gasp from Neala and Lilibet.

"That same morning, the young bride told her parents that the fairies had done it and that they had cast a spell on her. She said they had sprinkled her wedding gown with fairy dust, and told her that the first man she met was the man she would marry. He would be very, *very* wealthy and he would love her forever and make all her dreams come true. They told her to pass the wedding gown down to her own daughter, and on and on, generation after generation. The spell would hold true for whomever owned the dress. And that, Lilibet, is why I am giving this lovely gown to you."

Entranced, Neala moved to touch the bewitched gown. In places, she noted, the ivory silk did seem to sparkle. Was it true? Had the gown truly been sprinkled with fairy dust? Lilibet had also reached to touch the ancient silk but the look on her face said she was not quite as convinced as Neala.

"I still don't see why are you giving the dress to me," she whined. "Nealie should be the one to marry first."

Neala glanced up. She *was* the elder.

"I am presenting it to you," Lady Abercorn replied, matter-of-factly, "because it is already quite clear that Neala shall never

marry at all. She is far too plain. You are our only hope for the
future, Lilibet. With your golden hair and lovely blue eyes—"

"But I don't want to get married!" Lilibet cried. "Here—"
she tossed the dress to Nealie, "it's yours. I don't want it! I
don't want to be like Mama and Papa!"

"Lilibet!" Lady Abercorn scolded. "The spell has been cast.
You will *not* end up like me and Papa."

"But, you and Papa were not happy."

"Because, my dear, I married *against* the spell. I did not
marry the first man I met. Instead I married your Papa." Her
voice shook with bitterness. "Oh, I was taken in by the charming and handsome Sir Richard Abercorn, but if I'd had my wits
about me, I'd have turned and fled the minute I laid eyes on the
bounder. Instead, nothing would do but for me to marry the
wastrel! And you see where that led me."

Across the room, Grandma O'Grady was nodding wisely. " 'Tis
true," she said, "Fiona should have married Mr. Kennedy. Sure,
'an he weren't as handsome as Sir Richard, an' he dinna' have
a title. But, that all changed. Today, Mr. Kennedy is one of the
wealthiest men in all of Cork County. And last year was honored
for service to the King, he was."

Turning to gaze at her mother, Neala thought she saw the
glitter of a tear in Lady Abercorn's steel gray eyes. Yet the fiery
Irish woman merely squared her shoulders and brushed the of-
fending moisture aside.

"If I had followed my destiny, Lilibet," she said, "the three
of us would not now be penniless in the world."

Nealie considered that a moment, then said, "But if you had
not married Papa, then Lilibet and I should not even be here."

"Of course you would be here!" her mother snapped. "You
would just have a different papa, that is all. Now, you will do
as I say, Lilibet. You will marry the next man you meet and that
is the end of it."

Two

Two days later, Lilibet was still in a pet because her mother had said she could not leave the house or show her face in public until Saturday evening next.

"It would never do, Lilibet, for you to lay eyes on somebody's footman! Of course, in the end, he'd become rich and respected, but think of the bother while we waited," she declared that third morning at breakfast. "You shall stay indoors until we all attend Lady Sefton's musicale on Saturday evening."

"Am I to be blindfolded along the way?" Lilibet replied angrily, drawing circles in her porridge with a spoon.

One of Lady Abercorn's brows lifted. "I hadn't considered that, Lilibet. 'Tis quite a good idea, now that I think on it."

"Oh, Mama!" Lilibet cried. "What if the first man I meet is a . . . . a rotter? Or worse, what if he is old and ugly?"

"There is no chance of that. According to the spell—"

"But what if he doesn't want to marry me?"

Neala had wondered about that, as well.

"Of course, he shall want to marry you, Lilibet. What man would not want to marry you?"

Neala lowered her lashes, tried to force a mouthful of her lumpy oatmeal down. It was true. What man could resist Lilibet's lovely face and full figure? Lilibet had inherited Papa's golden good looks, while Nealie wasn't sure where her own mousey coloring came from. Even Mama's flaming auburn hair and snapping gray eyes had passed her by. Neala was simply plain, had plain honey-colored hair and plain brown eyes, though, unlike Lilibet, Neala was proud to be thought of as dainty and petite.

"Be a good 'un this morning, Nealie," her mother's voice jarred her senses 'round, "and set things to rights in the drawing room before my first sitting arrives today."

"Yes, Mama." Neala rose to clear away the breakfast dishes, then headed for the tiny parlor where her mother received her guests.

"Nealie," Lady Abercorn called after her, "did you send a note to Lady Diana? If I am to fashion her wedding gown, I must take precise measurements before I order the fabric. I shouldn't want any of it to go to waste."

"Yes, Mama. Diana will be here promptly at three." Lady Diana Brewster was Neala's closest friend. The two had attended school together in Bath, and even though the Abercorns had fallen on hard times, Lady Diana had not deserted Neala. Several of her school chums had not. Emma Chetwith was married now, but on occasion she still came calling. Almost a year ago, Mama had made Emma's wedding gown. It was the first one Mama had made, and after that, quite a number of Lady Abercorn's *ton* acquaintances had hired her to design and make special gowns for them. Neala usually drew up the initial sketch, then both she and Mama did the stitching. Lilibet watched.

A dejected look now on her pretty face, Lilibet ambled into the parlor where Nealie was fluffing the cushions. "Mama says I must keep Grandma O'Grady company again today," Lilibet muttered. "I don't see why I should. It's not as if a gentleman will come to call."

"Grandma enjoys having you nearby," Neala replied quietly. "She hasn't been feeling well since she arrived."

"All she does is sleep. I shall be obliged to sit about all day with nothing to do."

"You could read to her," Nealie suggested. "And there's plenty of mending to keep you occupied while Grandma rests."

"I don't like to sew! And I don't want to read. And I also don't want to get married," Lilibet added beneath her breath, but loud enough for Nealie to hear. "The wedding spell is silly. It can't possibly come true."

"Of course it will come true, Lilibet! Just look at Grandma and Grandpa O'Grady. They were very happy."

"But Grandpa wasn't handsome."

"He probably was when he was a young man."

"And Grandma's not wealthy."

"Perhaps not now. But they had a lovely house in Ireland, with plenty of servants and a fine carriage. If it weren't for Grandma lending a hand now, we would all be in high thicket."

"But Mama makes money with her sewing," Lilibet persisted.

Neala shook her brown curls with dismay. "Lilibet, making a new ball gown every second fortnight does not earn nearly enough to keep us in food and lodging. That is why one of us must marry!"

"Well, it shan't be me! I don't want to be like Mama. I want to be like Papa. I want to enjoy myself. So far as I am concerned, the wedding gown is yours!" Her chin at a tilt, she pranced across the room to deliberately peer from the window. "Now *you* must marry the next man you meet!"

Striding briskly into the room, Lady Abercorn sputtered, *"Lilibet!* Come away from that window! Grandma O'Grady is already asking for you. Now, go along with you!"

Neala glanced up, then shook her head as she watched her willful younger sister take her own sweet time about minding Mama. She certainly hoped the wedding spell worked soon. Even on a good day, Lilibet was difficult to live with.

This same day on the other side of London, in the fashionable section, Trench Lambert, Viscount Winterton, was at loose ends. Lord Winterton had arrived in England less than two weeks ago after serving a long and dangerous tenure of fifteen years in the army. Now, everyone in Town was of the opinion that the gentleman had sold his commission and had settled down to

live the life of a proper English gentleman. Everywhere Lord
Winterton went, Londoners heartily congratulated him on the
brave deeds of valor he'd performed while serving under Wellington. Trench took the accolades in stride. He knew he was
considered a war hero. But, unbeknownst to them, his work for
England was not yet done.

On this particular morning, since Lord Winterton couldn't
seem to get the hang of staying in bed til past noon, he had
risen early. He had enjoyed a hearty breakfast of eggs and kippers, perused the *Times,* called at his solicitor's office and long
before luncheon had even made some discreet inquiries regarding his secret military assignment and stopped in at Weston's
to order several sets of fashionable new clothes. He had selected
hats, gloves, seven pairs of evening pumps and two dozen
lengths of the fine white linen, which his valet, Rigas, had insisted was all the crack.

Now, tooling down St. James in the spanking new racing
curricle he had rushed out and bought the first day he arrived
in town, it was still only three of the clock in the afternoon.
Having lingered over luncheon at White's, Winterton had finally
got the idea to pop over to Tattersall's and pretend to inspect
some horseflesh, when just now, out of the blue, he heard a
delightful sound that could only be described as music to the
ears of a man who had not been privileged to hear such a mel-
lifluous ripple on a daily basis in years.

"*Trench!* Trench Lambert! Is that you? Why, it is! Trench!
Over here, on the flagway!"

Lord Winterton's dark head jerked round and sure enough,
hopping up and down on the flagway, hailing him with a scrap
of linen, was a pretty young lady whom Winterton did not believe he had had the pleasure yet of meeting. But, the young
lady seemed to know him, so who was he to quibble?

"Trench!" the little blond called again.

As quickly as he could manage, driving not being Winterton's
long suit, he headed his team and curricle alongside the curb
where the attractive miss stood. A glance at the equipage already

drawn up there revealed the reason for the young lady's distress. Her neat tilbury had suffered a broken axle.

Winterton swung his long legs to the ground, one hand touching the curly brim of his brand new black beaver hat. "Major Lambert at your service, ma'am. Though you seem to have me at a disadvantage."

"Why, Trench!" She giggled. "Don't you recognize me? But, how silly of me, of course you don't, I am all grown up now!" As if to prove her point, she twirled prettily in front of him. "See?"

Winterton grinned rakishly. A shrewd military man never passed up the opportunity to inspect the opposition's arsenal. "Indeed, you have, miss. But, I must confess I still do not know your name."

She giggled again "It's me, Diana!"

"Why, so it is," he muttered. "Little Lady Diana Brewster; all grown up. And very nicely turned out, too, I see."

"Why, Trench, you are as charming as ever." Diana's blue eyes danced. "And, I declare, even *more* handsome than I remembered!"

His lips twitching, Winterton sketched a polite bow, but at that instant, a crunching sound on the cobblestone street behind him caused him to turn that direction. Two of Lady Diana's liveried footmen and her coachman were busy wrestling with the lame carriage. "Perhaps I might be of assistance, gentlemen," he offered.

A scowl on his face, one of the footmen glanced up and at once, swept off his hat. "Why, Master Trench!" The man's face broke into a wide grin. "Welcome home, your lordship. I done heard it was you what won the war for us!"

Winterton grinned sheepishly. "I fear the war's not yet won," he said, his gaze falling again to the damage. "But looks as if you could use a hand here. Perhaps I might—"

"Not on me life, your lordship!" the man cried. "Would spoil your slap-up new finery. Would be obliged if you'd carry her ladyship to her appointment this afternoon, though. I shouldn't think Lord Brewster would object. Seeing as how it's you and all."

"Why, I'd be delighted." Turning again toward the attractive little blond, Winterton put out an arm. "Where are you off to this afternoon, Lady Diana?"

When Diana had given him the direction, Lord Winterton gallantly handed his pretty charge into his curricle and climbed in after her. "And what is the nature of this important engagement?" he asked indulgently, taking up the ribbons and checking the traffic before carefully heading the team into it.

"I am to be fitted for my wedding gown," Lady Diana replied archly.

"No!" Winterton replied. "You can't possibly be old enough to marry!"

Tossing her golden curls, Lady Diana giggled. She looked so young and happy, Winterton suddenly felt far older than his three-and-thirty years.

"Of course, I am old enough, silly. I suppose you would rather I had waited on the shelf for you to offer for me?" she teased.

Lord Winterton laughed. "I clearly recall telling you when you were a mere child of eight that I do not rob cradles. Last year I believe it was." His tone was playful. "So, who is the lucky chap?"

"Lord Edward Dunmore," Diana replied proudly.

"The Marquis of Marchmont's youngest? If I remember correctly the lad's still in leading strings!"

Lady Diana giggled again. "We have all grown up since you went away, Trench. I myself was three years in school at Bath. And following university, my brother Harry—"

"Don't tell me Harry is also married?" Winterton teased.

"Indeed, he is. Your best friend Harry was married ten years ago," she said, her tone chiding. "And he never forgave you for not being here to congratulate him."

"Was unavoidable, my dear. My commanding officer would never agree to me abandoning my post in order to attend a friend's wedding. I seem to recall that Harry removed to the family seat in Hertfordshire, that correct?"

"Hmmm." Diana nodded. "But Father is still living in Town."

"Ah. And how is Lord Brewster getting on, now that the family has all but deserted him?"

"Well enough, I suppose. Though I do worry about Father. Now that I'm to be married, I fear there shall be no one about to keep him company."

"Well then I shall have to pop 'round."

"Oh, Trench, he would adore seeing you again. He always thought of you as a son. In fact, I believe he preferred you to Harry!" She laughed gaily. "At least, Harry used to accuse him of that."

Winterton fell silent, then he said, "I shall always feel indebted to your father, Diana. It was he who bought my commission when my family turned me out." A trace of bitterness had crept into his tone, but still he wore a smile. "I shall make a point to call on Lord Brewster tomorrow."

"That would be lovely," Lady Diana said. "Did I mention I've a plan up my sleeve where Father is concerned?"

Just then, Winterton was distracted by the press of traffic on the narrow cobblestone street they had wheeled into. He did not hear Lady Diana's comment, so did not quiz her for details. "Must have taken a wrong turn," he muttered, gazing about at the less than elegant buildings lining both sides of the thoroughfare here. "This can't be—"

"Just there," Lady Diana said, pointing a small gloved finger at a two-story red brick building sandwiched in between a row of similar-looking ill-kept structures.

Lord Winterton pulled a face. "I say, does your father approve of you frequenting establishments in this sector of London, dear girl?"

"With two footmen and a driver, it is not as if I were not properly chaperoned!" Lady Diana protested.

"Nonetheless, I shall escort you safely inside and wait until your business here is concluded."

When the rap finally sounded at the door of their second story flat, Nealie and her mother both exchanged relieved looks.

"Be a good 'un and answer the door, Nealie girl," Lady Abercorn said, "I shall just go and get the inch tape."

Nealie moved toward the foyer, but when she swung open the door, was not the least prepared for the sight that greeted her. Raising her soft brown eyes to those of the tall, dark-haired gentleman hovering behind Lady Diana in the hallway, the oddest sensation—as if she were about to faint—beset her. Who was he? Not Diana's intended, Lord Edward. This man, with his powerful physique and ruggedly handsome face, in no way resembled the usual sallow-faced Englishman who whiled away his life in a gentleman's club or a stuffy drawing room. This gentleman was a . . . *man.*

"Do forgive me for being late, Nealie," Lady Diana said, sailing past Neala into the flat, "but my carriage lost a wheel and Lord Winterton was good enough to come to my rescue. Trench is my *almost* brother," she said with a laugh. "Actually he is an old friend of my brother Harry's," she clarified. "This is Miss Abercorn, Trench. Nealie and I were at school together," she told Trench.

"A pleasure to meet you, Miss Abercorn," Winterton said, smiling down into Nealie's upturned face as he entered the small flat, his large frame serving to make the tiny foyer seem even smaller.

"Oh," Nealie murmured. "Lord Winterton. I-I have read about you in the newspapers," she said, fighting to regain some control over her breathing.

A grin on his handsome face, Lord Winterton shrugged massive shoulders. "Mustn't believe everything you read, Miss Abercorn. I find newspapers often take liberties with the truth."

"Oh, pooh. Don't listen to him, Nealie. Everything they say about Trench is true and he knows it. It's what they don't say that we need worry about." Lady Diana playfully poked the tall man's ribs with a finger. "For instance, the *Times* would never report that the famous Major Lambert is also a frightful flirt. Or that he's left a trail of broken hearts all across the Continent."

"Why, you little minx!" Winterton said, encircling her shoulders in an affectionate hug.

Lady Diana squealed with delight and Nealie joined in the laughter. Indeed, it was not difficult to imagine this handsome man as a heartbreaker.

Neala led the way to the parlor. She had just offered her guests glasses of lemonade when her mother entered the room, a quizzical look on her face. "Why, I thought I heard a gentleman's voice," she said, eyeing Lord Winterton. "Lady Diana, do introduce me to your betrothed."

"Oh, this is not Edward, Lady Abercorn, this is an old friend of the family, Lord Winterton."

"Ah. Well, he doesn't look . . . old to me." She favored the gentleman with a bright smile, the same time pushing a stray lock of fiery auburn hair off her forehead.

Nealie winced. She knew exactly what Mama was thinking.

"I don't recall ever meeting a *Lady* Winterton," Lady Abercorn added, a sweeping gaze taking in the gentleman's impeccably-tailored clothes: the smart blue superfine coat, snug fitting beige breeches and pair of highly polished Hessians.

In the half-second of strained silence that followed, Neala said, "I shall just go and fetch Lilibet for you, Mama."

"What a good 'un, 'ye are, Nealie girl. I was about to suggest that very thing."

Odd indeed, mused Lord Winterton, as he surveyed the circle of women in the small drawing room that afternoon. Quite suddenly, as if he'd been struck by a thunderbolt—he knew exactly what he wanted to do with the rest of his life.

Perhaps the revelation was due in part to Lady Diana's incessant babbling about her forthcoming marriage. Or, perhaps it was due to Lady Abercorn's transparent ploy to interest him in her younger daughter, the lovely Miss Lilibet. But, regardless what prompted it, Trench Lambert suddenly knew that the time had come to get himself leg-shackled, something that until now he had avoided like the plague.

A grin softened his chiseled features as his eyes strayed to the pretty face of the young lady whose soft brown eyes made the hair on the back of his neck stand up. Another oddity, that. Miss Neala Abercorn, with her sweet heart-shaped face and honey-blonde curls, was not the least in his style. He usually gravitated to the more . . . worldly woman, voluptuous figure, that sort of thing. At first glance, Miss Abercorn was . . . well, just a bit plain, actually. She was trim, of an indescriminate height, yet she had an appealing air of vulnerability about her that made the war hero in him want to protect her from harm. Trouble was, so far this afternoon, he was having the devil of a time getting the young lady to look at him, let alone carry on a conversation.

"Lady Diana tells me the two of you attended school together, Miss Abercorn," he tried again.

As if stung, he watched Miss Abercorn's soft brown eyes fly to his, then flit nervously away. "Y-Yes," she murmured, lowering her long dark lashes, denying him the pleasure of drowning in those lovely brown orbs, "in Bath."

"Ah. And what did you study there?"

Miss Abercorn's nervous gaze now cut to her mother's face, as if seeking permission to speak. That such permission was not granted did not surprise Trench. Still, the young lady did manage, "Hm—the usual—geography, languages, music."

"Ah, music? Do you play then? Or sing?"

"Lilibet has a lovely voice," Lady Abercorn cut in shrilly. "I expect you will be attending Lady Sefton's musicale on Saturday night, will you not Lord Winterton? Lilibet is to sing, you know."

"Edward and I shall be there," Lady Diana interjected. "Perhaps you would accompany us, Trench? Would give you and father an opportunity to visit."

"I'd be delighted, my dear. You will be there, will you not, Miss Abercorn?"

Again, Miss Abercorn looked startled. "M-Me?"

Lord Winterton nodded, his gaze expectant.

"We shall all be there," Lady Abercorn said. "Though Neala is not the least bit musical. Not nearly so talented as Lilibet. Lilibet, play a piece for us now, won't you, dear?" Her eyes indicated the small piano tucked neatly in a corner of the crowded room.

"Of course, Mama! What shall I play?"

"Excuse me, Lady Abercorn," Lady Diana cut in, an edge of annoyance to her tone, "I have another engagement this afternoon and I expect Lord Winterton has pressing business, as well. Perhaps we could attend to my fitting now."

"Very well, Lady Diana." Reluctantly, Lady Abercorn rose to her feet. "If you will please excuse us, Lord Winterton? Neala, be a good 'un and chaperone Lilibet for me."

Springing to his feet as the ladies departed, Lord Winterton moved across the room to take the seat vacated by Lady Abercorn near her eldest daughter. "Now, Miss Abercorn," he began, the very nearness of her making him feel like the young pup he wasn't, "perhaps you will oblige by telling me—"

"I shall play *now*, Lord Winterton," Miss Lilibet said, from her position on the piano bench.

A half hour later, his ears still ringing, Lord Winterton was quite relieved to see both Diana and Lady Abercorn reappear. At the door, as they were all saying their farewells, he reached for Miss Abercorn's hand.

"Allow me to say how very much I enjoyed meeting *you*, Miss Abercorn," he said, aware of the delicate feel of her small hand in his large one. When the merest hint of a shy smile appeared on her face, he decided it was time to take a bolder step, alert the opposition to his intentions, as it were. Still holding her small hand in his, he exerted the veriest bit of pressure on her slender fingertips. "I assure you, we *shall* meet again, Miss Abercorn."

"Well, of course, we shall, silly!" Lady Diana interjected with a giggle. "We are all to be at Lady Sefton's musicale on Saturday evening." Shaking her head, she ushered Trench out the door, tossing a "Good bye, Nealie; thank you, Lady Abercorn," over her shoulder.

Beneath her long dark skirt, Nealie's knees felt weak. What did it mean? Why had the gentleman squeezed her fingertips? Was it true? Was he, as Diana had said, an unconscionable flirt? A libertine? Or was this simply the way *his* sort made a young lady feel? She had never met a man like Lord Winterton before. A war hero. He was so *very* handsome, so very dangerous, so—

"He is so *wonderful,* Mama!" sang Lilibet, dancing about the foyer. "How long must I wait to marry him? Oh, I cannot wait! I am already top over tail in love!"

"Do be still, Lilibet!" Lady Abercorn was tapping a forefinger to her cheek. "I must think."

"What is it, Mama? Is there something wrong? Did I say something wrong? I didn't, did I? Nealie?"

Neala slowly shook her head. "N-No. N-Not that I could see." Should she warn her Mama and sister about the man? Tell them that he had squeezed her fingertips?

Lady Abercorn's eyes narrowed. "You felt it too, did you not, Nealie?"

"F-Felt what, Mama?" Had the man also squeezed Mama's fingertips?

"Oh, Mama, don't spoil it for me," wailed Lilibet. "He is perfect and I love him. I must tell Grandma O'Grady! Does this mean our troubles are over, Mama?"

Neala cast a worried glance at her mother. She wasn't sure what it meant, but surely Mama would know.

Lady Abercorn still seemed deep in thought, but after a pause, she smiled. "Our troubles are, indeed, over," she called after Lilibet. "Come along, Nealie, we must begin at once on Lady Diana's wedding gown. We shall soon have a wedding of our own to plan!"

Neala silently obeyed, but following her Mama down the narrow corridor, her thoughts were not on Lady Diana's new gown. Not by a long chalk.

Three

Escorting Lady Diana down the stairs that afternoon, Lord Winterton had the niggling feeling his troubles had just begun. What had hit him? And why had he had such a difficult time makings his intentions known to the young lady he felt so unaccountably drawn to? Most women—young ones and older ones—reacted more to his masculine charm as did the silly chit, Miss Lilibet. What could it mean? Was he not to Miss Abercorn's liking? Was she already spoken for?

Reaching his curricle, he handed Lady Diana up. "Have you the time to stop at Gunter's for an ice, this afternoon, my dear?" Diana was well acquainted with Miss Abercorn, perhaps she could enlighten him regarding the young lady.

"Why, what a lovely idea, Trench. I should like an ice very much."

At Gunter's, Lord Winterton was far too intent on his mission—learning as much as possible about the enchanting Miss Abercorn—to take notice of his surroundings at the fashionable eating establishment. He didn't notice the colorful placards above the counter, the new chandelier the proprietor was so very proud of, the modern furnishings or the shiny new tiled floor. Also escaping his attention were the many coy glances and bright smiles directed his way from nearly every female in the place.

"They are all simply dying to meet you, Trench," Lady Diana whispered, dipping her spoon delicately into the frozen raspberry treat before her.

Winterton glanced up. "Excuse me?"

"Oh, Trench, you can be so oblique at times. Every young lady in the room, and their mamas—" she giggled "—are dying to be presented to you!"

An arched brow lifted. "Hmmm." Odd, indeed, was the fact that having met Miss Abercorn, the desire to meet other young ladies had simply vanished.

"What did you think of Nealie?" Lady Diana asked suddenly. Trench nearly choked on the sugary ice in his mouth. Had Diana read his thoughts?

"She is terribly sweet, don't you think?" the pretty blond went on. "Nealie has been my dearest friend in the world since we were little. I find it very distressing to see the family reduced to living in that part of Town. When her Papa was alive, they had a lovely house in Mayfair, quite near ours. Nealie and I used to play together in the garden." She delicately spooned another bite of pink ice into her mouth.

His ears standing at attention, Winterton had all but abandoned his dessert. Silently, he willed Lady Diana to continue. That she did so pleased him immensely.

"Nealie's Papa, Sir Richard, lost his entire fortune before he died. Gaming," Diana confided knowingly. "Nealie was so fond of her papa. I don't think she ever believed a word of the gossip, but it was all true. Anyhow," Lady Diana leaned over the table, her blue eyes sparkling, "you recall earlier, I said I had a plan."

Winterton didn't recall earlier. In fact, he had trouble recalling anything that had occurred much earlier in his life than about three of the clock this afternoon, when he'd met the charming Miss Abercorn. Mulling over the strangeness of that, he did not hear the first part of Lady Diana's next pronouncement.

"I have decided that Nealie would suit perfectly for Father," she said. "He is not too old for her. I think it shall be great fun to have her as my stepmother!" Diana giggled with delight.

Winterton shook himself to awareness. "Lord Brewster to be

married, eh? Capital. Am I acquainted with your new step-mama?" He tried to force an interest in what she was saying.

"Oh, Trench!" Lady Diana giggled again. "You haven't heard a word I've said! I said, Papa is to marry Neala!"

"Neala! I-I mean, Miss Abercorn! Why, he . . . why, that's—" he clamped his mouth shut.

"Oh, don't look so shocked, Trench. It wouldn't be the first May-December match to come along. There are plenty of others, there's Lord Ashworthy and Miss Amabelle, and Lord and Lady Tentrees . . ."

While Diana prattled on, Winterton's mind reeled. *His* Miss Abercorn and Lord Brewster! It was unconscionable! It was unthinkable! It was . . .

". . . a simply marvelous plan, don't you agree, Trench? Father will be *so* lonely once I am married."

Lord Winterton closed his mouth again. Lord Brewster lonely? Hardly fathomable that, but it wouldn't be proper to discuss a young lady's father's escapa—well, it wouldn't be proper. Not the least hungry, he covered his chagrin by feigning a renewed interest in the blueberry ice before him. He hadn't counted on pitting himself against his good friend Lord Brewster. He owed his life to Lord Brewster. That gentleman had been the only one to come to his aid when the unfortunate scandal involving Trench and the young lady he refused to marry fifteen years ago had been the *on-dit* of the season.

There had been nothing to the rumors, of course, unless one believed the gossip-mongers. Which is precisely what the young lady's mama had counted upon when she connived for a young Trench Lambert to be discovered alone with her rather homely daughter in the garden the night of the girl's come-out ball. Trench's parents had quickly sided with the irate woman and insisted that he offer for the girl. But Trench had refused, and though he knew it was a cowardly thing to do, had fled London that very night. Had saddled his horse and rode straight to the country home of his Eton schoolmate, Harry Brewster. A fort-night later, thanks to the connections and generosity of Harry's father, Lord Brewster, Trench had left England altogether, determined to prove to himself and to anybody else who'd take notice, that he was anything but a coward.

In the past fifteen years, he believed he had proved that and considerably more. And, he owed it all to Lord Brewster. It was inconceivable now that he could set himself against the very gentleman who had saved his life those many years ago.

Finished with his confection, Winterton angrily shoved his plate away. He had no choice but to step aside. Honor was a duty. "If you've finished with your ice, Lady Diana; I shall see you home," he said, his tone brusque.

Once they arrived at the Brewster town house, Winterton was vastly relieved to find Lord Brewster not at home. He was not in the least humor now to be cordial.

Preparing to leave for Lady Sefton's musicale on Saturday evening, the ladies of the Abercorn household were all a-twitter.

"Oh, Mama, I can barely contain myself!" gushed Lilibet. "I shall see him again tonight!"

Tying the pale blue satin ribbons of her bonnet beneath her chin, Neala had to admit that, she too, was looking forward to seeing the handsome war hero again. The infamous Lord Winterton had been the center of most every discussion between the Abercorn women since the gentleman appeared on their doorstep last week.

Mama was enchanted with him.

"Just think, Lilibet. A war hero! Why, I don't believe the spell has ever worked quite so grandly before!"

Even Grandma O'Grady was singing the gentleman's praises.

"The papers are full of his daring-dos on the battlefield, they are. Sure and ye' shall be happy as a lamb, Lilibet."

Lilibet had declared to anyone who would listen that she was in love.

"I am the luckiest young lady alive!" Neala had heard her tell Mrs. Montcreif only yesterday.

On the surface, Neala concluded, it did appear the wedding spell had worked perfectly. Lord Winterton *was* the first gentleman Lilibet had met. He *was* titled and wealthy. And Lilibet loved him. Yet . . . Neala couldn't stop thinking about how the tall man had squeezed her fingertips. Or about how very *warm* his skin had felt pressed to hers.

"Come along, Neala dear," Lady Abercorn called to Neala, who, still lost in thought, had trailed behind her Mama and sister down the walk to the closed carriage they'd hired for the musicale this Saturday evening. "We're late as i'tis."

"I know, Mama." Neala hurried up the creaking steps of the carriage and stepped inside. Because her mother was trying to conceal the fact that they no longer owned a coach, Mama had insisted that they arrive at Lady Sefton's a good deal, a *very* good deal, later than everyone else. That way the other guests would already be inside and would not see the Abercorn party arrive in a hired carriage.

When they reached fashionable Grosvenor Square, Mama's plan worked smooth as silk. Inside the brilliantly lit foyer of Lady Sefton's elegant house, Neala noted Mama's glittering gaze casting about for the towering figure of Lord Winterton. When she spotted him standing by the stairwell, she steered the girls that direction.

"Good evening, Lord Winterton," she began brightly. "You are looking quite well tonight. And, may I say, you are in for a treat. Lilibet is to sing this evening, you recall."

Lord Winterton sketched a slight bow. "Good evening, Lady Abercorn; Miss Lilibet." Though Winterton was doing his best to avoid meeting the appealing soft eyes of Miss Abercorn, the magnetic pull she had on him won out. "You look quite charming this evening, Miss Abercorn." And she did! His throat grew tight. Wearing a pale blue muslin gown trimmed in ivory lace, her neat figure looked both demure and alluring.

"Oh-h," Miss Abercorn murmured, lowering her lashes in a way Winterton found quite becoming. His normally very stout heart skipped a beat. The effect the young lady had on him was astonishing!

"Shall we all go inside?" The sound of Lady Abercorn's shrill voice brought him around.

"Ah, yes," said Lord Winterton, his smile still fixed on Miss Abercorn's pretty heart-shaped face. He fought a sudden impulse to take her arm when he felt someone at his other side slip an arm through his.

"Trench! You simply must come and say hello to Father!" Winterton glanced down at Lady Diana. "He and Edward are holding seats for us inside."

"*We* were all just going in," Lady Abercorn said pointedly.

"There are chairs aplenty for everyone!" Lady Diana called gaily over her shoulder, already dragging Lord Winterton away.

Apparently Lady Abercorn saw nothing for it but to join forces with Lady Diana. With a stern look, she indicated to her daughters to hurry along. They quickly caught up and filed into the spacious room on the heels of the pair ahead of them.

After Winterton and Lord Brewster had exchanged hearty greetings, Lady Diana took charge once again, and with a skill equal to, or surpassing, any matchmaking mama Winterton had ever seen, she put Miss Abercorn next to her father, herself beside her intended Lord Edward and Lord Winterton alongside the glowing Miss Lilibet. Lady Abercorn she left to fend for herself.

That woman slipped into a chair a few feet from her charges and wearing a smug smile of satisfaction on her face, settled back to enjoy the show.

It soon became apparent to Winterton the Sefton's had spared no expense in the evening's entertainment. Not only did the famous, exorbitantly expensive Catalani perform, but the popular Italian tenor, Tremezzani, also sang. Miss Lilibet was in good company. However, it was not until the end of the program that she was introduced. By then, a good deal of the guests—mostly gentlemen with a lesser tolerance for music than Winterton, who not being accustomed to such *fetes* in the army, was

enjoying himself immensely—had vacated their chairs and
headed for the card room.

When Miss Lilibet moved to the fore, Winterton almost
seized the opportunity himself to retreat to the game room. But,
as long as Miss Abercorn was still in the room, he was loath
to leave, so he simply folded his arms across his chest and
leaned back in his chair.

Yet, as fate would have it, a few moments after Miss Lilibet
opened her mouth to sing, Lord Brewster developed a frog in
his throat and, convulsed in a fit of coughs, slipped out the side
door. Winterton, unaware that his handsome features had relaxed into a broad smile, made haste to fill the empty seat next
to the charming Miss Abercorn.

So pleased was he, in fact, that once Miss Lilibet's song was
over, his applause for the young lady came out a trifle too exu-
berant.

Leaning close to Miss Abercorn's ear, he enthused, "You
must be quite proud of your sister, Miss Abercorn! She has a
lovely voice, indeed."

"Thank you, sir," Miss Abercorn said, then she turned her
head to look directly into his eyes . . . and smiled.

Winterton's gloved hands froze in mid-applause. Not a gun-
shot to his leg, not a cannonball to his heart, *nothing* could ever
affect him quite so strongly as did the charming smile he now
beheld on Miss Abercorn's face. It was like a ray of sunshine
piercing through the clouds on the morning after a bloody battle.

"Neala!" came a shrill voice in front of him. Winterton
nearly jumped. "Mama wants you!"

Blinking himself back to awareness, Lord Winterton discovered Miss Lilibet standing poised in front of them, the toe of
her slipper tapping impatiently on the floor. "Mama wants you,"
she said again, her blue eyes blazing.

Winterton sprang instantly to his feet, as did Miss Abercorn.
At that same moment, Lord Brewster reappeared. Minutes later,
when the troops had reassembled, both Lord Brewster and Lord
Winterton were on their way down the corridor to the card room,

while Lady Diana's intended had been sent to fetch glasses of madeira for the ladies who remained in the saloon.

"Charming young lady, don't you agree?" Lord Brewster began, pulling a fresh cigar from his pocket and lighting up. He was a good deal shorter than Winterton, had thinning gray hair and a paunchy middle.

Still reeling, Winterton's tone sounded absent. "I take it you are referring to the lovely Miss Lilibet."

"Miss Lilibet! Hell, no!" Lord Brewster threw his head back and guffawed loudly. "I mean the older sister, Miss Abercorn. Diana means to pair me off with the gel."

Lord Winterton was jarred fully alert now. "And . . . you object?" *He hoped.*

"Object!" Lord Brewster guffawed again, a stream of cigar smoke spewing from his mouth. "Take me for a fool, do you? Been a widower this age, Winterton. About time I found a pretty little thing to warm my bed nights."

Lord Winterton suddenly had trouble drawing breath, and cigar smoke, he realized, had nothing to do with it. If Brewster weren't the good friend he was, and he not the gentlemen he was, he would have knocked the man's lights out by now. Instead, still fighting the urge, he muttered, "Miss Abercorn is charming, indeed. Though, I find it difficult to believe you haven't had a bit o' lace in your bed these many years."

"Well, of course I have," Brewster bellowed. "But, I can hardly marry that sort, can I?"

"No," Winterton mumbled. "I expect not."

The gentlemen had now entered the card room and were casting about for the bar. "But why marry at all?" Winterton said suddenly. Perhaps he could dissuade the gentleman from the idea of marriage altogether.

Not to be swayed, Brewster countered, "About time *you* settled down. You could do worse than Miss Lilibet. The gel's a looker, and she seems quite taken with you. And Miss Abercorn seems not to object to me. Though I am a bit rusty in the courtship department. A demmed nuisance, that." He began to cough again. Regaining himself, he added, "Never know quite what to say to a young lady these days. I invited Miss Abercorn for a drive tomorrow. She accepted."

Suddenly the smoke and the deafening noise in the room seemed close beyond endurance. Winterton reached into his waistcoat pocket and withdrew a gold watch. Consulting it, he said brusquely, "Don't feel much like cards this evening, Brewster."

Lord Brewster looked up, then a knowing grin split his face. "Got a ladybird awaiting you somewhere, eh? Well, go along with you. Enjoyed seeing you again, my boy." He clapped Winterton on the shoulder. "Pop 'round anytime."

Lord Winterton exited the Sefton townhome, his lungs welcoming the crisp night air and pinpricks of cold rain that assailed him outdoors on the flagway. Wrapping his long dark cloak about himself, he opted for a walk home instead of taking his carriage. Something told him this long dreary night would go on forever.

Four

Viscount Winterton hated himself. Last evening after leaving Lady Sefton's, he had not walked home, but instead had walked to White's Club, where he downed a few. Then he'd left in the company of two gentlemen he hardly knew, and gone to the establishment of a certain Madame X, where he downed considerably more. Upon awakening this morning, he'd found himself lying next to a dimpled damsel he was certain he had never met before. He only hoped that, in his inebriated state, he hadn't got to know the girl better than he might now wish.

But, because he could recall very little beyond leaving White's Club last evening, he could not say for certain. He was certain this morning, however, that his head felt the size of a cannonball, and he could kick himself for behaving in such a cork-brained fashion.

In his own bed, where he had poured himself in the early dawn hours, he consulted his pocket watch, which, fortunately he still possessed, and which he apparently had had the presence of mind to place on the nightstand next to his cot when he fell into it this morning. Blinking cobwebs from his brain, he focused on the numbers, and shuddered when he saw it was nearly two in the afternoon. Falling back on the pillows, he groaned again.

Equally as foolish last evening was his besotted reaction to the lovely Miss Abercorn's sweet smile. What had come over him? He'd known—in *every* sense of the word—any number of

women far more beautiful than shy Miss Abercorn. Yet the pull
he felt toward that little miss was something he'd never experienced before. What did it mean?

Flinging the blankets back, he swung long legs over the side
of the bed, then following the sudden motion, grabbed his head
and groaned once again. Louder this time. Also ridiculous was
the turmoil he'd felt last evening when his good friend Brewster
made his intentions known regarding Miss Abercorn. Demme!
He should have congratulated Brewster—drunk a toast to him—
no, forget the toast. But, he could have at least congratulated
the man. A gentleman Brewster's age deserved accolades for
snagging a girl as young and as pretty as—*demme!* there went
the blasted churning in his stomach again! It was the same unsettling feeling he'd got when Brewster told him he meant to
marry the girl.

Angrier than ever, he got to his feet. The thing to do today
was congratulate Brewster, then get on with his own life. He
had important military work to do in London. Falling in love
would only tie him down. Make him unfit for service.

"Rigas!"

"Yes, my lord," came the immediate reply.

Winterton's disheveled head jerked 'round. Where had his
manservant been lurking? 'Til now, he had assumed he was
alone in quarters. His lips thinned. It was going to take considerably longer than a few weeks to become accustomed to the
ways of polite society again.

"I shall be going out, Rigas."

"Very good, sir. And where might his lordship be going?"

The scowl Lord Winterton turned on his manservant plainly
told the man his lordship's whereabouts were no one's business
but his own.

"I will need to know precisely what to lay out, sir," Rigas
said by way of explanation for his impudence. "If his lordship
is going to—"

"Lay out the usual, Rigas. Trousers, shirt, coat—and coffee."

Watching Rigas spring into action only made Winterton's head spin faster.

"Lay out the coffee first, Rigas."

Inside the Brewsters' drawing room, Lady Diana greeted Lord Winterton.

"Father left only moments ago to take Neala for a drive," she told Trench excitedly, a bright smile lighting up her pretty face.

Of course! Winterton hit his forehead with his palm—then wished he hadn't. Brewster had said last evening that he had invited Miss Abercorn for a drive today.

"Isn't it wonderful!" Lady Diana squealed. "I am certain we shall see Father and Neala wed before the season is out."

"Hmmm."

A scowl on his face, long strides carried Winterton back outside. He climbed to the platform atop his new curricle and scooped up the ribbons. He would drive to the Abercorn flat, say his piece to Lord Brewster, and be done with it.

At the Abercorn flat, despite the fact that a shaft of glorious sunshine was streaming through the long window of the tiny parlor and that four people of pleasant countenance were seated about the room, the prevailing atmosphere inside could be described in a single word. Glum.

Neala had never felt more uncomfortable in her life. Why was her good friend Lady Diana's father, the stodgy Lord Brewster, calling on her? The gentleman was . . . old. Not for the life of Neala could she conceive of Lord Brewster as a suitor. But it appeared Mama could. Mama was the only person in the room wearing a genuine smile although there was also a malicious grin on Lilibet's face.

"We are delighted to see you again, Lord Brewster," Lady Abercorn said, for the third or fourth time since the gentleman had arrived.

Neala knew Mama was having a difficult time keeping the conversation afloat, and she was being no help whatever. She was having enough of a time just keeping a smile on her face. Oh, why had she accepted Lord Brewster's offer last evening for a drive?

"Neala has always spoken highly of you," Lady Abercorn tried again. "Haven't you, Neala, dear?"

Neala nodded tightly.

"She did so enjoy your company last evening at the musicale." Mama gazed expectantly at her. "Neala?"

Neala wanted to crawl under the sofa. Instead, she murmured, "Indeed. Thank you, sir."

"Neala is such a good 'un," her Mama said, her tone a bit too stern to make her words believable. "She's been a great help to me these last months. She is very talented with a needle . . . and clever, too. It was Neala who sketched the design for Lady Diana's wedding gown, Lord Brewster. Neala, fetch the sketch and show it to him, dear."

"But, Mama . . ."

"Neala, be a good 'un and do as I say."

"Yes, Mama."

Neala left the room in search of the sketch, pausing on the threshold of Grandma O'Grady's room to check on her. Grandma was still feeling out of curl.

"Can I get you something, Grandma?" Neala asked gently.

From the bed where she was propped up on pillows, Grandma's wrinkled cheeks softened into a smile. "No, dear, it's doing fine, I am. Sure an' 'ye should be gettin' back to your young man."

Nealie winced. "He isn't young, Grandma."

"All the same, he's come a 'calling and 'ye mustn't keep him waiting. 'Twouldn't be proper."

With a sigh, Neala turned to go. In her own room, she had just located the sketch Mama had sent her to fetch when she heard a loud rapping at the door of the flat.

Moments later, when Neala reappeared in the parlor, it was

to an entirely different scene. Suddenly, everyone in the room was smiling. Lord Brewster was jovial. Lilibet was a bouquet of sparkling eyes and dimples. Lady Abercorn was near gleeful and catching sight of the tall gentleman who had just entered the chamber, Neala couldn't deny that her senses were now standing at attention. Lord Winterton looked a pattern-card of perfection today, as he had last evening, when he'd been dressed all in black. This afternoon the gentleman was wearing a beautiful bottle-green silk waistcoat and a matching frock coat. Tan breeches were tucked into a pair of shiny black Hessians. In his gloved hands, he carried a curly-brim black beaver hat and a cane. Just looking at him, Neala's breath grew short. The sketch in her hand wafted to the floor as she eased onto the straight-backed chair positioned just inside the doorway.

When he opened his mouth to speak, she felt chills creep down her spine. "Wanted to extend my apologies for deserting you last evening, Brewster."

"No harm done, Winterton!"

"Please do, sit down, Lord Winterton." Lady Abercorn indicated her chair, next to Lilibet.

Before he sat down, however, Lord Winterton's gaze swept the room, and Neala was certain he looked directly at her, then his gaze reverted to Mama. "You have two beautiful daughters, Lady Abercorn," he said. "I can't think when I've heard a lovelier songbird than Miss Lilibet." He turned a handsome smile on Lilibet.

She giggled. "I should be delighted to sing for you again, Lord Winterton. Now?"

"A-Another time perhaps." He rose again to his feet. "I should be taking my leave now."

Lord Brewster stood as well. "Miss Abercorn and I were set to take a drive in the park, Winterton. Perhaps you would join us?"

"What a splendid idea!" Lady Abercorn chimed in. "Lilibet, go and fetch your bonnet."

Lord Winterton's eyes cut 'round, then he politely murmured, "Indeed. Lovely day for a drive."

Long before the drive had concluded, Lord Winterton wished he had thought of a way to confine Miss Lilibet to quarters—perhaps for the remainder of her life—certainly for the remainder of his. With her fawning and gesturing, Neala's silly younger sister had tested his tolerance almost beyond endurance. She was as different as chalk and cheese from the serene Miss Abercorn. Lord Winterton cast a longing gaze at Brewster and the young lady seated next to him. Brewster was indeed a lucky man. And Winterton was a cad. In spite of his resolve to the contrary, he'd spent nearly the whole of the afternoon, gazing at Miss Abercorn. He had even tried to draw her out, asking question after question. But she would hardly talk to him. Either she was deeply in love with Brewster—to the point of not wishing to so much as speak to another man—or she was shy beyond anything Winterton had ever encountered before.

Upon arriving back at the Abercorn flat, the gentlemen politely showed the ladies up. Standing just inside the foyer, Lord Brewster seemed anxious to leave. "Must trot. Have an engagement this evening." He tipped his hat to the Abercorn ladies, and behind their backs, winked at Winterton, who surmised that the older gentleman would not be lonely tonight.

"But, *you* will stay, will you not, Lord Winterton?" admonished Lady Abercorn. "I have prepared . . . er, that is, Cook has prepared a lovely tea for us. You simply must stay."

"Of course, he'll stay," put in Brewster, his tone obliging. "Winterton would never pass up the opportunity to take tea with a roomful of beautiful women. Good day, ladies; Winterton."

Winterton shrugged. So, there it was. He had no choice. He had to stay.

After the three women and Lord Winterton had munched on

thin sandwiches and slices of somewhat stale lemon cake, Lady Abercorn filled everyone's cup again with tea.

"Lord Winterton," Lilibet said in a high-pitched tone, happily perched next to him on the faded mulberry silk sofa, "tell us about the time you led the attack on Napoleon in Italy!" Her face was aglow with pleasure.

"It wasn't Napoleon, Lilibet," put in Miss Abercorn quietly. "It was his brother Joseph, and it was Salamanca, which is in Spain. Lord Winterton served with Wellington."

Setting aside his teacup, Lord Winterton's lips twitched. "You have been reading the newspapers again, Miss Abercorn." A fresh article recapping his career had appeared in the *Times* only yesterday.

Miss Abercorn blushed and lowered her lashes prettily.

"Neala's *always* reading!" Lilibet pulled a face. "She is dull as dishwater."

"I do not find your sister dull, Miss Lilibet; on the contrary, she seems quite knowledgeable to me." Enjoying the tea party immensely, and the fact that, at last, Miss Abercorn was talking, Winterton turned her way again. "Other than exaggerated accounts of war battles, Miss Abercorn, what else do you like to read?"

He noted Miss Abercorn watching her mother gather up a few of the tea things, then quit the room. When she had gone, Miss Abercorn seemed to relax, then said, "I like to read adventure stories."

"Adventure?" Her answer surprised him. That she could surprise him made her seem all the more intriguing.

She nodded. "I like to read about men of courage and tales of their daring exploits." There was a wistful sound to her tone.

"She reads to Grandma O'Grady," Lilibet interjected, then added archly, "I don't like to read."

Winterton knew the girls' grandmother had recently arrived in London from Ireland. "Have you been to Ireland, Miss Abercorn?" He was making grand progress drawing her out!

"Yes." She nodded, and when that lovely Irish smile he had

witnessed the night before lit up her face again, Winterton grew warm inside. Even her brown eyes were sparkling. "I went there once, when I was a child."

"Neala went, but I didn't," Lilibet said flatly. "I was too little. Neala went with Papa."

Winterton noted the sad look that had replaced the glow on Miss Abercorn's face and fought a desire to draw her close and comfort her. "You must miss your father terribly," he said gently.

She nodded again, her smile completely vanished now. Though, her tone was nearly a whisper, Winterton was glad when she began again to speak. "My trip to Ireland with Papa was the most delightful time I have ever had. We went to see Grandma, but along the way—" some of her lightheartedness began to return "—we had so many adventures. Papa was . . ." she looked down, then some thought seemed to jar her, "—he was much like you, Lord Winterton."

"Oh? In what way was your papa like me, Miss Abercorn?"

Miss Abercorn suddenly seemed flustered. "Well, he . . . he was brave and courageous and—" she glanced up, her brown eyes soft, "—I don't mean to imply he was a war hero like you, sir, but he was . . ." she seemed unable to go on.

"Papa was a bounder," Lilibet said flatly.

"Lilibet!" Miss Abercorn's tone was as close to a scold as Winterton had ever heard from her before. "That is not what I meant at all."

Winterton couldn't help chuckling a bit. Did she think him a bounder?

"Well, he was, and he gambled," Lilibet told Winterton, still discussing her father. "Sometimes, Papa would be gone for days and we wouldn't know where he was."

Miss Abercorn lifted her sweet face to Lord Winterton's again. "Papa was a good, kind man, Lord Winterton."

"I'm certain he was, Miss Abercorn." A pause followed, in which Winterton toyed with the idea of assuring her that since making her acquaintance, he was no longer a rake or a bounder.

"Would you care for more tea, Lord Winterton?" The shrill sound of Lady Abercorn's voice brought him 'round.

Lord Winterton politely declined her offer, whereupon Lady Abercorn put down the pot and again took a seat near the window. Now that tea was done, he realized it was long past time for him to depart. He had well overstayed the accepted quarter hour that Rigas had informed him was allotted for a call. "I should be going now," he said.

"Oh, you needn't," Lady Abercorn said hastily. "Lilibet, why don't you fetch the pretty watercolor you painted yesterday and show it to Lord Winterton."

"Yes, Mama." Lilibet scampered from the room.

Having edged toward the doorway, Winterton eased into the straight-back chair positioned there.

"In addition to my daughter's lovely singing voice, Lilibet is also quite talented as an artist, Lord Winterton. Both my daughters are talented," she added.

"Indeed, madam," Winterton murmured politely, then his gaze fell to a scrap of paper lying on the floor at his feet. He bent to pick it up. It was of a feminine figure wearing a diaphanous gown decorated with lace and embroidered rosebuds. "Is this one of Miss Lilibet's sketches?" He glanced up.

Miss Abercorn was blushing. "No, sir. That is my drawing."

"Yours, Miss Abercorn?" He studied the figure afresh. "Well, you are *very* talented, indeed, Miss Abercorn. I am quite impressed."

"That is the final sketch I did for Lady Diana's wedding gown. Mama and I are making it."

"How clever you are!" he exclaimed.

As he was looking again at the drawing, another square of paper was thrust beneath his nose, obscuring the one in his hand.

"This is my picture, Lord Winterton."

Winterton drew back, but Lady Abercorn was hovering over him as well, pointing to one or another aspect of Miss Lilibet's rather amateurish watercolor of pink flowers in a patterned vase.

"Just look at the detail in the petals," Lady Abercorn pointed out.

Winterton felt his stomach muscles tighten. It was the exact same feeling he got on the battlefield when the enemy had ventured too close for comfort. He needed air. Lots of it.

After Lord Winterton had departed, the three Abercorn women remained in the parlor ruminating over the day's events.

"But he hardly talks to me, Mama!" wailed Lilibet.

"Of course, he talks to you, my pet."

"No, he doesn't. He is always asking Neala questions. He much prefers talking to her!"

"That is because he is a gentleman, Lilibet. A gentleman will always endeavour to make the less pretty young lady feel attractive. That is the only reason he addresses Neala."

Lilibet pouted. "I don't think he likes me, Mama."

"Of course, he likes you, darling. He loves you! Why else would he come calling today? And stay such a length, too."

Lilibet's lower lip protruded noticeably.

"He was obviously quite taken by your performance last evening, and now he is aware that you are a talented artist, as well. He shall come up to scratch in no time," Lady Abercorn said with conviction, then turned to look at Neala, who stood gazing from the long window at the top of the room. "As, I am certain, will Lord Brewster," she added.

Neala wasn't listening. In the gathering shadows of evening, she had watched the imposing figure of Lord Winterton climb atop his curricle and drive away. An odd longing filled her, much like the tug at her heart she'd felt when she watched her Papa drive away. She'd watch him go, and wonder when, and sometimes if, she'd ever see him again. How odd to experience those feelings about a man she barely knew . . . .

Five

Driving away from the Abercorn flat, Lord Winterton felt as if he'd narrowly escaped with his life. Calling there today had been a poor choice, indeed. Not only had he not accomplished his mission—congratulating Lord Brewster on his good fortune—he feared his lengthy stay had only fed the flames of what could soon become a scandal similar to the one he'd escaped fifteen years ago. Clearly evident now was the fact that Lady Abercorn meant to legshackle him to the birdwitted Miss Lilibet. Which would never happen, not in a pig's eye! On the way home, Winterton felt a sense of dejection settle about him, but unable to think why he should be feeling so downcast, he decided he'd simply had too much to drink the night before, and it was showing.

Still, it took considerable effort to turn his mind to the matter he'd been assigned to investigate here in London. The disappearance of highly confidential documents in both the War Office and the admiralty was growing at an alarming rate and if England entertained any hope at all of winning the war, the treasonous activity must be curtailed at once. Because Winterton had been instrumental in apprehending a double agent in Spain who for months had travelled freely between English and enemy lines, he had been summoned by the prime minister to handle this particular assignment. But it had been days since Winterton had received any clues or definitive word in regard to the secret agent's whereabouts, so other than making a few discreet inquiries on his own, he had been at a loss as to how

to proceed. Yet time was of the essence. He knew he should do
something right away.

The next morning at breakfast, he was vastly relieved when
Rigas entered the room carrying a thick packet beneath his arm.

"This just arrived for you, your lordship."

"Thank you, Rigas." Winterton hastily set aside his coffee
cup and tore into the package his manservant had handed him.
At the same time he couldn't help noting that Rigas had stepped
to the sideboard and was now depositing several neat white
letters atop a pile of others that was so high the stack seemed
to teeter on the tray beneath them.

"And to whom might those letters be directed, Rigas? I was
under the distinct impression that I was the only person in resi-
dence here."

"These are for you, your lordship."

Winterton's brows pulled together. "And when, may I ask,
am I to be permitted to read them?"

With no indication at all that anything was amiss, Rigas replied, "Whenever you choose, your lordship."

Winterton glanced down at the missive in his hand, wondering what about it that had prompted Rigas to bring it directly
to him while bypassing the others. "Was there some urgency
about this particular one, Rigas?"

Tending to his duties at the sideboard, Rigas didn't even look
up. "It simply looked urgent, your lordship. The others are
merely invites."

"Invites?" Lord Winterton glanced again at the pile. "Invites
to what, Rigas?"

"The season is in full swing, your lordship. You are considered a prime *parti.*"

Winterton's countenance darkened. "I see." Deciding against
asking Rigas how he had arrived at that learned conclusion, he
returned again to the business at hand. Inside he found several
handwritten pages, all at the moment undecipherable. His work
was cut out for him today. It would take hours to translate the
gibberish into recognizable language, but it was necessary that

1e and his contacts communicate in code. Winterton pushed
away from the table. He had a full day's labor ahead of him if
1e planned to translate all of the missives.

At the doorway of the dining room, however, something
:aused him to pause. His gaze fell again to the stack of unread
mail. Perhaps attending a *soiree* or two, and dancing attendance
1pon a number of young ladies, would go a long way in dis-
)elling whatever rumors may already be circulating about him-
elf and Miss Lilibet. "Do you suppose I should attend a rout
)r two, Rigas?"

"Couldn't hurt, your lordship," Rigas replied from across the
oom where he was now handing Lord Winterton's soiled dishes
o a housemaid.

"Very well then, select a suitable few for me and I shall
attend."

Several days later at the Abercorn flat, the ladies were just
oncluding an early supper of boiled fish and potatoes.

"But, I don't see why *I* cannot attend!" wailed Lilibet. "If
Neala is to go, I don't see why I cannot!"

"Because, my dear," her Mama began patiently, "you have
1ot been presented at court and are not officially out."

Glancing up from her plate, Neala fully expected Mama to
.dd that Lilibet never would be out until she married. And, as
he often did, to loudly bemoan the fact. There simply wasn't
:nough money now to give Lilibet a proper season, whereas
Neala had already had two. And felt supremely guilty because
•f it, since the effort had netted nothing.

"But I have been invited elsewhere," Lilibet persisted, "Lady
;efton invited me to the musicale."

"That was different, Lilibet," Neala put in quietly. "You were
nvited there to sing. And Mama and I were only invited because
.ady Sefton is so very kind-hearted."

Lady Abercorn cleared her throat, and said nothing.

Neala knew it still hurt Mama that since Papa's death the

majority of her *ton* acquaintances shunned her shamelessly. Neala felt bad because of that, too, but of course nothing could be done about it. She sincerely wished her younger sister could have a proper season, but that couldn't be helped either. Yet now that Lord Winterton had come along, perhaps a season for Lilibet wasn't necessary.

"But, what if *he* is there, and I am not? I shan't want some other young lady to catch his eye."

"Lilibet," her Mama said sternly, "you are forgetting the force of the wedding spell. Once it has been cast, it cannot fail. You are to marry Lord Winterton, and that is all there is for it. We have now only to wait."

"Well, I still say it isn't fair," Lilibet muttered. "If Nealie is to go to the ball tonight, I should be allowed to go, as well."

With a sigh, Neala rose to clear the table. She knew full well that Lady Diana was responsible for her invitation to Miss Wentworth's come-out ball tonight. Along with the invitation yesterday had been a note from Diana saying that she and her father would call for Neala in their carriage on the night of the ball. Both Neala and Mama had been glad for that.

As Neala was getting dressed a bit later, both Mama and Grandma assisted her. Lilibet was still sulking in the parlor.

"Now, then," Mama said, once Neala had donned her favorite peach-colored silk gown and the matching overdress, which Mama had hastily sewn several rows of new blond lace upon this morning, "you must remember to be pleasant and to smile often, Neala dear. You were quite remiss in that department when Lord Brewster was here on Sunday last. No gentleman will wish to marry a sullen young lady."

"I'll try, Mama," Neala murmured.

"Sure an' she'll remember to smile at the ball," Grandma O'Grady said, favoring her granddaughter with a wrinkled grin. "Neala's a good 'un, she is."

Good 'un or not, Neala thought to herself, the bald truth was she didn't want to go to the ball. She didn't want to smile for

Lord Brewster, and she most certainly didn't want to marry the man. No matter how happy that prospect made Mama.

"Once you are married to Lord Brewster and Lilibet to Lord Winterton, we shall all be set once again! Now, come along, Neala girl, I am certain I hear Lord Brewster's carriage now!"

Mama was right and in only moments, Neala was being handed into the shiny black coach awaiting her at the curb.

"How pretty you look tonight, Nealie!" exclaimed Lady Diana, making room for Neala on the cushioned bench of the coach. "Doesn't she look pretty, Father?"

Neala kept her lashes lowered, but all the same felt herself color when Lord Brewster returned gallantly, "Miss Abercorn always looks charming."

In the grand saloon at the Wentworth ball, Lord Winterton was unprepared for the uproar his presence caused. In the few weeks since his arrival in Town, most of the gentlemen he had chanced upon at White's or Boodles, or during his occasional visits to Tattersall's, had ceased to fawn mercilessly over him. Not so the ladies.

Tonight, the vast number of introductions he'd received, accompanied by a dizzying whir of fan fluttering and high-pitched giggling, had already brought on a case of the megrims—something 'til now Winterton had not thought gentlemen experienced. Equally as off-putting was the blatant forwardness of some of the older women, most of them married ladies, a few of them widows. More than once, as Winterton made his way through the squeeze, he was startled by the 'accidental' pressing of a breast against his arm. Before a full hour had passed, the thought crossed Lord Winterton's mind that if he so desired, he could have his pick of almost any female in the room!

A few months ago, nay, even a few weeks ago, that thought may have taken root in Lord Winterton's mind and blossomed, but not now. The extra attention he was receiving only irritated him. His long gaze kept scanning the smiling faces of the glit-

tering crowd in search of a certain shy young lady who, no
matter how hard he tried, he could not dismiss from his mind.
Not seeing any sign of her, his irritation grew.

This afternoon at Gentleman Jackson's, where he had gone
for a bit of exercise, he had run smack into Brewster who had
mentioned that he and Lady Diana would be escorting Miss
Abercorn to the ball this evening. Winterton's long gaze once
again reverted to the arched doorway of the saloon. What was
keeping Brewster tonight?

To pass the time, Winterton stood up with several insipid
misses of varying size and coloring. During a rather lengthy
gavotte, he, at last, caught sight of Lord Brewster standing inside the doorway. And, on the turn-about, caught a glimpse of
Miss Abercorn's slim form. Instantly, he felt his heart lodge
uncomfortably in his throat.

The dance concluded, he hastily returned the young lady on
his arm once again to her chaperon, the voluptuous Lady Renfrow, a widow with dark ringlets and porcelain skin. But placing
a gloved hand on his arm, that lady successfully prevented his
immediate escape.

"I am told, Lord Winterton," she began, the other hand tapping her chin coyly with a folded fan, "that the entire country
owes you an enormous debt of gratitude."

Lady Renfrow waited for the tall gentleman to respond.

When only a cool smile was forthcoming, she stood on tiptoe
in order to whisper in his ear. "I should be delighted to person-
ally show *my* gratitude, my lord . . . if you are interested."

A raised brow, and a disinterested rake up and down her form
sufficiently exhibited the extent of Lord Winterton's interest.

Apparently mistaking the rebuff for acceptance, Lady Renfrow smiled brightly. "I shall have my card sent 'round tomorrow, my lord."

"And I shall put it with the others," Winterton replied coolly.
With a polite nod, he stepped past her.

His jaw set, he had almost decided to take his leave of the

party altogether when Lady Diana, her intended, Lord Edward, and another young lady approached him.

"Trench!" called Lady Diana, "I should like you to meet another dear friend of mine, Miss Belinda Morganstern. Miss Morganstern and I were at school together."

A set smile on his face, Winterton greeted the young lady properly, but wishing not to stand up with her, he turned to speak to Lord Edward. It was then that Lord Brewster, on a promenade about the room with Miss Abercorn on his arm, stepped up to greet them.

" 'Evening Winterton, enjoying yourself, eh? Quite a selection of lovelies to choose from, I see." Lord Brewster coughed, then tempered his somewhat crude remark with a candid wink at Miss Abercorn.

She blushed.

The portly gentleman coughed again. In the course of his coughing, he had to extricate himself from Miss Abercorn's arm. Then, while she was engaged in conversation with Lady Diana and Miss Morganstern, he motioned for Winterton to step aside with him. Safely out of earshot of the others, he began, "Be much obliged, Winterton, if you'd stand up with Miss Abercorn. I admit I'm finding this courtship dashed awful business. Having a blasted time getting the young lady to talk to me. If I didn't know better, I'd think she was mute. Which is not to say I don't want to marry her. But once the ceremony is over with, there won't be much need to talk, will there?" Brewster began to cough again, then managed, "I could stand something to wet my whistle."

Winterton did the polite thing and commandeered a passing footman carrying a tray. Handing Brewster a glass of champagne, he said, "You may count on me, Brewster. I shall be delighted to stand up with your Miss Abercorn, and—" he said without really thinking what he was saying "—do whatever else in the way of squiring her about that you'd like me to."

Lord Brewster's grey eyes lit up. "Bloody splendid idea, Winterton! I had wanted to go to Newcastle tomorrow for the races.

May be gone quite a spell. Be much obliged if you'd do the pretty for Miss Abercorn in my absence." Lord Brewster puffed his chest out.

"It's the least I can do," Winterton said, a rare smile, for this evening, suddenly appearing on his face. "Considering the debt I owe you, sir."

Brewster clapped him on the back. "You owe me nothing, my boy! But, if you did, and I'm not saying you do, this would surely cancel it!" He dove into his pocket for a fresh cigar, and twirled it in his pudgy fingers.

Feeling only a prick of guilt at what he had inadvertently set into motion, Lord Winterton directed a long gaze at Miss Abercorn. She looked a picture tonight in a peach-colored gown that seemed to accentuate the ivory smoothness of her arms and throat. Her soft curls were brushed to a sheen and when she turned her head, tiny diamond earbobs sparkled at her ears.

Apparently Brewster noticed the direction of his gaze for he said, "I know she ain't the least in your style, Winterton, otherwise I'd be a fool to turn her over to you. But, for that reason, I know she'll be safe in your care."

The prick of guilt Winterton had experienced earlier escalated to a pang, but with practiced military discipline he put the pang aside. He was to repay his debt to Lord Brewster and that was the whole of it.

Upon returning to the others, Lord Brewster told his daughter and Miss Abercorn that he wished to try his luck in the game room and that he needed a smoke. With a quick nod, he disappeared into the crowd.

Hearing the music start up, Winterton moved to stand next to Miss Abercorn. He was pleased when she looked up and favored him with a shy smile. Aware that the top of her head just barely reached his shoulder, he realized he had not noticed before just how petite she was. At length, he said, "Do you waltz, Miss Abercorn?"

She nodded, a small smile of pleasure playing at her lips.

"Neala is an excellent dancer!" Lady Diana, who was standing next to them, put in brightly. "At school, Neala was always the quickest study in the class." Turning to her betrothed, she said, "I should like also to dance, Edward."

Neala felt Lord Winterton's warm hand at her back, as he propelled her toward the floor. Being asked to dance by Lord Winterton tonight was beyond anything she could have hoped for. He was by far the most dashing and handsome man in the room. That he had actually come to stand beside her was compliment enough. That he'd share a waltz with her was a dream come true! She felt near to trembling now, but when he reached to encircle her waist and whirled her into the dance a sudden, unexpected shortness of breath overtook her. What was the meaning of it? Never had she felt breathless at the top of a dance before!

While she was wondering if she could last 'til the end, Lord Winterton leaned down to whisper in her ear. Feeling his warm breath fan her cheek almost made her stumble. "You are light as a feather in my arms, Miss Abercorn!" he said.

She was far too overcome now to speak. Only a small gasp escaped Neala's lips. Then she felt his hand tighten at her back and he drew her even closer! Feeling the hard wall of his chest pressed against the softness of her breasts, Neala was certain she would faint from the dizzying, delightful sensations that spiraled through her. Alarmed beyond measure, she wondered if Lord Winterton affected every young lady he danced with as he was now affecting her? Indeed, he was a *very* dangerous man!

Eager to make the most of the few precious moments he held Miss Abercorn in his arms, Lord Winterton lowered his head to speak to her again. "Lady Diana was right, Miss Abercorn, you are a wonderful dancer! You are like a will-o'-the-wisp in my arms."

Over the waves of the music, Lord Winterton couldn't hear her response, but he felt the sudden quiver in her breast. *She was delicious!* He wanted the dance to last a lifetime! Tightening his grip on her, he twirled her faster and faster, losing himself in the intoxicating feeling that being with her brought. Yet, all too soon, the music stopped and he was compelled to return her again to the sidelines.

Once there, neither Lady Diana nor Lord Edward were anywhere to be seen, so, with Miss Abercorn still on his arm, he headed for the refreshment table to procure them both glasses of fruit punch.

After taking a delicate sip of hers, Miss Abercorn murmured, "Lilibet will be sorry she was not here tonight, sir."

Having not the least desire to discuss Miss Lilibet, Winterton replied a bit absently, "I hope your sister is not ill, Miss Abercorn."

"If she is, it would be because she was not allowed to attend the ball," came the quick reply.

Winterton turned to look at her. "You make your sister sound a bit like Cinderella," he said dryly. "I find it quite difficult to imagine Miss Lilibet among the ashes."

To his delight, Miss Abercorn laughed aloud. It was the first time he had heard her laugh, and it struck him with such a degree of pleasure, he joined in. Looking at one another, they laughed and laughed. The sight of Miss Abercorn's sparkling brown eyes set up such a longing in Winterton's breast that he could barely stop himself from gathering her into his arms and hugging her on the spot.

With sudden decision, he set aside both their glasses and led Miss Abercorn once again to the dancefloor. He knew he shouldn't be dancing with her again, but if he were to repay this debt to Lord Brewster with any degree of completeness, the gossip his actions caused on Brewster's behalf would only help further the gentleman's cause.

On the way home that night, Neala wasn't sure what anything meant anymore. On the one hand, she had never had such a gay time in her life, on the other hand, what would Mama say when she found out that Lord Winterton had shamelessly monopolized her time for nearly the whole of the evening? It was shocking indeed!

Six

Winterton knew he was flirting with danger, but all his life he had lived on the edge. The exhilaration kept him young. Springing from his bed the next morning, he was determined to do the courting of Miss Abercorn, on Brewster's behalf, of course, up to snuff. And if in the end the young lady decided she preferred him to Brewster, well, what could anyone say to that?

After downing his coffee in a gulp, he dressed quickly and set out, his destination this crisp, clear morning: the flower market at Covent Garden. Though he had a bit of trouble maneuvering his team through the maze of traffic there, he managed well enough. Without a thought to extravagance, he bought the complete inventory off the first vendor he saw. After depositing the armful of pink and yellow blossoms on the seat of his curricle, he headed for Wright's bookshop and perused the shelves 'til he found the sort of story he thought Miss Abercorn would enjoy. Selecting the first two volumes of *The Mysteries of Ferney Castle,* he decided if she liked these well enough, he would buy the remainder of the set at a later date.

His next stop was Fortnum and Mason's, where he purchased a decorated box of chocolate bonbons for Miss Abercorn and her mother.

Climbing back into his vehicle, he pulled out his pocket watch to check the time and was dismayed to note that it was only eleven of the clock in the morning.

Far too early for a call.

Unless the gentleman in question was head over ears in love.
Which, of course, he was.

Therefore . . . eleven of the clock would suit perfectly.

Scooping up the ribbons, he slapped them over the backs of
the matched pair of chestnuts and was pleased to watch the
team—obviously growing more accustomed to his less than excellent driving skills—did, indeed, trot off down the street with
precision.

Arriving at the Abercorn flat, Lord Winterton took the narrow
stairs inside the ramshackle building two at a time, his progress
not the least hindered by the armload of flowers he carried, the
box of bonbons tucked under one arm and the two thick books
in one hand.

It pleased him immensely when Miss Abercorn herself an-
swered his eager rap. "Good morning, my dear!"

"Er . . . good morning, sir." She looked quite taken aback to
find him standing there. In fact, his presence must have ren-
dered her speechless for she said nothing more and he had to
ask if he might be let in.

"O-Of course." She stepped aside to allow him to enter.

"These are for you, Miss Abercorn," he announced proudly,
handing over the books, then laying the flowers and the box of
bonbons atop the pile.

"F-For me? But . . . but—"

"From Lord Brewster," he added quickly. "The gentleman
asked last evening if I might deliver them to you today. He
sends his best regards."

"Oh. I see, is he . . . ?"

"Gone. Left town on business. Will be away quite a spell, I
understand."

"Oh." She looked a trifle perplexed. "I don't recall him saying as much last evening, but then—" she looked down, shifted
the box of bonbons so as not to crush the flowers.

"Allow me to help you, Miss Abercorn." Winterton reached
again for the flowers and the bonbons, then looked about for a
likely spot in the tiny hall to deposit them.

At precisely that moment, Lady Abercorn appeared. "Why, Lord Winterton! What a pleasant surprise." She reached to tuck a stray auburn curl beneath her cap. "Lilibet will be pleased you have come to call. She should be returning from her errands very soon!"

"Lord Winterton did not come to see Lilibet, Mama," Neala said quietly.

Lady Abercorn cast a puzzled gaze from her daughter to the tall gentleman standing before them, then fixed a gaze on the bouquet of flowers and large box of chocolates he carried.

Winterton grinned disarmingly. "I am simply delivering today, Lady Abercorn. These are for Miss Abercorn, from Lord Brewster."

"My . . . how very thoughtful of Lord Brewster, I'm sure. We shall have to send notes 'round, Neala." She looked again at the load now in her arms, then at Winterton. "Would you like to step inside, sir? As I said, Lilibet should be returning shortly. She and her grandma have gone to Pearson the Laceman for a length of lace. For Lady Diana's wedding gown."

"Ummm—" Winterton fought to conceal his relief over the fact that Miss Lilibet was not at home "—perhaps, another time, Lady Abercorn. I thought perhaps, that is, Lord Brewster requested that I take Miss Abercorn for a drive, in his stead, of course. Is that agreeable with you, Miss Abercorn?"

Neala looked to her mama, who after a pause, nodded—a bit tightly Winterton noted—but the result was all the same. Miss Abercorn went to fetch her bonnet and reticule.

Feeling quite pleased with himself, Winterton handed his pretty charge into the carriage, then climbed in after her and scooped up the ribbons . . . then realized with a start that he had given no thought whatever to where he might take her.

"Have you a preference for our drive this morning, Miss Abercorn?" he asked.

Because the better part of her face was concealed behind the long-billed bonnet she wore, she had to completely turn her

head in order to look at him. "Green Park is quite lovely this
time of day."

"Green Park, it is." Winterton snapped the ribbons, and was
relieved once again when the action elicited the correct response
from the team. Shouldn't want Miss Abercorn to think him ill-
equipped to handle his cattle. "We are quite a distance from
the park, Miss Abercorn, so that should give us plenty of time
to take in anything of interest along the way."

For the first several minutes, they jostled along in compan-
ionable silence, then when Winterton felt firmly in control of
the team, he turned his attention to Miss Abercorn, asking her
a number of questions in an effort to draw her out. He asked
after her grandma, who he recalled had not been feeling well
since her trip from Ireland.

"Grandma is doing much better, thank you. She has resumed
her habit of taking long walks of a morning, which is why she
and Lilibet set off for Pearsons today. Usually it is I who shop
for the trimmings. Lilibet too often forgets the ticket."

"The ticket?"

"Oh—" Miss Abercorn ducked her head and Winterton per-
ceived that he, or she, had said something that embarrassed her.

"What is it, Miss Abercorn?"

There was a pause, then finally she said, "I—Mama would
not have wanted me to mention the ticket, sir."

He had no idea what she was talking about. "Forgive me,
Miss Abercorn, I am at a loss."

She turned to look up at him again. "The ticket, sir. The
lottery. Since Papa died . . . well, Mama believes that her luck
has now turned, and she'll soon be a winner. There is a winner
every week, you know."

"Oh, I see." Winterton tried not to laugh. He could clearly
recall a time in his life when winning the lottery would have
been just the thing. But instead, his good friend Lord Brewster
had stepped in. Brewster. A sinking feeling overtook him, reminding him of his mission this morning, courting Miss Abercorn on Lord Brewster's behalf.

"Well," he began roundly, "your mama must think Lord Brewster quite the catch. I expect she thinks you a winner in that department, Miss Abercorn."

Winterton was certain he heard her quick intake of breath and wondered again what he had said to upset her. This time he did not ask. He had to be truthful with Miss Abercorn, had to be certain she understood that all his actions, both last evening and today, were on behalf of Lord Brewster.

"Did you enjoy yourself at the ball last evening, Miss Abercorn," he began again.

"Oh, yes!" she exclaimed in a rush. "That is, I enjoyed . . ."

"Enjoyed . . . what, Miss Abercorn?" His tone had grown a trifle husky. He waited, almost forgetting to pay attention to his driving. They were nearing the busy intersection of Holbern Street and Drury Lane. Traffic here was thickening, the cobbled streets a tangle of gentlemen on horseback, lumbering carts and other carriages. On the narrow flagway, noisy hawkers and a stream of pedestrians jockeyed with one another for space enough to pass.

Trying to maneuver his team through the gnarl of traffic in order to turn at the next corner, Winterton was chargrined when his team trotted clean past it. Feeling some embarrassment over his inability to drive to an inch, he hastened to cover his humiliation by picking up the conversation he had left dangling. "May I say, I especially enjoyed our dances last evening, Miss Abercorn?"

Behind her bonnet, Neala smiled. "As did I, sir. Every young lady at the ball wished to dance with you."

Recalling that he had stood up with Miss Abercorn far too many times to be considered proper, he said, "Well, I shouldn't think our impropriety will cause a scandal, will it?"

"No, of course not," she said solemnly. "Not if you were standing up with me on Lord Brewster's behalf." She paused, then brightened a bit. "Lord Brewster speaks very highly of you, sir. I believe he is proud to count you as a friend."

"And I him," Winterton said with sincerity. "And how do you feel about me, Miss Abercorn?"

Tilting her head to one side, she slanted a look at the gentleman beside her. "Are you asking how I feel in regard to yourself, Lord Winterton; or are you posing that question on behalf of Lord Brewster?"

"If I am asking as Lord Brewster, Miss Abercorn, it is simply to ascertain if perhaps I have a rival for your affections in myself." With a start, he realized that he sounded like an arrogant nodcock. Equally as startling was the realization that his breath had grown short while awaiting her answer.

She considered a moment, then replied quietly, "Every young lady in England is a bit in love with you, sir."

It was not the answer he hoped for, but for now it would have to do. Glancing about at the unfamiliar surroundings he'd driven into, he muttered, "Wrong turn back there must have got us off the path."

"Are we lost?"

"Of course not, Miss Abercorn, we are in London!"

Still, it was an unsavory part of Town, and one that Winterton would never have knowingly brought a lady to. Casting a glance at the street marker, he could just barely make out the name, but it did jog something in his memory. Indeed! it was the last word he had deciphered on the page of information he'd received only yesterday from his contact regarding the suspected traitor's whereabouts. Glancing again at the flagway, something untoward there caught his attention. A gentleman wearing a bright red waist coat, which identified him as a member of the Bow Street Foot Patrol, was conversing with another man whom Winterton recognized as the young clerk he'd seen only last week at the Admiralty. In this neighborhood, where every other man sported wardrobes straight from the rag picker's barrel, the fashionable cut of the clerk's coat stood out as loudly as the Patrolman's red vest.

His curiosity fully aroused now, Winterton cast another glance over his shoulder, in time to see the clerk surreptitiously pass a package to the patrolman, who without pausing to examine the contents, slipped the bundle to an inside pocket. Aware that in their quest to prosecute criminals patrolmen often bought and sold information, Winterton wondered what of import would a rosy-cheeked young clerk at the Admiralty have to sell? Winterton's mind reeled. Had a wrong turn into a backstreet of London led him to the very link in the chain of deception he sought? If so, this was no time to loiter about asking mental questions, he had to act! Precious minutes had already slipped by.

"Miss Abercorn," he said abruptly, "look over your left shoulder and tell me if the gentleman in the red waistcoat is still standing on the flagway?"

Without question, she did as he requested. "The Bow Street Runner? Yes, he is. Shall we ask him for directions?"

"My thoughts exactly, Miss Abercorn," he lied, grateful to her for supplying him with a diversionary tactic. Wouldn't do to involve Miss Abercorn in this dangerous spy game.

She was still watching. "The gentleman with him has gone, but the patrolman is getting into a cab. He appears to be headed back the way we just came. Should we follow him?"

"You've read my mind again, Miss Abercorn. Hang on!" Giving a quick jerk to the ribbons, followed by a rapid succession of this-and-that way pulls, Winterton finally persuaded the chestnuts that he meant them to travel in the opposite direction. Thank Heaven the cobbled street here was not teeming with other vehicles or horses, and that he had purchased prime goers and someone else had trained them well! Winterton made a mental note to take a few more driving lessons before applying for membership in the Four-Horse Club.

Aware that during the less than smooth turn-about, Miss Abercorn had grabbed his arm and was still clinging so tightly to it he now feared loss of circulation, he asked, "Are you all right, Miss Abercorn?"

Her other hand holding her bonnet in place, Miss Abercorn replied rather breathlessly, "I-I think so." She glanced down as if to ascertain whether or not all four wheels of the carriage were indeed still rolling along on cobblestones. "It was a bit of a bumpy ride," she murmured.

"Sorry, Miss Abercorn, I fear I am sadly out of practice driving. Didn't do much in the army, most of my getting about there was done on horseback, or on foot."

Catching sight of the patrolman's blue-coated shoulder in the open cab a few blocks up ahead, Winterton turned his attention to the chase, a flick of his wrists successfully urging the beasts in front of him to trot at a swifter pace.

Just as he was gaining on the cab, it careened 'round a corner. Muttering a curse beneath his breath, Winterton prayed he could follow suit. When the horses seemed not to understand his command and the corner where he meant to turn was fast approaching, Winterton reached for the spanking new whip which 'til now he'd had no reason to use. His first attempt to communicate a need for urgency to the team met with little success; the second caused one horse to rear its head, then to Winterton's immense surprise, both animals skirted 'round the corner in perfect concert and charged down the street. In seconds, they were fast nearing the hackney cab jouncing along on the cobblestones a few yards ahead of them.

"Are you all right, Miss Abercorn?" he asked again.

Her answer this time was more of a squeak really. But, Winterton noted she had let go of his arm and now appeared to be trying to right herself, patting the long folds of her skirt back into place and untangling the ribbons of her reticule which he clearly recalled had lobbed him on the cheek in the midst of the last turn.

Hitting a large cobble in the road, Winterton again felt Miss Abercorn bounce against him.

"Oh, dear!"

"Hang onto my arm, Miss Abercorn," he said. "You are such a tiny thing, I shouldn't want you to go toppling sideways."

Neala instantly obeyed, twining both hands around his arm this time and clinging tightly to it.

Feeling her soft little body tucked close to his side, Winterton was unable to suppress a rakish grin. Since he seemed to be getting the hang of this driving thing, he wouldn't object greatly if the chase went on a spell.

But, as luck would have it, in only minutes, the cab turned down a narrow alleyway—too narrow for Winterton's coach—and though he slowed his team almost to a crawl, he lost sight of both the cab and its passenger.

"I think I know where we are now, sir," Miss Abercorn said presently.

Hearing her voice, Winterton dismissed his chagrin at losing his prey. Later today, he would double back and see what he could uncover. For the moment, however, he had far more pleasant business upon which to attend. "Very good, Miss Abercorn. I admit I am still at a loss."

"Just across the way is the piece goods shop, and over there is the fish market." A small gloved finger pointed across the street, directing Winterton's attention to a neat row of small shops. The traffic here was thicker, pedestrians were squeezed onto the flagway and both sides of the street were littered with vegetable and flower carts. "We are quite near Covent Garden," she added.

"Ah, yes." Winterton said, though he still didn't recognize a thing. "You are quite right, Miss Abercorn. I was at the market only this morning, to purchase the flowers I delivered to you from Lord Brewster."

"Hmmm," she murmured, then after a pause, said, "I trust you will remember to thank him for me, sir."

"Indeed, I will," he returned, still attempting, while driving, to ascertain precisely where in this labyrinth of narrow side streets they were.

Suddenly, Miss Abercorn cried, "Look out!"

Winterton's head jerked 'round just as his curricle and both horses collided with some obstruction on the street below. To a loud cacophony of whinnys and shouted curses, the horses reared up, wildly pawing the air in their fright. Winterton saw a blur of pedestrians scatter in all directions, then there was a deafening crash and both he and Miss Abercorn were pelted all over with a shower of something that felt rather wet and clammy.

Not taking the time to find out what they had hit, Winterton shoved aside whatever it was that drooped from the curly brim of his black beaver, and yelled "Whoa-there!" to the team while at the same time pulling taut the ribbons.

Luckily, the beasts responded, all eight of their hooves hitting the pavement and settling down to a sideways dance. Springing to his feet at once, Winterton first looked to see that Miss Abercorn was unharmed, then a glance toward the street told him he had caused no additional human casualties. However, the flower vendor whose cart he had overturned seemed a bit worse for wear. A few feet away, he was picking himself up from the pavement.

"I shall take the lot!" Winterton called gallantly to the man, and to prove his point, pulled his purse from his pocket.

"Right 'ye will, 'ye bloody block!"

When Winterton had paid the man—for the flowers and the demolished cart—he turned again to Miss Abercorn. She was a riot of color. Violets dripped from her bonnet, pink-tipped daisies sat askew on her shoulders, and periwinkles and primroses lay scattered at her feet. She had gathered a large assortment of blossoms and was holding them before her like a bridal bouquet. She was such a sight, he could not hold back the hearty laughter that bubbled up inside him.

"You're a picture, Miss Abercorn!" he exclaimed, brushing loose petals and wet leaves from his coat and breeches.

Looking up at him, Miss Abercorn's pretty face also wore a smile. "You're a picture yourself, Lord Winterton. The violets perched atop your hat are quite becoming."

"Why, thank you, my dear!" In a flourish, Winterton swept off his hat and dusted it over her head.

Miss Abercorn laughed gaily as violets rained down upon her again. Then she fixed Lord Winterton with a saucy look. "Must I also thank Lord Brewster for these pretty flowers, sir?"

Winterton threw his dark head back and laughed aloud. "On the contrary, Miss Abercorn, this bouquet was entirely my doing!" With an arm, he swept the bench free of flowers before he sat down and took up the ribbons again. "Now, then, shall we see if I can get you to Green Park all in a piece?"

Seven

Compared to overturning the flower cart, the rest of Neala's drive that morning with Lord Winterton proved uneventful. With the exception, that is, of the impromptu picnic in Green Park. Once in the park, Lord Winterton announced that he was hungry and spotting a pie man his lordship promptly purchased two. Then finding a shady spot beneath a large oak tree, he spread out his handkerchief for Neala to sit upon and they ate their pies together on the grass.

Neala enjoyed every last morsel of the flaky crust and the delicious filling, but not nearly so much as she enjoyed Lord Winterton's delightful company. She marveled over how relaxed she felt with him. She even felt free enough to tell him one of her favorite tales about her Papa, about the time they had been on their way to Ireland and on the last leg of the trip, had missed the stage and had to ride part of the way on a farmer's cart piled high with pumpkins. When a wheel broke, they and the pumpkins had rolled helter-skelter into the road. It was one of the most fun times Neala ever had with her papa. And being with Lord Winterton today felt every bit as lighthearted and enjoyable.

Winterton told her about some of his war experiences and how Lord Brewster had bought his commission for him those many years ago. Listening raptly to him, Neala realized that she would never grow tired of hearing the gentleman talk. She had never met anyone like Lord Winterton before!

She hated for the picnic to end, but end it did and afterwards, he drove her home. As she walked beside him up the stairs that afternoon, she felt loath to bid the charming gentleman good-bye. At the door, she turned to him. "Thank you for the lovely drive, Lord Winterton. I can't think when I have enjoyed myself quite so much."

Winterton politely tipped his hat. "Lord Brewster will be pleased to hear that, Miss Abercorn." His tone was low, and the deep sound of it sent a thrill coursing through Neala.

"However—" Lord Winterton's lips began to twitch "—I shan't tell Brewster about the extra bouquet I presented to you."

This brought a laugh of delight from Neala, and Winterton joined in as well. Neala loved hearing him laugh and watching the corners of his eyes crinkle when he did so.

"Would you be good enough to accompany me to the opera tomorrow evening, Miss Abercorn? I understand Brewster has a box at the King's Theatre. He had an idea you might find an evening at the opera entertaining," he added.

The second mention of Lord Brewster's name caused Neala's smile to fade a bit. Still, she managed an agreeable nod. "I should like that very much, sir. Thank you, indeed."

"Splendid! We shall make a party of it; Lady Diana, Lord Edward and the pair of us. Perhaps your mother as well? Until tomorrow then." With another polite nod, the handsome man turned to go.

Neala watched his backside disappear down the stairs, then let herself into the flat. Inside, she was so overcome from the delightful morning spent with him that she could only lean dreamily against the closed door, the huge garland of flowers Lord Winterton had presented to her clasped to her breast. Never had she had a real suitor. Dancing with Lord Winterton last evening and spending time with him today was the most thrilling thing that had ever happened to her. Not even the fact that her joy was due entirely to Lord Brewster's generosity made the events of the last two days any less memorable. And, now, a secret smile softened her lips, she had the opera with Lord Winterton to look forward to.

Her heart lighter than it had ever been, Neala pushed away from the door. Making her way down the narrow corridor, she paused when she saw Lilibet coming toward her.

Spotting the immense bouquet of colorful blossoms in Neala's arms, Lilibet cried, "Lord Winterton has given you *more* flowers? *Mama!*"

Neala felt her stomach muscles tighten.

Lady Abercorn stepped into the hallway from the small workroom beyond the kitchen. Neala knew her mother had been hard at work all day on Lady Diana's wedding gown.

"What is it, Lilibet?" Mama's tone was irritable.

"Neala has *more* flowers! And Lord Winterton has gone and Neala did not invite him in to see me!"

Lady Abercorn turned a disapproving look on Neala. "You should have invited the gentleman in, Neala. Lilibet is quite distressed that she missed seeing him this morning, to say nothing of the rumors that she heard circulating at the lacemakers today."

"It is all over Town!" Lilibet cried, her tone hurt and accusing.

"What is all over Town?" Neala asked quietly.

"Everyone is saying that you threw yourself at Lord Winterton's head last night at the ball!" Lilibet wailed. "That you danced with him a vast number of times and that he brought you punch and took you into supper!"

Lady Abercorn pinned Neala with a hard look. "Is this true, Neala?"

After a pause, Neala nodded. "Yes, Mama. But, Lord Winterton stood up with me only because Lord Brewster asked him to. The same as he came calling this morning. Lord Brewster is away, and he asked Lord Winterton to take me for a drive and to—" she paused, then decided against mentioning the invitation to the opera just now "—and to keep an eye out for me."

Lady Abercorn considered a moment, then said, "I see." She turned to Lilibet. "It is just as I thought, Lilibet. You have nothing to fear. It is unthinkable that Lord Winterton would prefer Neala to you. It would go against the spell. He is simply doing a good turn for Lord Brewster. Now," she said to Neala, "give the flowers to your sister and be a good 'un and help me with this lace. Lady Diana will be here shortly and I am not yet ready for her fitting."

When Lady Diana arrived that afternoon, she quickly reaffirmed all that Neala had said regarding Lord Winterton's actions of last evening and today.

"Father is quite taken with you, Nealie," she added, preening before the ornate mirror that looked sadly out of place in the tiny workroom. "So much so that he cannot bear the thought that another gentleman might snatch you from beneath his nose. Why, just this morning at breakfast, before he left for Newcastle, he told me he felt you'd be quite safe in Lord Winterton's care."

Neala lowered her lashes.

"How long will your father be away?" Lady Abercorn asked absently, removing a pin from her mouth and inserting it into the hem of Lady Diana's wedding gown.

"Only a day or two, I should think. Then we shall all be leaving again for the country." She turned to Neala, who was hovering close by with the inch tape and the paper of pins in her hands. "You are invited to come as well, Neala dear. There shall be quite a party of us. I've a fortnight of activities planned, and on the final day, Edward and I shall be married in Gloucester Cathedral. Father is especially looking forward to your being there. You must come!"

"Of course, she will attend," Lady Abercorn said around the pins in her mouth. "Neala, be a good 'un and hand me the scissors."

When the fitting was concluded, and they were all again assembled in the foyer, Lady Diana hugged Neala. "Thank you for everything, Neala dear. My wedding gown is beautiful! I am so happy the way things are turning out. We shall be friends forever, I am certain of it!"

"I am happy for you as well," Neala murmured, unable to summon the same degree of enthusiasm as Diana, but pleased nonetheless that her friend was happy.

Tying the pink ribbons of her bonnet beneath her chin, Diana added, "Don't forget, Edward and Trench and I shall call for you promptly at seven tomorrow evening."

"Tomorrow evening?" said Lady Abercorn, her face a question as she looked from Lady Diana to Neala.

"We are all to attend the opera together, Lady Abercorn. Trench said he had asked you this morning, Neala." Diana glanced at Neala for confirmation.

She flinched.

"Neala?" Her mother's tone was stern.

"Yes, Mama. Lord Winterton did mention our going to the opera together. I expect I forgot to tell you."

"I see," Lady Abercorn said tightly.

"Good bye!" Diana called as she left the flat, accompanied by her abigail and a footman, who had been waiting patiently for her outside on the stairs.

"Oh!" Lilibet wailed, appearing in the foyer the very second the door had shut behind their guest. "Now, Neala is to attend the opera with Lord Winterton! It isn't fair, Mama. I should be the one on the gentleman's arm, not Neala!"

After depositing Miss Abercorn at her flat that morning, Lord Winterton doubled back to the alleyway where he had lost sight of the Bow Street Patrolman and the war office clerk. The more he thought about it, the less he suspected the young clerk was the traitor he sought. More than likely the young man was an intermediary, unaware of what sort of secret information he was passing along. The real spy would stay hidden, shielded behind a long line of others who would be apprehended and punished long before the true culprit could be found.

Since the alleyway where the hackney cab had disappeared this morning was still too narrow for Winterton's coach this afternoon, and he did not think it wise to leave his new curricle and team unattended in order to sleuth about on foot, he decided to make a fresh start in the investigation in the morning. Tonight he would finish decoding the information he'd received from his contact yesterday. Perhaps he might glean some clues from it that would help him tomorrow.

Awake at first light the next morning, Winterton hastily consumed a hearty breakfast with only a cursory glance at the *Times*. Then he hurried back to his bedchamber and varied his normal routine by declining Rigas's offer for a shave.

"Not shave, your lordship!" Rigas tone was incredulous.

"Not today, Rigas." Winterton knew this went against everything his manservant stood for, but it couldn't be helped. He also refused to don the fashionable clothes his manservant had meticulously laid out for him and opted instead for a pair of tattered trousers that had weathered many a hedgebush and muddy roadway during the war. The wrinkled shirt and worn coat he chose to complete the outfit hadn't fared much better. Capital, Winterton thought, viewing his unkempt appearance in the cheval glass as behind him, Rigas shook his head with wonder.

In the mews Winterton traded a coin for the dirty wool cap one of the stablelads habitually wore and, without a backward glance, set out. On foot. The trek from fashionable Belgrave Square to Covent Gardens seemed like nothing compared to the long distances he had previously traveled afoot between battlefields in Spain. And to limbs already grown stiff from too much city living, the exercise felt inordinantly good.

Once he had reached the Rookery and Seven Dials, where Winterton was now aware he had stumbled into yesterday, his senses became fully alert. They always did when he felt danger lurking 'round every corner. The exhilaration peaked in him here just as it had on the battlefield, when he'd balanced on that thin line between life and death. Then, he'd wonder when the first shot would be fired, if the bullet would fell his own body or that of a respected comrade. Today, however, he was aware of other emotions, feelings he had never experienced before. The simple newness made them impossible to name. With mild irritation, he brushed aside the oddity, trying to focus instead on the familiar, the titillating danger, the breathless anxiety.

But after a long day spent on the filthy streets, dodging footpads and pickpockets, and eavesdropping on the conversations between boisterous patrons in crowded ordinaries and flash houses in the area, all of Winterton's efforts netted nothing. Except a bruised jaw. In spite of the disguise he'd donned this morning, the flower vendor whose cart he'd overturned yesterday had recognized him today. The man had proceeded to knock his lights out.

"Should've done it yeste'dy!" the irate man shouted, taking another wild swing at Winterton's prickly jaw.

Not expecting fisticuffs, Winterton only had time to turn his head. The man's second blow landed a bit right of its mark. Winterton was quick to react, and flattened the man with a single punch. Then he ducked out of sight and disappeared down the street. Soon after that, he decided to head for home.

Rubbing the sore spot on his chin now as he entered his bedchamber, Lord Winterton addressed his longsuffering manservant. "I shall be going out this evening, Rigas."

Still wearing the disapproving look on his face, Rigas glanced up from his work, neatly folding a stack of freshly laundered neck cloths. "And will we require a shave this evening, sir?"

Winterton smothered a grin. "Of course, we shall require a shave, Rigas. A gentleman can hardly be seen in public in a slovenly state, can he?"

Winterton squelched another smile as he watched Rigas's eyes roll skyward.

That evening the door knocker at the Abercorn flat sounded promptly at seven of the clock. Neala had been ready since six. Tonight she was wearing a lovely new gown of lavender sarcenet that she and Mama had fashioned from a length not used in

Lady Stanhope's ball gown last month. With tiny cap sleeves and rounded neckline, it was the latest style, and wearing it, Neala felt almost pretty.

"My, how charming you look this evening, Miss Abercorn!" Lord Winterton exclaimed, extending an arm to escort her down the stairs and into the Brewster carriage awaiting them at the curb.

Neala felt breathless with excitement as she settled herself beside the tall gentleman inside the dimly lit coach. Never in her life had she dreamed she'd be going to the opera with such a distinguished and attractive man. Not even Lilibet's fit of disappointment earlier was sufficient to dampen Neala's spirits tonight.

Once Neala and her fashionably attired companions were ensconced in the Brewster box on the second tier of the King's Theatre, Neala gazed wide-eyed around the enormous auditorium where a noisy crowd was gathering for tonight's performance. The interior of the building was lit with hundreds of glittering candles. Shadows danced on the ceiling where a beautiful mural of mythological figures had been painted in the clouds. In addition, the ceilings of all the boxes were painted sky blue, and scarlet draperies at the rear of the small enclosures matched the theatre seats in the pit. There the fops and dandies were already parading up and down, showing off their riotous finery as they quizzed the theater patrons and one another.

"Look, just there!" squealed Lady Diana at Neala's side, trying not to point a small gloved finger. "It's the Prince Regent. And, he's looking this way!"

Indeed, at that very moment, the Regent did stand and looked straight toward their box. Neala's breath caught in her throat as all eyes in the theater followed those of the Regent. She watched the corpulent Prince lift a gloved hand and, with an admiring gesture, salute the war hero, Lord Winterton. At once, she and every other patron in the huge theater sprang to their feet as pandemonium broke loose. Cheers, shouted accolades and wild applause feted the tall gentleman standing at Neala's side. Neala had never felt so proud in her life.

Lord Winterton, with only the hint of a smile on his handsome face, took the adulation in stride, at times nodding this way or that. When the noise and excitement finally died away, they all resumed their seats and at length, turned expectant eyes upon the stage.

Neala felt Lord Winterton lean toward her. "Have you heard Miss Billington perform before?"

Neala shook her head. "No, sir, I have not, but I am quite looking forward to it. I understand her voice is exquisite."

"Indeed, it is," he returned. "I was fortunate to hear her sing last summer in Venice."

"Oh," Neala breathed, her tone impressed. "I have never been to Venice, nor anywhere on the continent."

Winterton fixed an intent gaze on her. "I would love to take you there one day, Miss Abercorn. There is nothing quite so enchanting as an evening stroll along a moonlit canal."

"Oh!" Neala's eyes widened and she felt herself color deeply. How *very* romantic he was!

For a moment, she could almost believe that the gentleman was being sincere, that he truly meant what he had just said to her. But, of course, he could not really mean he wished to take her to Venice. He was merely being a gentleman, repaying the debt he owed Lord Brewster in a grand fashion. How thoughtful of Lord Winterton to try and make her feel special. He was very like Papa in that respect, too. Papa liked to make other people feel good, and he always repaid his debts in a grand fashion. Papa was honorable to a fault.

Neala recalled the time her father had lost two prize geldings to a gentleman whom everyone acknowledged had cheated him at cards. But, Papa stood by his word and though he prized the animals highly, he gave them up, and did so with a smile on his face.

Neala stole a peek from beneath her lashes at Lord Winterton. The tall gentleman actually looked pleased, even *happy,* to be here with her tonight. Neala's breath caught in her throat again. Lord Winterton could have his pick of any woman in London. Since the Prince had called the entire theater's attention to Lord Winterton's presence here this evening, a vast number of quizzing glasses had been turned on their box. Most especially, Neala noted, that belonging to a dark-haired woman in a crowded box across the way. She had hardly stopped looking at him.

Winterton had noted as well the dark-haired beauty quizzing him from the opposite box. Though for the entire first act of the performance, he was unable to recall where he had last seen the woman. That is, until raptly holding his gaze, she began to coyly tap her chin with her fan. Then the recollection came to him. She was the chaperon who had waylaid him at the Wentworth ball. Lady Renfrow, he believed her name was.

She looked quite attractive this evening in a low-cut green velvet gown that left very little to a gentleman's imagination. But Winterton wasn't the least interested in the woman, so merely cleared his throat and turned to place an arm across the back of Miss Abercorn's chair.

During the first intermission, Lord Winterton gallantly procured glasses of champagne and plates of strawberries for Miss Abercorn and Lady Diana. After the curtain had gone up again, they all settled back to enjoy the remaining act of the opera when a noisy disturbance in the box across the way caused Winterton to glance that direction again. A gentleman had apparently elbowed his way into Lady Renfrow's box and was now insisting that he be allowed to sit beside her. In the brilliantly lit theatre, Winterton easily recognized the young man as being the youthful clerk from the war office. Winterton's brows pulled together. What business could the young pup have with the seasoned widow?

She and the gentleman now had their heads together, apparently involved in a lengthy discussion behind the shield of the lady's fan. Making no attempt to hide his interest in the proceedings now, Lord Winterton suddenly grew very interested in the beautiful Lady Renfrow. But how to ask questions or learn more about the woman without causing notice or undue alarm?

He glanced toward his lovely companion, the serene Miss Abercorn. She looked sweet and delicate this evening in a silky-looking lavender gown with an ivory shawl draped across her smooth shoulders. Listening to the *prima donna* Billington sing, the rapt expression on Miss Abercorn's face was near angelic. Winterton felt his breath grow short just watching Miss Abercorn's enjoyment of the music. He would like nothing better than to spend the remainder of this evening in her delightful company, but . . . his long gaze flitted across the theater again. Like it or not, he did have official military business to attend to.

Gazing still at Lady Renfrow's box, he watched the young clerk rise and prepare to take his leave, nodding his head repeatedly as if assuring the dark-haired woman he'd been conversing with that he understood . . . something. For a fleeting instant, Winterton considered following the young man, but he dismissed the notion. Instinct had told him before that the boy was not the quarry he sought. His gaze fell again to the porcelain-skinned beauty who, as if sensing Winterton's intent gaze upon her, now fastened one upon him. This time, Winterton responded to her look with a slight incline of his dark head.

When the long intermission between the opera and the ballet ensued, Winterton reached a decision. Rising to his feet before the final applause reached a crescendo, he had taken several steps toward the scarlet curtain at the back of the Brewster box, when Lady Diana's voice halted him.

"Trench! We are not to leave just yet! The ballet is still to come and I should like to see it, wouldn't you, Neala?"

Also on her feet, Miss Abercorn turned toward him. "Indeed, I should like that very much, sir."

Winterton moved back toward the trio still standing near their chairs. "We shall stay as long as you like," he assured Miss Abercorn, who rewarded him with a sweet smile. How he hated to leave her now, but it could not be helped. "I . . . just mean to pay my respects to someone. I shall return straight away." In the saying, his gaze had flitted across the theater.

Following it, Lady Diana giggled. "Oh, Trench! You are not being the least bit circumspect. Lady Renfrow has been quizzing you all evening. We have all seen her."

Winterton paused. What did Lady Diana know of the woman? Perhaps he could gain a bit of foreknowledge before he barged into her box. "So—" he assumed a casual air, leaning against the side wall of the enclosure "—you have found me out. What do you know of her? I made her acquaintance at the Wentworth ball the other evening, but other than the fact that she is a widow, I know nothing about her."

"Save that she is a great beauty!" enthused Lord Edward, who until now had remained silent, who nearly *always* remained silent.

"Ah, yes, she is that indeed," Lord Winterton murmured, hating to hurt Miss Abercorn's feelings by dancing attendance upon another woman, but under the circumstances saw no other way for it. "What do you know of her late husband?"

Again, it was Lord Edward who spoke up. "Killed by the French while on official government business in Paris last year. Gentleman was to have been protected, immunity, that sort of thing, but apparently his bodyguards were a trifle remiss. Some said it was an accident, but Lady Renfrow would have none of it, was quite put out about it. Left virtually without funds, don't you know."

"Why, Edward!" Lady Diana cried, "how is it you know such a great deal about the widow Renfrow?"

When the poor fellow colored deeply, Winterton wisely refrained from asking any further questions of him. Already, he knew enough to be suspicious of Lady Renfrow. She not only had strong motives to betray her countrymen—revenge *and* a need for the ready—she also had the military connections to carry off any sort of espionage. Again, the exhilarating feeling of danger beset him. He itched to apprehend her. "Ah, well," he pushed himself up from the wall, "if you will excuse me please, Miss Abercorn, Diana? I shall only be a moment."

At the curtained door to the box, however, he turned again to Miss Abercorn. "Might I bring you another glass of champagne, my dear?"

Miss Abercorn shook her soft brown curls. "No, thank you, sir." A gloved hand indicated the half-empty glass on the railing near them. "There is plenty left in my glass."

"But I expect it is flat by now. I shall bring you another." Saying that he was gone.

When the ballet had concluded and Lord Winterton had not yet returned to the box, Neala found herself fighting back tears of disappointment. Throughout the long performance, she had tried not to direct a gaze across the way to Lady Renfrow's box, where it had been plainly evident at the outset that Lord Winterton's sudden appearance there had caused quite a stir. During most performances, the theater was usually noisy, with fops and dandies calling to one another, trying to direct patrons' attention to themselves instead of to the play, but tonight the disturbance in Lady Renfrow's box easily outweighed the noise on the floor, or on the stage. And, at the center of it was Lord Winterton himself.

Because the entire audience, including Lady Diana, seemed to enjoy the additional spectacle, Neala had said nothing. But she had felt plenty. Every time another young lady, or two or three, had crowded into the Renfrow box, jockeying to sit or stand next to the illustrious war hero, Neala's heart had grown heavier. How he must have *loathed* being with her tonight! He had not even looked her direction since he entered Lady Renfrow's box! It was obvious he had completely forgotten her.

When the ballet was at last over, Neala lost sight of her escort entirely. Her footsteps heavy, she, Lady Diana and Edward made their way down the winding staircase to the crowded foyer. Outside on the cool damp flagway, they waited for the carriage to be brought 'round. Once, Neala thought she heard the deep rumble of Lord Winterton's laughter. Unable to keep from looking about, she caught only a fleeting glimpse of his handsome face before he disappeared again from sight.

Hardly able to swallow around the huge lump forming in her throat, Neala bit her lower lip to keep it from quivering. When she was safely inside the dark interior of the coach, and the carriage finally jerked forward, she felt one stinging drop of moisture trickle down her cheek. In the darkness, she hastily brushed it aside and tried to join in with Diana's gay chatter. Prattling on about tonight's performances, both on and off the stage, Diana had snuggled closer to Edward.

"Did you not enjoy the ballet, Neala?"

"I am quite certain Winterton did," Lord Edward muttered, casting a bemused gaze from the coach window.

"Oh, Edward!" Diana squealed, "how you do go on! I think Trench and Lady Renfrow would suit perfectly. They are both very attractive. What do you say, Neala?"

Neala couldn't think of a thing to say, but knew that her silence didn't matter a whit to either Diana or Edward.

"Well, if you want to know what I think," Lord Edward began, "I think it not the least bit sporting of him to abandon us entirely."

"Oh, I don't think that at all," Diana retorted. "Trench did what he told Father he would do, he escorted Neala to the opera. He was not obliged to see her home. She is quite safe with us. Gentlemen often go their own way after arriving at a *soiree* or a ball. Neala doesn't mind, do you, Neala?"

Her breath short, Neala shook her head. It was true. Lord Winterton had sufficiently repaid his debt to Lord Brewster. He owned *her* nothing. From the outset Neala had known that Lord Winterton was a flirt. Diana had said he was a heartbreaker. Still, at the top of this evening . . . as well as, at the Wentworth ball, and on their drive through Green Park yesterday, he had seemed genuinely pleased to be with her.

Remembering the laughter they'd shared, she felt moisture well again in her eyes and fought to control the overpowering sadness that filled her heart. What was wrong with her? Why did Lord Winterton's actions tonight hurt her so? She wasn't in love with him. She could never be that silly. She wasn't a bit like Lilibet. Oh, poor, dear Lilibet. She hadn't the least notion what sort of man she was set to marry. What should she say to Lilibet now?

Eight

Over the next several days, Neala failed miserably in pushing away the painful sadness that had settled about her the night she went to the opera in the company of Lord Winterton. Not even making plans for the upcoming houseparty at Lady Diana's family estate in the country could take her mind off how badly she felt. Though she knew that daydreaming about the delightful times she had spent with Lord Winterton was useless, she couldn't seem to stop herself. Both Mama and Lilibet persisted in speaking of the handsome gentleman, Lilibet wondering why he had ceased altogether in calling upon her.

"No doubt, he has important business to attend to," Lady Abercorn assured her youngest daughter. "He will call again. I am certain of it. You forget, Lilibet, once the spell is cast, it cannot fail."

"But, how can you be so sure, Mama?" Lilibet wanted to know, her lower lip protruding in a decided pout.

"Because, I *am* sure, Lilibet! Now, hush!"

On the evening before Neala was set to depart for Ross-On-Wye, the small market town near Brewster Hall, the three Abercorn women and Grandma O'Grady were gathered, as was their custom, in the tiny drawing room following an early supper.

"Neala," began Lilibet, her blue eyes trying to pin those of her older sister, whose brown head was bent over her work, stitching a pretty feathery plume to the crown of the new green riding bonnet she intended to take to the country with her. "I rather expect Lord Winterton will be present at Lady Diana's houseparty, don't you?"

Neala did not look up. She had no desire to speak about Lord Winterton. Though she knew she had no right to feel as she did, the pain she had suffered the night he abandoned her at the opera still felt as fresh as if it had happened yesterday. She had begun to wonder if the wound would ever heal.

"Neala!"

Neala bit her lip. She knew she must eventually answer her sister. Lilibet was not one to give up without a struggle. "I-I cannot say for certain, Lilibet," she mumbled. "Diana has not mentioned whether Lord Winterton will be present or not."

"Well, of course, he will be there! He and Lord Brewster are the best of friends," Lilibet persisted, her tone quaking with anger. She turned to her mother. "I still say Diana should have invited me! Can't you *do* something, Mama?"

"Now, Lilibet, we have discussed this matter at length. You will have plenty of time to spend with your young man once you are married." Lady Abercorn shook out the garment she was working on, a pretty Spencer jacket to match the new riding dress she had made for Neala. The jacket was the same shade of forest green as the hat Neala was working on. "Quite possibly Lord Winterton is busy with Parliament or some such. Gentlemen carry a lot on their minds these days. Neala, I should like you to slip this on now." She put aside her needle, then addressed the pouting Lilibet again. "Throughout the whole of your marriage, sweetheart, your husband will stay busy with gentlemanly concerns. After all both he and Lord Brewster sit in the House of Lords. You should be listening to this, as well, Neala, dear."

Neala was listening. But being reminded of the nature of Lord Winterton's current 'gentlemanly concern' did little to lift her spirits. She shifted uncomfortably on the sofa, wishing with all her soul the Abercorn women would find another topic of conversation to fill the long evening hours.

"Be a good 'un, Neala, and slip this on," her mother said again. "I must check the length of the sleeves before I stitch on the piping."

"Yes, Mama." Neala obediently set her own work aside and rose to her feet to put on the pretty new jacket. She had needed a new riding habit for quite a spell, her old one was in tatters. When he was alive, she and Papa often spent long hours riding together. Papa's horseflesh had been the talk of Mayfair. Pulling the double-breasted Spencer snug about her, she began to feel quite the thing wearing so stylish a garment. She wondered if Lord Winterton would think she looked attractive in her fashionable attire? Oh! Why did thoughts of that gentleman persistently intrude upon her mind?

"You look very pretty, 'ye do," murmured Grandma O'Grady from her comfortable chair near the fire. A smile of contentment played at her thin lips. "It's sure I am your young man will offer for you 'afore the week is out."

Hearing Lilibet's malicious little chuckle from behind her, Neala pressed her lips together. She did not wish to be married to Lord Brewster, no matter what Grandma, or Mama, or anybody said!

"Lady Diana certainly expects her father to offer for you soon," Mama added, turning up the long fitted sleeve of the jacket so it hung just right and inserting a pin to mark her place on the edge. "Why, only yesterday when Diana came to collect her wedding gown, she told me as much herself. You are a fortunate young lady, Neala dear."

Neala did not think so. But what could she say to it? Mama had made it quite clear if she were to be married at all, she had no choice but to accept Lord Brewster's suit. And, though Neala did not doubt for a second the veracity of the wedding spell, if it did not work soon, the well-being of the entire Abercorn family rested on Neala's head. Already, their pockets were to let. It would not be long now before . . . at any rate, it was beginning to look as if the sooner Lord Brewster offered for her, the better off they would all be.

* * *

Soon after noon on the following day, five carriages, carrying
Neala, Lady Diana, Lord Edward, Lord Brewster and two other
couples, friends of the Brewster family, plus assorted servants
and baggage, set out for Ross-on-Wye in Hertfordshire. By five
of the clock that evening, the coaches rattled across Magdalen
Bridge into Oxford and drew up before The Star Inn. It had
been pouring rain all day, delaying the party's departure that
morning and impeding their progress throughout the long hours
on the road that afternoon.

Once the bedraggled group had assembled inside the cozy
inn and shaken the raindrops from their cloaks and wraps, they
all took seats around a long wooden table in the near-deserted
common room to partake of a quick meal. Over slices of cold
roast beef and bowls of steaming soup, thick with chunks of
potatoes and onions, the conversation among the gentlemen
centered around whether or not to proceed in light of the inclement weather. It was finally decided to push on, at least as
far as Woodstock, where they could spend the night in a comfortable hostelry that Lord Brewster was familiar with.

Climbing back into the coaches, Neala realized that so far
today she hadn't minded the rain, it suited perfectly the dejected
spirit that persisted in dogging her steps. Assigned to the carriage carrying Lady Diana and Lord Edward, she had spent
most of the long rainy afternoon reading one of the two books
Lord Winterton had given to her. Diana and her intended were
not terribly good company, for anyone other than themselves,
that is, so Neala was doubly glad she had brought along her
new books.

By the next day, as the carriages approached the Cotswold
hills, rumbling through such picturesque villages as Lower
Slaughter and Upper Swell, the rain had let up a bit. Upon
reaching Shipton Sollers the hungry travellers disembarked
again, this time at The Frogmill Inn situated on the banks of
the usually peaceful river Coln. Again the gentlemen expressed

concern over the wiseness of continuing or passing the night here while they awaited sunnier skies.

"The two-mile descent onto the Gloucester vale can be quite treacherous," said Mr. McGill, a longtime friend of Diana's older brother Harry. A tall man, Mr. McGill seemed always to be taking care of his little wife, Elizabeth. "It is not uncommon for passengers to be required to make the descent into the city on foot," he added, casting an anxious glance at his plump wife, who was seated beside him.

She glanced up to smile at her husband, but apparently the action distracted her from the task at hand—eating the meal in front of her—and a wayward hand successfully knocked over an entire mug of ale onto the scarred tabletop, which only moments before had been hastily covered with clean linen. The innkeeper had unearthed it from Heaven only knew where once he ascertained that Quality had come to dine.

"Oh. Dear me." The little woman cast an anxious gaze at her husband, who had jumped at once to assist her.

Both Neala and Lady Diana offered up their napkins, while Lord Edward sprang also to his feet to avoid being dribbled on by the river of ale which had been quickly soaked up by the cloth and was now moving precariously close to the table's edge.

Slapping at his thighs with his napkin, he remarked, "Dash it all! First the rain all but destroys my new trousers, and now this!"

"The rain appears to be slackening," Neala put in quietly. "Though, I daresay, I can't say the same for the ale." A round of good-natured laughter followed her last remark.

Mr. McGill had moved to escort his wife to the hearth so she might stand in front of the low-burning fire in order to dry out. While still on his feet, Lord Edward glanced past the elderly Lord Tentrees to gaze from the diamond-paned window at that gentleman's elbow. "By Jove, I do see sunlight just beyond that stand of trees. If need be," Lord Edward continued, resuming his place at the table and some of his good cheer, "I could carry

Diana pig-a-back down the mountain." Winking at his pretty bride-to-be, a certain rakish look twisted his mouth.

Across from him, Lady Diana giggled with delight.

"Pitch is quite perilous," muttered Lord Brewster, his jowls full of the spicy sausage and black bread he had especially ordered from the innkeep. Neala noted the unfortunate ale spill hadn't interfered one bit with his hearty enjoyment of his meal. Judging from his shape, not much else had either.

"Oh, it would be great fun!" Lady Diana enthused. "I should like us stay the night at The King's Head Inn in Gloucester. Edward and I first met in Gloucester." She reached across the table to clasp Lord Edward's long slim hand, being careful to avoid the damp spot on the cloth. "Tomorrow I should like us to walk to the cathedral where Edward and I are to be married." Her blue eyes sparkled with happiness as she locked gazes with her husband-to-be.

"Sounds like a good plan to me," remarked Lord Tentrees dryly, his mouth barely moving as he talked. He was a tall man, about Lord Brewster's age, and had a long, pinched nose and thinning yellow hair. Acquainted with his much younger wife, Helene, Neala had felt rather sorry for the girl when she first learned of her marriage to the much older Lord Tentrees. Like her, Helene's family hadn't a feather to fly with. Now, Neala realized, she and Helene may have a bit more in common than she first thought.

After luncheon, the travellers climbed back into the coaches, and by the time the party arrived at Crickley Hill, which overlooked the Gloucester plain and the pretty city of Gloucester, its cathedral spire rising like a sentinel from the midst of the muted tapestry below, the rain had indeed let up. The spring air was still cool, however, and the sun had not yet dried up the muddy ruts or deep puddles of rain water. Though the entire party did have to alight and make the perilous descent into Gloucester on foot, Neala found she rather enjoyed the trek downwards. The rain-washed breeze sweeping past them felt far more refreshing than the strenuous walk was tiresome.

She also found she quite enjoyed the half day spent in Gloucester. Apparently all she needed to forget her despair over Lord Winterton's abandonment of her was a simple change of scene. She had never been to this part of England, nor had she seen the tiny town of Ross-on-Wye. The Brewsters' estate was situated a bit south of the village, near the winding Severn River. On the following day, as the caravan of coaches drew nearer the house, Lady Diana grew increasingly more excited.

"We are to have such fun this week, I can barely contain myself for thinking on it! I have not seen my brother Harry in ages, nor my niece and nephew."

"How old are the children now?" Neala asked, her tone pleasant.

"Julie is nine and little Harry is five. Father dotes on them. And I am sure you will, too, Neala."

"Hmmm." Being linked with Lord Brewster again made Neala feel a prick of . . . something. She had rather enjoyed not being in close contact with the cigar-smoking gentleman the past two days. He had chosen to ride in the carriage with his friend Lord Tentrees.

"Does Harry still hunt?" asked Lord Edward a bit absently.

"Oh, I expect he does. Harry was always an avid hunter. And Melinda enjoys the sport, as well. You remember Harry's wife, don't you, Neala?"

"Hmmm." Neala nodded. She barely remembered the woman, she and Diana had been little girls when Harry married and removed to the country.

"Oh, I do wish Emma Chetwith and her husband could be with us for the entire fortnight," Diana went on. "Emma's husband has a living near here," she told Edward, "but, of course, we shall see the both of them the day we picnic on the River Wye."

"I am looking forward to seeing Emma again," Neala said. "It has been over a year since I last saw Emma. The day she came to collect her wedding gown."

"Which was not nearly so lovely as mine! Not that, your

mother did not do a splendid job on it, Neala, it's just that—"
Diana snuggled closer to Lord Edward, supreme joy evident on
her face "mine is so *very* special. Anyhow, as it's turned out,
there will only be married couples here for the entire week, or,
at least," she cast a sly gaze at Neala, *"soon* to be married
couples." She giggled prettily as Edward patted both her small
gloved hands which were now clasped tightly about his arm.

Across from them, Neala realized she suddenly felt extremely
uncomfortable.

"What about Winterton?" Lord Edward asked dryly. "He
ain't married."

Neala felt a fresh pang shoot through her. Was Lord Winterton to join them after all? She waited breathlessly for Diana's
response, but when the carriages rounded a sweeping curve in
the winding road and drew up before an imposing country
home, the conversation was dropped.

Neala had never been to Brewster Hall before either, but all
her life had heard Diana speak lovingly of the house and the
surrounding grounds. To the north of the estate lay the Forest
of Dean, the bank of dark trees making a lovely backdrop for
the ancient red brick and buff stone building. Before the house
in the distance lay the rolling hills of Wales. Lush green meadows flanked either side of the house, which Neala knew had
been in the Brewster family for generations. New additions to
it branched off in several directions, added, she correctly assumed, by subsequent families who had resided there. Behind
the house lay a network of out-buildings, the stables and a beau-
tifully laid out rose garden.

Neala was assigned to a bedchamber on the second floor.
When first she stepped into the room, the sight of it, with its
green silk draperies and matching bed hangings took her breath
completely away. Even her parent's lovely house in Mayfair had
not been quite so grand as this. Her brown eyes round, she
circled the room, pausing to gaze at many of the large ornately
framed paintings that graced the green and gold striped silk
walls. In addition to the canopied bed, the other furnishings in

the chamber consisted of a magnificently carved armoire, a small writing desk, several side chairs and two green silk sofas positioned before a large hearth with an elegant mantelpiece.

Adjoining her bedchamber was a small, but prettily appointed sitting room and a neat dressing room with a beautiful lacquered table, blue brocade chair and a gold framed looking glass.

Neala untied the ribbons of her bonnet and had no sooner dropped it onto the bed before one of a number of servants bustling about the room snatched it up and put it on the top shelf of the clothes press. Then, she set about putting away the rest of Neala's things, while another maid tended to the low-burning fire, and still another filled the wash basin that stood near the bed with fresh water. With all the efficient help about, Neala felt at loose ends with herself, so decided to walk across the way to Diana's suite.

She was surprised to note that it was not nearly so large or as grand as the one assigned to her. Had Lord Brewster chosen the finest chamber in the house especially for her? She felt another twinge of anxiety assail her.

For the first two days Neala spent in the country, she managed at times to put aside her troubled feelings and enjoy the long leisurely hours. She found she especially enjoyed mealtime. Always, the house seemed full of wonderful smells wafting from the kitchens, and at luncheon and dinner, the array and variety of delicious foods spread before them was something she had not seen in quite a spell.

Both days, the party was blessed with sunny skies and unseasonably warm weather. Activities ranged from bowling on the lawn, to long rides through pretty meadows ablaze with scarlet pimpernel, sweet-smelling clover and chamomile. Still, as evening fell each day, Neala was dismayed again when the now familiar cocoon of melancholia settled about her. She could not think what was the matter. She refused to admit that Lord Winterton's absence from the group was contributing to her low spirits. It had been more than a week since the incident at the opera, surely she was not still smarting from the gentleman's rebuff. By the second evening, however, as the group assembled after dinner in the drawing room, she felt near to despair.

Five gentlemen, fashionably turned out for the evening, were now clustered about the hearth—Lord Edward lounging against the mantelpiece, Lord Brewster sprawled in an overstuffed chair, Harry standing straight and tall behind his father, and Mr. McGill pacing a bit in front of the fire. Lord Tentrees was seated in a straight-backed chair a bit apart from Lord Brewster.

Nearby, five ladies, just as fashionably dressed, were comfortable on a grouping of maroon silk sofas and gold brocade chairs. While having a second cup of tea, four of the five were engaged in lively conversation. Try as she might, Neala could not feign an interest in the proceedings tonight, but wished only to escape from the party altogether and retire again to her bedchamber, where she might take up her book and read herself into a deep, drugging sleep. Just then, however, she caught a snippet of conversation from the gentlemen's corner and could not help turning her head a bit to listen.

". . . no doubt, the infamous Lord Winterton is up to his old tricks again," Lord Edward mused.

As if she fully expected to see the gentleman being discussed suddenly appear in person, Neala turned full around to fix a gaze on the gentleman speaking near the hearth. Instead, she caught only the wicked gleam in Lord Edward's gray eyes as he twirled the remaining inch of brandy around in his glass.

"Daresay I thought Winterton would have joined us by now," remarked Lord Brewster. "Perhaps he has found a new ladybird in Town, eh?"

"Or one in the country," Lord Tentrees dryly remarked.

A chorus of hearty laughter followed.

Neala colored deeply and turned back around, while beside her, Lady Diana giggled.

"Edward must have be telling the gentlemen what happened last week at the opera. You recall, don't you, Neala."

Neala felt stung to the quick. She knew she couldn't speak if she wanted to.

"Oh, do tell us!" squealed Lady Tentrees.

"Yes, please do go on, Diana," said Melinda. "We so rarely hear *ton* gossip this far removed from Town."

Both Melinda and Lady Tentrees had drawn their chairs closer to the sofa where Neala and Diana sat. Poor little Mrs. McGill seemed a bit confused, without her husband to tell her what to do. More than ever, Neala wished to be excused from the party.

But, Diana would have nothing for it but to recite the entire story, every last lurid detail accompanied by "oohs" and "ahs" from all three women.

"Edward said he later bumped into the pair at a rout hosted by the songbird Billington. Edward said the Prince Regent was in attendance *and* a goodly number of—" Diana's voice lowered to a mere whisper *"—undesirables."*

"No!" The ladies marveled. "How fortunate you were not along, Diana," said her sister-in-law. "Your reputation would be in shreds."

"Oh, I would never attend such an *affaire,"* Lady Diana replied loftily, then giggled. "At least, not now. After I am married, of course, I intend to go about quite freely."

"Oh, Diana!" squealed Lady Tentrees, who knew quite well Diana's penchant for larking about.

"I also heard," Diana went on, again lowering her voice to a whisper, "that Lord Winterton was seen the following day emerging from Lady Renfrow's house. At seven of the clock in the a.m.!"

This time it was Mrs. McGill who remarked, "Do you suppose he had been there the entire time?"

Diana shrugged, her blue eyes twinkling merrily.

Beside her on the sofa, Neala felt crimson with embarrassment. She hated listening to such coarse talk, though she knew married ladies often indulged in this sort of gossip.

Apparently Diana noticed Neala's silence, for she remarked upon it. "I fear we have put Neala to the blush! I am so sorry, dear—" she laughed gaily "—but, it isn't as if you did not know. You were there!" With another laugh, she reached to hug her friend.

To Neala, the women's laughter began to sound over-loud, as if they were trying to lure the gentlemen their way. The ploy must have worked, for in only moments, all five of the men ambled over.

"Well," began Lord Edward, sounding a trifle off-put as he perched on the arm of the sofa where Diana sat, "appears you ladies are having a vastly amusing time without us."

"Indeed," Mr. McGill said, taking up a protective stance behind his little wife. "I can't think when I've heard Mrs. McGill laugh so heartily."

Mrs. McGill cast a guilty look upwards. "Forgive me, husband. I did not mean to be vulgar." As she spoke, the teacup in her hand teetered precariously.

Mr. McGill reached to steady it. "Quite all right, m'dear."

"So, what were you ladies discussing?" Lord Tentrees asked, looking the length of his pinched nose at the women.

Trying to curb her laughter, his attractive wife, younger than her husband by at least fifteen years, cast a coy glance his way. "What do you suppose women speak of when their gentlemen are not present, my lord?"

Lord Tentrees shrugged his disinterest, but Lord Edward's brows had lifted as if truly pondering the question. Finally he looked down at Diana. "Well, I for one haven't the least notion. Do tell us, Diana."

Lady Diana and two of the women dissolved again into laughter. Even Neala managed a weak smile.

"I say," Harry interjected brightly, "what say we play a game of charades?"

"Splendid!" Lord Edward enthused. "We'll give you ladies a further opportunity to confound us!"

The game lasted several hours, stretching long past the time Neala usually turned in for the night. She was glad when, at last, the elderly Lord Tentrees pleaded exhaustion and ushered his young wife away from the lively group in the drawing room.

"I am also feeling a bit overtired," Neala murmured to Lord Brewster, whom Neala felt had been sitting in her pocket all evening, much of the time coughing loudly in her ear.

"Very well." Lord Brewster sprang to his feet to clasp Neala's hand tightly between his. "Good night, m'dear."

Neala managed a thin smile as she shyly extracted her hand, then cast a glance at Diana and Edward, who were busy making sheep's eyes at one another. "Good night Diana, Lord Edward."

"Sleep well, dear," put in Harry's wife, Melinda. "Don't forget, we have a gay time planned for tomorrow."

"Oh, indeed!" Diana exclaimed, dragging her eyes from her intended's. "I am *so* looking forward to our picnic on the River Wye! And, do not forget that Emma will be there!"

Managing an agreeable smile, Neala turned to make her way abovestairs, the laughter and good-will of the others receding in the distance behind her.

In her own bedchamber, Neala undressed quickly, and as soon as Peggy, the lady's maid who had been assigned to assist her had left the room, she climbed into the canopied bed and pulled the satin coverlet to her chin. Just as she was drifting off to sleep, however, a loud commotion coming from belowstairs jarred her to consciousness again. Neala raised up on one elbow to listen, but hearing only the muffled sounds of voices intermingled with deep male laughter, she decided nothing was amiss and lay back down again to sleep.

Early the following morning, she awoke feeling quite hungry, and after dressing quickly, hurried downstairs to the dining hall for breakfast. Reaching the arched doorway to the room, which was already beginning to fill up with guests, she beheld at once the reason for the late night disturbance.

Lord Winterton had arrived.

Nine

Standing before the sideboard, Lord Winterton towered head and shoulders above the other gentlemen gathered there. About his powerful physique—massive shoulders, broad chest and well-muscled thighs—was an aura of masculinity that in the other gentlemen was sadly lacking. The classic lines of his tanned face—straight forehead, aquiline nose, the elegant planes of his cheekbones—seemed to draw Neala like a flame. Suddenly, she felt a compelling urge to run to him, to fling herself into his arms! But . . . what was the matter with her? Alarmed at the reaction the mere sight of the gentleman stirred within her, she instead uttered a small cry, and turned and fled from the room.

Lord Winterton, as always alert to his surroundings, heard the frightened intake of breath coming from the direction of the doorway. But his quick gaze was swift enough only to catch a fleeting glimpse of swirling skirts and the back of . . . *Miss Abercorn?*

Puzzled, Winterton's dark brows drew together. What could have caused the young lady to flee from the room? In truth, Winterton had not wanted to come to the country, had decided it best not to see Miss Abercorn again lest an overlong look or a too gentle word betray his deep feelings for her. However, as if fate, or destiny itself had had a finger in it, his presence here had been decided, not by him, but by Lady Renfrow, in whose company Winterton had spent the bulk of last week.

He had been correct in his assessment of the beautiful widow.

She was indeed involved, up to her pretty neck, as it were, in the dastardly spy scheme. Uncovering her part in the elaborate network had actually proved easier than Winterton had imagined. Though to gain her confidence, he had had to engineer an undercover game of his own. The result was that Lady Renfrow now believed Winterton to be a turn-coat, that he had sold his commission in the army and returned to civilian life because of a deep-seated grudge against the British monarchy. All of the above he had fabricated, of course, but during certain intimate situations, Lady Renfrow had proved far more gullible than she was intelligent.

Never would Winterton have fallen prey to the woman's seductive trap if it had not been essential to insuring the security of England's war effort. Besides, in light of Winterton's reputation as a womanizer, to have refused her would have aroused the lady's suspicions. Therefore, Winterton regarded the weeklong sexual interlude as a necessary adjunct to his secret military assignment. It had surprised him, however, to find the task considerably more distasteful than he recalled that sort of work, if one could call it work, ought to be. In a word, making love to Lady Renfrow was . . . boring. He was aware that since he was London's current nonpareil, she regarded him as a challenge. And, now that his name had been added to her list of conquests, she was using him to promote her own cause.

To that same end, Winterton had readily fallen in with the plan. He would do whatever it took to save his country. However, it had not seemed within the realm of possibility that the doing of it would return him again to Miss Abercorn's side. As it happened, however, due to a chance conversation overheard by Lady Renfrow between Lady Diana's intended, Lord Edward, and Winterton, at the rout they'd all attended that night following the opera, Lady Renfrow had become aware of Winterton's forthcoming plans to attend the houseparty in the country. Then when Winterton had sprung his double agent game on her, Lady Renfrow had jumped at the opportunity to arrange a secret meeting between Winterton and her primary contact near the

French agent's point of entry to England in Gloucestershire. Since Winterton had plans to be nearby, anyhow, Lady Renfrow reasoned, it would arouse less suspicion if he simply carried on as normally as possible.

"I never change my plans," she bragged to Winterton, as he left her bed that last evening. "I always meet with my contacts in public places—"

"Like the opera?" Winterton regarded her with a cool gaze as he drew on his trousers.

"Precisely! Why, I all but wave the most sensitive documents right under their stupid noses. I am far too clever to ever be apprehended."

In the dim light of her bedchamber, Winterton watched the beauty, stretched out languidly on the crumpled white satin sheets of her canopied bed, her long black hair cascading in ringlets down her bare back. "I am sure you are, my dear. You are far too clever for me."

"Oh, Winterton—" she rolled onto her back, her ample breasts gleaming in the candlelight "—you are like most gentlemen I am acquainted with. You simply need a woman to guide you, both in, and . . . out of bed."

Reaching for his coat, Winterton merely lifted one dark brow. Even if the snare he was setting killed him, too, he would see the entire traitorous lot of them captured and brought to justice. He had never been instrumental in sending a woman to gaol, and in truth, he found the idea of a rope around Lady Renfrow's neck as distasteful as he found the act of making love to her, but in this case, both appeared to be unavoidable. He had completed one task, now it was time to finish the job.

Lord Winterton's ruminations on the past week were interrupted by the sound of Lady Diana's voice.

"Father!" Lady Diana's blue eyes were a question as she approached the gentlemen at the sideboard, who were filling their plates from the sumptuous feast spread before them. "Did you say something to upset Neala?"

Lord Winterton's ears perked up, but Lord Brewster merely

glanced at his daughter, then back to the plate he was heaping high with ham, kippers, eggs and hot buttered scones. "Miss Abercorn? No, of course, not. Haven't yet seen the young lady this morning. Not ill, I hope."

"Has Miss Abercorn been ill?" Winterton interjected hoarsely, not even attempting to conceal the concern in his voice.

Both Diana and Lord Brewster gazed quizzically at him, then Diana said, "I saw her a moment ago on the stairs and she seemed quite overset. I paused to inquire after her health, but she dashed right past me as if I weren't even standing there. I thought perhaps you had said something untoward to her, Father."

"Indeed, I did not, my dear." Having dismissed both his daughter and the subject at hand, Lord Brewster walked to the long mahogany table in the center of the room and deposited his plate at his customary place, at the top of the table. "Winterton!" he called over his shoulder, "Come sit here, and catch me up on the doings in Town."

Winterton did as his host requested, but as he was cheerfully obliging the gentleman and renewing his acquaintance with his schoolchum, Harry, his thoughts were not entirely on the proceedings at the table.

Abovestairs in her bedchamber, Neala's heart was pounding so loudly she could barely think. Why had she run like a frightened rabbit from the mere sight of Lord Winterton? What was happening to her? The gentleman would soon be married to her sister, she could not flee from her brother-in-law every time she saw the man! She simply must control her racing heart and pounding pulse. To behave in such an unseemly fashion was ridiculous.

She collapsed in a heap on the bed, then sprang to her feet again and paced from there to the window and back again. What did it mean? Why was Lord Winterton's presence so unsettling to her? She thought back to the day she had first met him, how her knees had grown weak beneath her skirt. He had squeezed her fingertips that day, and afterward, they seemed to burn overlong with fire. Then she recalled how breathless she had felt dancing with the gentleman at the ball. Startling sensations had assailed her then, an odd quivering in her mid-section, a fierce inability to breathe. What did it all mean?

Lord Brewster did not affect her in such a strange fashion. Except for his frequent coughing fits, which she sometimes found annoying, his presence did not affect her in any way at all. The gentleman rarely addressed her directly, hardly ever asked a question of her, or tried in any way to draw her out. In that respect, he was also unlike Lord Winterton, who seemed always to wish to talk to her. And, to say truth, she rather liked that. If fact, she loved conversing with Lord Winterton. She hadn't felt that way about anyone before. If only she could understand what this . . . this . . . she simply had no name for what this feeling was!

She flung herself onto the green silk sofa. What was she to do? She simply had to calm herself before she returned again to the dining room. Today, the group planned to go to Ross-on-Wye for a picnic on the river. She would hate to miss that. Oh, why had Lord Winterton turned up?

As if seeking divine guidance, Neala's frightened gaze drifted upward. There, her eyes focused on the lovely oil painting hanging above the mantelpiece. It depicted a cozy family scene, complete with a pet dog curled up asleep at his master's feet. When first she saw the picture, Neala thought the gentleman in the painting resembled Lord Brewster. But, of course, it wasn't him—there were four children positioned about the room, instead of three, and the woman in the picture was not Diana's mother. Still, gazing at the quiet family scene now made Neala feel peaceful inside. And it told her what she must do.

She must marry Lord Brewster. It was the only way to silence the disquieting fluttering in her heart that she experienced every time she saw Lord Winterton. He and Lilibet would be married soon and according to the ancient wedding spell, they would be very happy together.

Neala pulled her shoulders back. It was the only way, she

told herself again. It did not matter that she did not love Lord Brewster, or that he did not love her, for she was certain that he did not. She had to marry him. Rising heavily to her feet, she moved to the lovely dressing table in the small anteroom adjoining her bedchamber. There, she gazed at her own reflection in the mirrored glass. Beneath the bodice of her peach-colored morning gown, she saw that her breasts were still rising and falling with each fitfull breath she drew. Her cheeks were flushed a deep rosy pink and her brown eyes still glittered brightly.

Lifting her chin, she willed herself to take several deep, calming breaths. For the remainder of the week, she would avoid Lord Winterton entirely. Beyond the required civilities, she would not even speak to him. She would reserve all her energies for her future husband, Lord Brewster.

A half hour later, Neala's resolve to avoid Lord Winterton was shattered. The entire group, save Neala, had already assembled in the marble-tiled hall awaiting the carriages to take them to Ross for the excursion down the River Wye.

Slowly descending the carpeted staircase, Neala noted that the large party was quite noisy and excited. Everyone seemed to be talking at once. In the general confusion, she hoped that she might join them unnoticed, most especially by *him*. But, alas, it was not to be. Rounding the curve in the staircase, she saw that Lord Winterton was standing on the bottom step, his long legs wide apart, arms folded across his broad chest. He wasn't talking to anyone. In fact, he appeared to be . . . waiting.

Neala drew a last breath of courage but before she reached Lord Winterton, Lady Diana spotted her and called out to her. "Neala! Do, come quickly, we are all set to go!"

At once, Lord Winterton turned about, an intent gaze fixed on Neala. "Ah, Miss Abercorn, I had about despaired of you."

Neala willed herself to remain calm. But, as she drew near the gentleman, he surprised her by putting out a hand to assist her to the ground floor, though, of course, she did not require assistance. It was only one step. But since it would seem a cut direct if she did not take his hand, she reluctantly did so, murmuring, "Thank you, sir."

"Feeling better, I hope?" he asked, the rich timbre of his voice more pleasant than Neala remembered. Truly, she had missed the gentleman.

"I am quite well; thank you, sir," she said. Though, she desperately wanted to, she refused to look directly at him.

He released her hand. She was now standing beside him in the foyer. "Lady Diana mentioned that you were feeling a bit out of curl earlier. Said she had passed you up on the stairs and you seemed in too great a hurry to tell her what was amiss. I am pleased to see you have recovered nicely from whatever ailed you."

"Hmmm." Neala still had not looked full at the gentleman, and she did not now. Instead, she cast nervously about in search of Lord Brewster. She spotted him standing before the wide double doors engaged in animated conversation with Lord and Lady Tentrees. She wondered if she should be so bold as to join them? But, as Lady Diana appeared to be treading her way toward Neala, she stood still, her eyes cast down, her hands nervously clasped in front of her.

"Neala," began Diana when she had reached them, "you still look quite pale to me. Are you certain you are well enough to join us? It shall be quite a long day. We shall not be returning home until late." Her sweet tone was solicitous. "Trench, will you be a dear and look out for her?"

Neala's stomach lurched afresh as beside her, Lord Winterton exhaled a hearty, "It will be my pleasure, Lady Diana. I shall protect Miss Abercorn with my very life, if need be."

Lady Diana giggled as she turned again to Neala. "Isn't he simply the most outrageous flirt you have ever met? It is not the least surprising that every young lady he meets falls top over tail in love with him!"

Her heart pounding in her ears, Neala dared not speak. But

Diana was still not done. She turned again to Winterton, but at least had the breeding to lower her voice when next she spoke. "For your information, Trench, Father and Neala have been getting on famously. I expect him to come up to scratch any day now! I am so happy for you, Neala!" She gave her dear friend a quick hug, then flitted off.

Neala was glad when from the doorway, Lord Brewster next addressed the group, his voice quite loud so as to be heard over the general gaiety and laughter. "Coaches have arrived! Everybody out! Set to!"

Outdoors, Neala did manage to extricate herself from beneath Lord Winterton's nose. As everyone piled into one of the four carriages, the last one reserved for a number of servants and the huge hampers of food and wine that had been specially prepared for the picnic, Neala skirted round the company and headed for the small barouche that she saw Melinda and the children climbing into.

Melinda seemed pleased to see her. "Ah, Miss Abercorn, you are brave, indeed, choosing to ride with us."

Neala smiled agreeably. "Oh, I shan't mind sharing with the children. On the contrary, I should quite enjoy it."

"And I shall be glad enough for the company of another adult!" She laughed.

Neala quickly scrambled into the coach and was glad when the footman let up the steps and closed the door. Lord Winterton, she saw, peeking from the tiny window behind her, was assisting young Lady Tentrees into another of the coaches, but before he climbed into one himself, she thought he appeared to be looking about. Perhaps for her? A small smile of satisfaction on her face, Neala turned back around, grateful to be free of the gentleman, at last.

"I feel I must warn you," Melinda began, "we shall be taking on another pair of children. Julie has invited a little friend, and of course, when Julie invited someone, Harry would not be outdone. It is not too late to change your mind about riding with us."

"Oh, no, ma'am. I am quite happy to be here."

It was not a lie.

The journey to the picturesque hamlet of Ross-on-Wye took about an hour. Once there, the passengers alighted on Dock Street for the quarter mile walk to the river where the pleasure boats awaited. The empty carriages and the one bearing the picnic were to travel on ahead, the servants and food veering off at Coldwell to meet up with the hungry tourists. The remainder of the coaches would go on to Monmouth to be waiting at the end of the excursion to carry the party back again to Brewster Hall.

As everyone began to troop down the sun-dappled cobblestone street, Neala thought the cool air wafting in off the water felt good and fresh. The shops were open this morning, with busy shopkeepers and townfolk milling about. She was struck by how peaceful and quiet the tiny village seemed, a decided contrast to the noise and constant bustle of London's crowded streets.

Though she was quite enjoying the sights in the small market town, she did not forget her primary intent which was to reach the pleasure boats and procure a lone seat on one of them as far away from Lord Winterton as possible. In her singlemindedness, she was not aware that Harry's little friend, Robert, had approached her from behind. Not until the child slipped a tiny warm hand into hers did she look down.

"Why, Robert, I daresay, you startled me!" She smiled at the boy, a pretty child of about five with dark curls and large blue eyes.

"I should like to walk with you, ma'am. Harry's mama is holding his hand."

"Then I shall hold yours!" Neala tightened her grip around the little boy's palm.

Apparently this pleased the child, for he began to skip alongside her and Neala turned her attention again to the three boats bobbing below in the sea-green water.

"Well, I see I have been replaced as your guardian for the day," came a deep voice beside Neala.

At the sound of it, Neala's heart did a quick flip-flop. To know that it was Lord Winterton who had come up beside her, she did not have to turn around. "You could never be replaced, my lord," she said quietly.

"Well, it pleases me to hear that," he said, his words in perfect concert with his tone.

Nearing the water's edge where the pleasure boats were being readied for them, Neala caught sight of Lord Brewster conversing with one of the boatmen. Gesturing with a hand and arm, Lord Brewster was obviously telling the oarsman the direction the party wished to travel down the river.

When a salty breeze wafted by, Lord Winterton sniffed the air. "Smells fresh and clean here, does it not?"

Neala could not conceal a smile. "Indeed, it does. Only a moment ago, I thought that very thing."

"There, you see. How like-minded we are!" He gestured toward the boats tethered in the water up ahead. "Which vessel shall we board? The larger one, or would you prefer the smaller of the three?"

Neala thought a minute. The smallest boat would quite cozily accommodate herself and Lord Winterton, and also Melinda and the two little boys, for she rather expected Melinda and Harry would find their way to her and Robert. Though that arrangement was not entirely undesirable, she quickly decided it would place her far too close for comfort to Lord Winterton's side. She tilted her chin up. "The larger boat will do nicely."

"Ah, now there's where we differ. I was certain you'd say you preferred the smaller boat."

"I wants to go on the little boat!" Robert piped up, who until now had walked quietly alongside Neala. He pointed a chubby finger at the smallest of the three crafts. "It looks like my boat at home. Papa lets me float it on the fish pond."

"The small one it is, then!" Lord Winterton said, stepping

around behind Neala and scooping up the curly-headed little
boy into his arms. "You've made a fine choice, lad."

"I'm Robert!"

"Hallo, Robert."

"This gentleman is Lord Winterton," Neala said politely. "He
is just home from the wars."

Jouncing along in Lord Winterton's arms, the child's eyes
were round. "Did you kill the Frenchies?"

Winterton laughed. "I shall tell you all about it while we
float down the river." With that, he loped on ahead of Neala to
commandeer the vessel of Robert's choice.

Watching them, Neala could not suppress a smile. In spite
of her resolve to avoid the enigmatic Lord Winterton, she was
already enjoying herself immensely. By contrast, Lord Brewster
had not so much as looked her way today.

When Melinda and little Harry joined them at the water's
edge, Lord Winterton handed them one by one into the boat.

"Do you suppose we need another gentleman aboard?" Melinda asked, glancing anxiously at the two small boys who were
already leaning over the side trying to dip a hand into the sparkling green water.

Winterton quickly assesed the situation, taking in both the
boys and the pair of oarsmen positioned at the bow and stern.
"We would need another gentleman only if a team of horses
were hitched to the craft and I was expected to drive." His lips
twitched as he climbed in and promptly took a seat beside
Neala.

She could not resist a smile as the three vessels moved away
from shore and began to drift lazily downstream. It was difficult
not to relax and enjoy the gentle lolling of the boat beneath her.
Though Lord Winterton's nearness was as intoxicating as ever,
she soon discovered that the children kept him so occupied answering their incessant questions about all and sundry, that he
hadn't a spare minute to devote to her.

A quarter hour into the jaunt, the gentleman and Melinda
traded places so that Winterton could more easily keep the lively

little boys in tow. Despite Melinda's constant remonstrations, they were all but hopscotching from bench to bench in their curiosity about everything to do with the vessel.

Winterton was, at last, able to hold them in check by launching into a lengthy war story, drawn out and embellished upon, Neala suspected, so as to make it last as long as possible.

Presently, the small boat approached the ancient ruin of Goodrich Castle, situated high atop a hill overlooking the water. In light of this new wonder, Winterton's war tale was completely forgot.

Neala and Melinda also craned their necks to gaze upward at the imposing structure. The crumbling keep and the tower walls, with their strange wedged spurs, were all but covered over with ivy.

"I say, the castle looks to be growing from the rock!" observed Harry, his little voice quite serious.

"Papa says the castle is haunted," Robert announced.

"Your father is quite right," said Harry's mama. "Goodrich Castle is said to haunted by a maiden named Alice and her sweetheart named Clifford. In the thirteenth century, I believe it was, the castle came under siege and the two tried to escape, but both were drowned in the river."

Harry's eyes widened. *"This river?"*

"The very one."

Robert had leaned over the edge of the boat as if to plumb its depths for the hapless pair. "Not there now," he pronounced solemnly.

"Of course, not." Melinda looked upward again. "They are both haunting the castle."

Throughout the discourse, Lord Winterton said nothing, was leaning back, both his hands clasped comfortably behind his head. Watching him, Neala thought he seemed grateful for the respite from entertaining the children.

"Do you believe in ghosts, my lord?" she asked quietly.

A small smile played at his lips. "No, Miss Abercorn. I believe only in what I can see and hear."

Smiling, Melinda remarked, "I am told Alice and Clifford can make a jolly good disturbance."

Winterton wasn't convinced. "I am a soldier, ma'am. As such, I have been trained to rely solely upon my senses. I find the thought of trying to capture or shoot a ghost, ludicrous, indeed."

Both Harry and Robert were listening intently.

"I don't believe in ghosts either," Robert announced proudly.

"What about you, Harry?" Winterton asked.

The blue-eyed child gazed solemnly from Lord Winterton to his mother, then without a word, crawled into his Mama's lap and buried his blond head in her ample bosom.

Neala watched Lord Winterton cast another lazy glance up at the castle. If the gentleman did not believe in ghosts, did that mean he also did not believe in magic? What bearing, she wondered, might his disbelief in magic have on the ancient wedding spell?

Ten

By the time the three pleasure boats washed ashore at Coldwell, most everyone in the party had begun to proclaim how hungry they were.

"I expect the children are famished," Melinda said. "I should have brought along a piece of fruit or cheese for them."

"The wind and the water spur one's appetite," Lord Brewster proclaimed jovially, assisting his pretty granddaughter Julie and her friend Susan to shore. Both girls had elected to ride with Julie's grandfather in the larger craft.

"Wind and water have nothing to say for it, Father, *you* are always hungry." Diana tossed teasingly over her shoulder as she set foot on solid soil.

Since Neala had completely missed breakfast, she realized she was feeling quite peckish, too. Glancing past the sandy stretch of ground where lappets of water licked the shore, she saw several long tables set up on the grassy knoll at the foot of the cliff. An army of servants were busy laying out platters of cold chicken and ham, huge wedges of cheese, freshly baked bread, small meat pies and bowls of wrinkled russet apples. Frosty pitchers of lemonade and wine stood at each end of the tables, and for dessert, Neala spotted plates of blueberry tarts. Her stomach growled as she and the others streamed toward the tables and began to fill their plates from the laden tables.

Waiting her turn, Neala glanced toward first one and then another of the gnarled old elm trees, beneath which comfortable looking rugs had been spread on the ground for the picnickers to sit upon while they ate. Which inviting looking spot, she wondered, would Lord Winterton choose? Though she had enjoyed the ride down river in his company, she renewed her vow to avoid the gentleman now that they were on shore.

Beneath the furthermost tree, she saw Melinda speaking with the children's governess, Miss Phelps, who had apparently travelled with the servants. All four children were already seated beneath the tree, a footman stationed nearby to see to their needs. Moving toward another rug, Mrs. McGill was close by her husband's side—so he might dust her off after she ate, Neala thought. Harry and Lord Edward seemed to be trailing along after Mr. McGill. Perhaps the gentleman would congregate together and leave the ladies to themselves.

After helping herself to the tasty-looking luncheon, Neala spotted Diana heading for a rug quite apart from the gentlemen and quickly fell into step behind her. In moments, Lady Tentrees appeared and asked if she might join them and the three of them settled down to enjoy the feast. Neala had no sooner removed her gloves and reached to pick up a cold chicken leg to nibble on when the sound of a carriage rattling into the clearing claimed everyone's attention.

"It is Emma and Mr. Chetwith come to join us!" Lady Diana exclaimed, scrambling again to her feet.

She ran to the coach, squealing her delight at seeing her girlhood friend once again. Harry, as well, moved to greet Mr. Chetwith, with whom he was well acquainted. The two girls embraced and her arm about Emma's shoulders, Diana escorted Emma back to the girls' rug, on the way instructing a servant to fetch the new arrivals some sustenance.

Neala rose to her feet to embrace her friend. "I am so happy to see you again, Emma! You look lovely! I daresay, your new life suits you."

Emma drew back. She was almost as petite as Neala, with short reddish curls and hazel eyes. "And you, Nealie, look positively radiant!" Surprise was evident in her tone.

Neala smiled and knelt again to her knees while Diana introduced Emma to Lady Tentrees, then they all settled down again to eat.

"It has been an age since last we saw you, Emma, tell us everything that has happened!" Diana demanded.

Neala thoroughly enjoyed the hour spent in the company of her friends. However, every now and again, her long gaze travelled across the lawn to the rug where Lord Winterton sat. More than once, she caught him looking her way and their gazes locked for the merest second. Without fail, Lord Winterton always smiled and nodded, but Neala looked quickly away.

She had about concluded her meal when from the corner of her eye, she saw the tall gentleman approaching. When he came to stand by her side, she had no choice but to look up. "Might I get you another glass of lemonade, Miss Abercorn, and perhaps a tart?" he asked pleasantly.

"Oh," Neala murmured, so alarmed that he had singled her out that she could not think of a thing to say.

As if also awaiting her answer, conversation among her companions had also ceased.

"We would *all* like lemonade and tarts, Trench," Lady Diana finally replied, a bit crossly. "And," she added, her customary merriment returning, "you have my permission to fetch them for us."

Winterton's dark eyes twinkled as he nodded solemnly her direction. "As you wish, Lady Diana. I shall just be off then."

Giggling, Diana held up a hand to delay his departure. "Not just yet. I should first like you to meet my dear friend, Mrs. Chetwith. Emma, this is Viscount Winterton, the unconscionable rakehell who broke my heart into a million pieces when I was a little girl. You *must* have heard me speak of the wastrel."

Winterton laughed aloud.

"Indeed, I do recall the name," Emma said, smiling prettily. "And even if I had not, word is already about in the countryside that Lord Winterton has arrived for a visit."

"Indeed?" Winterton seemed surprised.

"Quite," Emma replied. "Gloucestershire has not had so dis-

tinguished a visitor since Admiral Nelson and his party toured
the area in oh-two."

Smiling his pleasure, Lord Winterton folded his arms across
his chest. He leaned back against the tree trunk. "And what do
the locals have to say about me, Mrs. Chetwith?"

"Oh, they are very complimentary, my lord. Most especially
regarding the tales of your war escapades. I daresay, you must
be quite a courageous man."

Winterton's lips twitched. "Perhaps. If all they say about me
is true. I expect it far more likely that with each of the tellings,
my bravery multiplies by leaps and bounds."

"You are much too modest, my lord," Emma murmured.

"Trench!" Diana put in, mock exasperation in her tone.
"Neala and I are near to dying for want of a tart! Pray, bask in
the glory of your silly war escapades another time and tend to
our needs now!"

Winterton did not leave, instead he pushed himself from the
tree and gazed down at Neala. "Is this true, Miss Abercorn?
Are you near to starving for a tart?"

Neala was unable to suppress a smile. And, going along with
the lark, she cocked her head to one side, and replied smartly,
"In truth, my lord, I am near to famished for a tart, in fact, I
am so hungry, I should like two."

They all laughed as Winterton sprang instantly to attention
and saluted her. "Major Lambert at your service, my lady!" The
ladies were still giggling, as Winterton spun about to go.

When he was safely out of earshot, Emma turned to Neala,
admiration in her eyes and her tone. "Why did you not tell me
you had a suitor, Nealie, dear? And such a glorious man!"

Neala looked stricken. "Lord Winterton is not—"

Emma was patting her breast as if to still her pounding heart.
"Neala, he is so charming and so *handsome!* Why, all the tales
I have heard about him must be true!" She turned next to Diana.
"It is no wonder that your heart was broken into a million
pieces! He is top o' the trees!"

"Emma," Diana began firmly, "Trench is not Neala's beau, she and—"

At that moment, Winterton reappeared with two servants trailing on his heels, one carrying a pitcher of lemonade, the other a platter heaped high with delectable pastry. Winterton instructed the footmen to place the platter in the center of the rug and to refill the ladies glasses. As they carried out his orders, Winterton sat down on the grass beside Neala. While the other ladies busied themselves with the refreshments, he leaned over to whisper in her ear.

"You look as pretty as a daisy sitting beneath this tree, Miss Abercorn."

Shocked by his unexpected words, Neala colored deeply. Involuntarily, she reached for her bonnet both to cover her hair and to shield her flushed face. But Winterton took the straw confection from her and tossed it aside, then leaned again to her ear.

"Pray, leave it off a bit longer, Miss Abercorn, your shining hair is far too pretty to cover."

Neala blushed all the way to her toes. Why was he—?

Just then, the tray of tarts was passed to Neala. Winterton reached to hold it while she nervously helped herself to one, but she couldn't eat it, her hand was shaking far too greatly. Beside her, Winterton scooped one up and popped it into his mouth.

A moment later, he said, loud enough for everyone to hear, "I had thought to take a walk along the shore. Miss Abercorn, will you join me?"

She wanted to. *Oh, she wanted to.* No gentleman had *ever* whispered such lovely words into her ear before! She was saved from a reply when little Robert came running toward them from out of nowhere. Neala had noticed he and the other children standing close to the shore, watching a flock of ducks paddling in circles in the water.

"Sir!" the child said, "I wants a ducky!"

Winterton turned to the boy. "A ducky, you say?"

"Yes! Just there!" Robert pointed to the water's edge. "There's a mama ducky and all her little wadlings."

"Don't you mean ducklings?" Winterton asked, smothering a laugh.

All the young ladies turned to gaze that direction. On the sandy shore, little Harry was dancing up and down, both his sister and her chum also enthralled by the spectacle. Miss Phelps, the children's governess, appeared to be trying to keep Harry from leaping into the water to go after a duck.

"Shall we all go and look at them?" Lady Diana said, scrambling quickly to her feet.

Emma and Lady Tentrees at once followed suit. Lord Winterton reached to assist Neala. Not wanting to take the hand he offered, she pretended a preoccupation with brushing the pastry crumbs she had scattered on her skirt. Then, trying to ignore the gentleman entirely, she busied herself retying the ribbons of her bonnet beneath her chin.

"Hurry, sir, please!" Robert pulled impatiently at Winterton's trouser leg. "I want a ducky to take home with me!" Grabbing Winterton's hand, he began to drag the gentleman toward the shore.

Neala brought up the rear as the ladies walked toward the water's edge. As Lord Winterton approached, Miss Phelps looked up at him.

"The children wish to take a duckling home, my lord," she told him.

Towering above the rather thin, spinsterish-looking woman, the excited children dancing at his feet, Winterton assessed the situation. "Well, the ducklings don't appear to be too young to be removed from their mother."

"No, not at all," Miss Phelps agreed.

"One already got et! We saw it!"

" 'was eaten', Harry," Miss Phelps corrected the boy.

"It is true, sir," Julie said, gazing up at Winterton. "A big fish gobbled it up as we stood and watched. It was quite a gory sight, indeed."

"I'm sure it must have been, Miss Julie." Winterton shaded his eyes to gaze out over the sparkling water.

"Can you get one for us, sir?" Robert asked. "I wants to put it on the fish pond at home."

"I wants one, too!" Harry cried.

"What's this?" It was little Harry's father come to join in the confab.

"The ducklings, Harry," Diana said to her brother. She pointed toward the water. "Look! Just there, by the thrushes, there are more of them coming!"

"They are darling," Lady Tentrees said. "I should like to take one home, as well."

Diana looked appalled. "But, where would you put it, Helene? They are charming to look at, but I shouldn't want one waddling about the house."

Lady Tentrees shrugged. "I would just like to have something . . . small to stroke and cuddle."

Standing beside Helene, Neala heard the wistfulness in the girl's tone. Judging from the cool way Lord Tentrees treated his young wife, she felt it was no wonder Helene was starved for affection. "Perhaps we might toss bread crumbs to them," Neala suggested quietly.

"That's a splendid idea, Miss Abercorn," Winterton said. He turned to a footman who was hovering nearby and requested a loaf. When it arrived, he broke off chunks of it and passed it among the children, who took great delight in throwing the pieces onto the water and watching the ducks dive for it.

"Look, that one is turning a somersault!" Robert squealed, flirting with danger as he ran close to the water.

"Hallo! What have we here?"

Neala turned to see Lord Brewster approaching the noisy group. So far, today, the gentleman had not so much as acknowledged her presence. Feeling somewhat annoyed by that, she decided to force the older man to speak to her. "Good afternoon, Lord Brewster," she said, willing unnatural volume to her voice.

Neala thought he seemed startled that she had addressed him

at all, much less loud enough to be heard. "Why, Miss Abercorn. Enjoying yourself, I hope?"

"Indeed, sir. Thank you," she returned, but because little Harry chose that moment to run up to his grandfather, he ignored her reply.

"Grandfather, grandfather! I want a ducky! The fishes are eating the ducklets for dinner. Help us, Grandfather!"

Neala felt rather than saw Diana move closer to her. "We mustn't let Father go into the water, Neala. He might slip, or catch his death."

Her eyes a question, Neala turned toward Diana. "But . . ." What could *she* do about it?

Diana's mouth firmed. "You should be the one to stop him, Neala."

"Me? But, I-I wouldn't know what to say to him," Neala replied. Lord Brewster was a grown man. She could not tell him what to do! It would be like telling her own Papa what to do! Neala would *never* do that!

As it turned out, Neala's intervention was not necessary. Near the water's edge, Lord Winterton had already removed his boots and stockings and, at this moment, was rolling his trouser legs up as far as his knees.

"Never mind, Neala. Trench appears to be going in." Lady Diana folded her arms across her bosom. "I hope he falls. It would serve him right for the time he pushed me into the stream when I was little. He probably doesn't even recall . . ." her voice trailed off as she moved closer to where Lord Winterton was now tramping into the water.

Watching Lord Winterton, Neala's breath caught in her throat. She had never seen a man's naked limbs before. She could not pull her eyes from the sight of his muscled calves and bare ankles.

Near the shore, Lord Brewster called to Lord Winterton and Neala turned toward him again. Gazing at the portly older gentleman, she tried to imagine how she might feel if she were watching him wade naked into the water instead of Lord Winterton.

For Lord Brewster, the comparison did not bode well.

"He is a *very* handsome man, Neala." The sound of Emma's voice interrupted Neala's thoughts. "It is easy to see how you might fall in love with him," she said quietly.

"Emma!"

Emma smiled secretively. "He appears quite smitten with you, Neala."

Neala felt her breath grow fitful. "Emma, I am not in love with Lord Winterton! I could *never* be in love with him!"

Undaunted, Emma sipped an arm about Neala's waist and gave her a small squeeze. "You mustn't fear what others will say, Neala. Mr. Chetwith says we cannot help our feelings."

Neala tried desperately to calm herself. This was becoming the most horrid day of her life!

When, at last, Lord Winterton emerged dripping from the water, he had captured two fuzzy ducklings, carrying one in each hand. Speaking quietly to calm the children, who were hopping up and down with glee, he instructed them how to gently pet the baby ducks, then he carefully deposited the small creatures into a wooden bucket that a servant had brought to the shore. Winterton clamped the lid on tight and knotted the rope securely to hold the lid in place.

"There," he said, addressing the two little boys, "you each have a baby duckling to raise. And—" he glanced behind him, "—the fish in the river have two less to eat."

Lord Brewster moved to clap the children's newfound hero on the back. "You're a sport, Winterton."

Neala and the other young ladies had also moved nearer the gentleman, hoping for a closer look at the ducklings.

As Winterton began to pull on his boots, Diana's brother approached. "You up for a hike this afternoon, Winterton?"

He groaned, then a grin split his handsome face. "I assume you mean old Symonds Yat?"

Harry gestured to the ledge, looming high above the grassy

knoll that overlooked the river. "Rock is still there, beckoning to us the same as it did the last time we were here. What do you say? I haven't hiked to the top of Symonds Yat since we were boys."

Winterton rose to his feet, shaking his trouser legs back into place. "Why not? Exercise should suit after all the food I consumed." He turned to Lord Edward, who was speaking with Lady Diana. "Coming with us, old man?"

Edward pressed his lips together with distaste. "Absolutely not! Climbing to the top of that ridge is pure folly. It would accomplish nothing beyond rending my clothes or soiling a coat sleeve." He flicked an imaginary speck of dust from his lapel and adjusted his impeccably tied cravat. "I shall stay behind and keep the young ladies company."

For a split second, Neala thought Lord Winterton seemed torn. His quick gaze flitted to her, then he turned again to the gentlemen.

"How about you, McGill? Coming with us?"

Mr. McGill had only just lumbered up, having sat out the excitement in the company of his wife, who had fallen fast asleep following her meal. He glanced anxiously at her now. Her bonneted head was lolling uncomfortably against the tree trunk against which she was leaning. "I suppose I could leave the missus for just a bit," he mused.

"We shall keep an eye out for her," Diana said, reaching to claim Lord Edward's arm. "Go and climb your silly mountain. Edward will stay behind and amuse us. Nealie—" she turned suddenly to where Neala stood "—persuade Father to join us. He should not go rock climbing. The sport is far too dangerous for a man of his years."

A bit alarmed, Neala did not know what to say. But, again, that she say anything at all turned out to be unnecessary, for Lord Brewster decided of his own volition to stay behind.

"Take care not to fall, gentlemen!" he said, then trudged toward the tree where Diana and Edward were headed.

Neala fell into step alongside Lord Brewster.

The next hour seemed to drag on interminably. After Emma and Mr. Chetwith departed for Monmouth, conversation between the two couples remaining on the rug grew decidedly thin. Even Diana seemed to grow weary of trying to keep it afloat. She looked to Neala to say something fresh. But, after exhausting the few questions she had thought of to draw Lord Brewster into conversation, she couldn't think of a word else to say to the gentleman. He, in turn, said very little to her.

Both Neala's gaze and her mind wandered incessantly. Helene, she noticed, also appeared at loose ends. Lord Tentrees had apparently opted for a stroll by himself, for Neala spotted his angular form several yards off. Left to herself, Helene made straight for the bucket and began to stroke the baby ducks. Farther afield, the children—after both a hearty luncheon and an abundance of excitement—had all fallen asleep at Miss Phelps feet. Nearby, Melinda was taking advantage of the stillness to also nap on a rug. And little Mrs. McGill had not yet awakened from her snooze.

A good hour later, Neala was vastly relieved to catch sight of the three gentlemen returning from their hike. Again, she was struck by Lord Winterton's masculine attractiveness. Next to Harry, who was lean, but not nearly so powerfully built as Winterton, and the slim and pale Mr. McGill, Lord Winterton looked as if the perilous climb upward had required no more exertion from him than a stroll on the lawn.

Moisture gleamed on both Harry and McGill's foreheads. They were puffing as if thoroughly winded, their shirts and coats rumpled. A streak of dirt slashed the front of Harry's breeches, and Mr. McGill had apparently torn his coat sleeve, for he kept looking at it. On the other hand, Winterton was walking straight and tall, turning his face to the wind which blew off the water and breathing deeply of it. He had shucked his coat, which he now carried hooked in one finger over his shoulder. He had also rolled up his shirtsleeves and loosened his neckcloth. His dark hair was ruffled and the rosy color that shone on his sun-bronzed cheeks only added to his virile good looks.

Neala watched the gentlemen pause at the picnic table, where Winterton downed two large goblets of water. Then, when he made straight for the rug where she sat, she felt her heart begin to beat with heightened anticipation.

"You should have come along!" Winterton said to Edward, as he plopped down beside Neala, draping his bare forearms across his drawn-up knees. Turning to Neala, he said, "The view from atop the hill was splendid, Miss Abercorn! Wish you could have seen it."

Aware of the fresh out-doorsy scent that accompanied him, Neala drew in several deep breaths while next to Diana, Lord Edward turned a look of disgust on the gentleman.

"You look an absolute fright, Winterton."

Neala didn't think so. She thought he looked . . . splendid. She stole another peek from beneath her lashes at the gentleman seated next to her. Suddenly he yanked off his neckcloth and popped open the top two buttons of his shirtfront! Neala gulped! Like a magnet, her eyes were drawn to the vee below his neck. And there, she saw *hair!* Dark, curly hair, as visible as daylight, across his strong chest!

Her eyes darted quickly away. But not quickly enough to stop the tingling sensation that began in the pit of her stomach and crept upward to her throat. In an attempt to curb it, she swallowed hard. What was happening to her?

"Hummph," Lord Brewster muttered, "you do look unkempt, Winterton." With some effort, he managed to get to his feet. "Time we pressed on. Must see to the boats." With that, he was gone.

Quite against Neala's will, her gaze again reverted to Lord Winterton. No comparison between that gentleman and the stodgy Lord Brewster would ever fadge. Unlike Lord Brewster, Winterton's masculine appeal *demanded* her attention. She couldn't stop herself from asking, "Did you enjoy your climb, sir?"

Winterton's dark head turned her way again and she watched a slow, deliberate smile lift the corners of his mouth. "Not half so much as I enjoy sitting here with you, Miss Abercorn."

Neala felt her heart flutter wildly in her breast. It was not what she had expected the gentleman to say.

Eleven

That night as Neala lay abed, thoughts of Lord Winterton continued to haunt her. His bravery, his heroism, his gentle way with the children. Her fascination with the dashing major seemed to grow with each time she saw him. The pull he had over her defied reason, his presence seemed to draw her like a magnet, and once she succumbed to his unflagging charm, it held her captive against her will.

This evening the two of them had sat before the fire in the drawing room and for a full quarter hour, had quietly conversed with one another while sipping their tea. They had spoken of nothing of consequence—remarking in passing upon the lovely time they had had on the outing today, of the children's delight upon the rescue of the ducklings, of the lovely sunshine they had all enjoyed—yet for Neala, the short interlude had been the highlight of the evening. Especially when Lord Winterton had complimented her again, telling her that she looked lovely in her lavender sarcenet with the matching plume in her hair.

Recalling the intent way he had gazed into her eyes, Neala felt her pulse quicken again with remembered pleasure. Why did the gentleman's very words set her heart thumping in her breast? In truth, they were but empty words for, she was certain he did not mean them. Nor had he meant what he said to her this afternoon at the picnic. How could he enjoy sitting beneath a tree with her *more* than he enjoyed the climb up the mountain or the spectacular panorama he had viewed amongst the clouds?

Neala could make sense of none of it. Yet, one thing was

perfectly clear. She admired Lord Winterton immensely. He was a hero of the first order. And, not only to England. He had endeared himself to all of them today, most especially to the children. Neala could easily imagine the dashing war hero with children of his own. They would love him as dearly as she had loved her Papa. When thoughts of her beloved Papa flooded her mind, she felt the familiar moisture begin to well up in her eyes. Seeing his face before her—his eyes twinkling, the everpresent smile on his lips—it was almost as if . . . as if he had come to bid her farewell, a fond but, *final* farewell.

When the warm vision vanished, Neala realized an odd, but comforting feeling of peace had settled about her. Papa was indeed gone and she and Mama and Lilibet must carry on without him. Drawing in a long breath, Neala decided that Papa's coming to her tonight meant that he knew his family would be well provided for now. Somehow, Papa knew of the magic wedding spell, Neala decided, and his smile meant that he approved of the match between Lilibet and Lord Winterton. And surely, it also meant that Papa approved of her match with Lord Brewster.

Neala tried to draw another deep breath, tried again to feel the same peace that had settled about her a moment ago. But, this time, peace would not come. Instead, she was assailed with a vivid image of Lord Winterton wading into the water, his trousers legs drawn up to his knees! *Oh!* She covered her face with both hands. She knew she should not be refining upon so delicate a subject as a gentleman's nakedness, but as with anything that concerned Lord Winterton, she seemed unable to stop herself. What was happening to her? What did it mean? Suddenly, she felt as tortured as the darkness that engulfed her. Very like the strange way she had felt when first she beheld Lord Winterton in the dining hall this morning. What was she to do?

The next morning, Neala awoke from a fitful sleep, determined afresh to avoid the dashing war hero. Gathering all the strength she could muster, she descended the staircase, her heart heavy with unease. What new occurrence today would wreck havoc with her resolve?

When she reached the dining hall, she was instead surprised to find only Lady Diana and Melinda at breakfast, and not in the large dining hall, but in the small nook adjacent to it. Upon learning that the gentlemen had arisen early and set out for a day of angling and rabbit hunting, an enormous feeling of relief washed over her.

"I rather expect the impromptu hunting party was Harry's idea," Diana said, leisurely spreading blackberry jam onto a warm scone.

"I expect he will return with a brace of rabbits and insist that Cook prepare them for dinner," her sister-in-law replied, then with a laugh, added, "There was a time last summer when we had a rabbit dish every night for a week. Rabbit pie, rabbit stew, rabbit salad. During partridge season we eat squab with equal regularity."

Diana sighed lazily. Neala noticed that without Lord Edward hovering about, her friend seemed somewhat at liberty herself. Her blond curls were not coiffed nearly so fashionably as they usually were, and at present, Diana was licking the sticky sweet jam from her fingertips, something she would *never* do if the gentlemen were at table. "At least with the gentlemen away, we can finalize our plans for our *soiree* of Thursday next. Were you successful in securing the musicians from Gloucester, Melinda?"

Her sister-in-law nodded, reaching again for the teapot. "Would you care for more tea, Neala?"

Neala nodded, quite enjoying her breakfast without Lord Winterton's disturbing presence about. As Melinda filled Neala's tea cup, Lady Tentrees joined them.

"Ah, good morning, Helene," Diana said. "I trust you are aware that our gentlemen have deserted us for the whole of the day."

Even the usually demure Helene wore a bright smile as she

took a plate from the sideboard and delicately lifted a hot buttered scone onto it. "Indeed, my husband was up quite early this morning," she replied agreeably. "And I daresay, I have been enjoying quite a refreshing nap since." Then, realizing what her remark could have meant, she colored deeply and tried to hide her embarrassment by quickly asking, "Is Mrs. McGill not with us this morning? Surely she is not off hunting with the gentlemen."

This brought a round of merry laughter from the ladies, then Diana said, "I presume her to be still abed. Without Mr. McGill to awaken her and see that she is properly clothed, it would not surprise me if she did not join us at all today."

The ladies tittered again, Neala covering her mouth with her napkin. It was true. Poor Mrs. McGill did need looking after. Yesterday at the picnic, she had awakened from her nap some time before Mr. McGill was back from the climb and apparently decided to have a blackberry tart. The purplish streaks visible on her upper lip and cheek remained in place until her husband returned and the smudges mysteriously disappeared.

"Oh, Diana!" Helene said, amusement still playing at her lips, "it is not nearly so bad as all that."

"You saw the remains of the tart yesterday the same as the rest of us did."

"In regard to our entertainment today," Melinda said, in an obvious attempt to divert everyone's attention from the hapless Mrs. McGill, "we have been invited to take tea with the Hamilton's this afternoon. They are our closest neighbors," she told Neala and Helene, "they were friends of Lord and Lady Brewster when the boys and Diana were little. The Hamilton's have a lovely picture gallery," she added.

Neala set her tea cup down. "Perhaps I should awaken Mrs. McGill. She would not want to miss seeing the pictures."

"What a good 'un 'ye are, Nealie, girl," Diana said, grinning at her friend as she pushed away from the table. "I was just going upstairs myself, if you are finished with your breakfast, I shall accompany you to Mrs. McGill's suite."

"How very thoughtful of you, Diana. Thank you."

On the way abovestairs, however, Diana revealed the real reason she had agreed to come along with Neala.

"I should like to speak privately with you, Nealie, dear."

Thinking that perhaps Diana wished to discuss some detail regarding the plans for her lavish country wedding, or perhaps the *soiree* of Thursday next, Neala followed her friend into Diana's blue-walled bedchamber. Diana closed the door behind them and indicated the matching pair of blue striped silk sofas, similar to the green ones in Neala's room, for them to sit upon.

Once they were seated comfortably before the hearth, Diana's countenance turned solemn, the look telling Neala something was amiss.

"I trust I have your permission to speak plainly, Neala."

"Of course, you do, Diana." Neala's eyes were a question. "Is something troubling you?"

"Indeed, something is troubling me greatly. It concerns you and Father." Diana paused to clear her throat, during which time Neala wondered again what was the matter. "Judging from your behavior at the picnic yesterday, Neala, I am convinced that you are not . . . well, putting your best foot forward in regard to encouraging Father."

Neala's brows pulled together.

"Even Emma remarked upon it."

"Remarked upon what, Diana?" Neala was at a loss to understand what was the trouble.

"I am referring to the manner in which you seem to blossom in Lord Winterton's presence, Neala, and when Father is about, you turn quite clammish again. What can be the meaning of it? Father was quite upset last evening when he spotted you and Winterton enjoying a coze by the fire. To the point that he asked if I thought you were still receptive to his suit. If you had made your feelings known to him, Neala, he would not have had to ask."

Neala winced. Of course, Diana was right. She had been woefully remiss in her behavior toward Lord Brewster. If only she could . . .

"Neala, your actions regarding Lord Winterton are unseemly, indeed. Surely you do not harbor the notion that the gentleman is singling you out. It cannot be true! Trench shows the same face to everyone; to every female, that is. I recall telling you at the outset, Neala, that he was responsible for a string of broken hearts across the continent." She waited. "Can you not say something on your own behalf, Neala?"

Neala wished with all her heart that she could.

"Then, at least assure me that you are not foolish enough to believe that a gentleman of Winterton's stamp would find you to his liking. I do not mean to rip up at you, Neala, quite the contrary. It is plain as a pikestaff to anyone with eyes that you are simply not in Winterton's style."

Anger suddenly flared within Neala. She had never fancied herself to be in Winterton's style! "I would never be foolish enough to link myself romantically with Lord Winterton, Diana. It would be the outside of enough." Neala felt her bosom rise and fall. For a twopence she would tell Diana about the wedding spell and how Lord Winterton was destined to marry Lilibet. But Mama had sworn them all to secrecy on the subject and Neala would do nothing, *nothing* to endanger the magic spell.

"Indeed, Neala," Diana returned quietly, "you coupled with Winterton would be the outside of enough. As is your behavior toward the gentleman. If you can forgive me for saying so, Neala, you are acting like a silly nodcock where Winterton is concerned. Much as I must have acted when I was a child of eight and fancied myself in love with him." Diana sniffed. "But, of course, I was a little girl then, whereas you are a grown woman." She paused, then at length, smiled for the first time since the girls had sat down. "I implore you, Neala, to make more of an effort where Father is concerned. You are a charming girl, but I fear Father has yet to see evidence of it. It is true you have done nothing scandalous, or given Father cause to think ill of you, but you have also not given him reason to approach you with an offer. And, my dear, that is our objective, is it not? You know I cannot go off and leave Father unattended, Neala. You must marry him, you must!"

Neala was listening carefully. She could easily understand Diana's deep desire to look after her father. If Papa were still alive, Neala would feel the exact same way about him.

"Consider your options, Nealie, dear."

Neala had considered them, and had reached the grim conclusion that she hadn't many.

"I am not pressing for a love match between you and Father. I want only to insure that you are well cared for and that Father does not grow lonely in his mature years."

Diana rose to pace a bit in front of the ornately carved mantelpiece. "Take a look about you, Neala." A sweeping gesture encompassed the elegant surroundings. "Father can provide very well for you and your family. I can quite easily picture your Mama and Lilibet, here. Though I rather expect with Lilibet's smashing good-looks, she will make a splendid match once she is out. She was quite commented upon, you know, at Lady Sefton's musicale. Though——" she laughed, as if some absurdity had struck her "——I believe Lilibet harbored the same silly notion as you, that because Trench was seated next to her, he *fancied* her."

Neala colored visibly, but quickly bit her tongue.

"Once you have married Father, Neala, he will give Lilibet a season and settle an allowance on her. As Lady Brewster, you will be in quite a good position yourself to sponsor your younger sister. Surely, Neala, you can see the advantages of encouraging Father." She turned an expectant gaze upon Neala. "Can you not?"

Neala quickly nodded.

"Splendid. Father further confided to me last evening that he means for our *soiree* to double as your engagement party!"

"Oh!" Neala sucked in her breath.

Diana beamed. "I thought that would please you, Nealie." Absently, she twirled the gold filigree ring on her own finger, the one Edward had given to her to seal their betrothal. "So, you see, you must pay court to Father, Nealie, and do all in your power to discourage Winterton! It is quite clear that Trench is only amusing himself with you. He has always been a bit of a rake, though among friends, he is a gentleman and would not think of pressing himself upon me, or Melinda. And, of course, he would never flirt with Mrs. McGill," she paused to laugh, "and Helene is too much beneath her husband's thumb for another gentleman to approach her. So, there it is, you are the only unattached female here, Nealie. That can be the only reason Trench has taken it in his head to shower you with attention."

That and the fact that Lord Brewster persists in asking it of him, Neala thought angrily, but she did not voice her thoughts. She knew Diana was right. Instead, she murmured, "Indeed, that is it."

"Most assuredly, it is."

Diana was right. "I must have appeared quite foolish, Diana. I am sorry, indeed. Can you forgive me?"

Diana moved to sit on the sofa next to Neala. "There is nothing to forgive, Nealie, dear. At one time or another, every young lady fancies herself in love with the dashing Major Lambert. Why—" she laughed self-consciously "—perhaps I am still a bit in love with him, myself."

Neala gazed up at Diana as Diana sprang nervously to her feet. "Of course, I am only larking," she said, flouncing to position herself before the mantelpiece again. "I am top over tail in love with Edward. Though, at the picnic yesterday, Trench did look . . ." she chewed fretfully on her lower lip, "that is, with his trouser legs rolled up . . ." her voice trailed off. She quickly recovered. "Say you will heed my advice, Nealie. I wish only to see matters set to rights between you and Father."

Neala smiled sweetly at her friend. "You are a dear girl, Diana, for caring so deeply about your father, and about me."

"Oh, Neala!" Tears shone in Diana's bright blue eyes. "I do so wish to see you and Father wed. You will endeavor to encourage him, will you not?"

Neala nodded again.

Still, as the two young ladies quitted the room to go and awaken Mrs. McGill, Neala wondered what precisely she must do in order to encourage Lord Brewster to come up to scratch?

The question was still uppermost in Neala's mind the following evening after dinner, when Lord Brewster made the observation that since it was quite a clear night, they might all enjoy gazing through his powerful new telescope which was set up on the south lawn. Neala had noticed the metal cylinder just beyond the garden and had longed to view the moon and stars through it.

"On a cloudless night, one can actually see bumps on the moon!" Lord Brewster enthused, ushering the entire group through the drawing room to the double doors that gave on to the terrace.

Moving toward the marble steps that led to the garden, Neala became aware that their host had lagged behind a bit, to especially escort her to the star-gazing apparatus, she wondered? Sure enough, as she neared the railing that lined the stairs, Lord Brewster reached to place a large hand at her back and the two descended the stairs alongside one another. Contrary to the sensations that spiraled through her at Lord Winterton's touch, Neala had to fight off the urge to squirm away from the offensive feel of Lord Brewster's hand. But, reminding herself of Diana's plea, she refrained.

It was quite balmy outdoors, the air felt fresh, almost humid. The gentle breeze that wafted past them carried with it the sweet scent of roses and honeysuckle. The party meandered through the garden, coming upon a circular clearing in the center that featured a large marble pond, round in shape. Neala had been here before, and knew that it was now stocked with one lone baby duck as well as a profusion of gold fish. Glancing down, she saw the shiny scales of the fish gleaming brightly in the moonlight.

Jutting outward from the pond were several narrow paths, much like spokes of a wheel, that led to different parts of the garden. Lord Brewster directed the party down the widest path, passing beneath rows of giant poplar trees. Amid the long shadows cast by the full moon, Neala became aware that Lord Winterton had jockeyed to walk along her other side. She felt small between the two gentleman, though her head was nearly on a level with the thickset Lord Brewster.

She was grateful when Lord Winterton made no attempt to speak to her but instead directed a few comments over her head to Lord Brewster. Neala turned her attention to the soothing sounds of evening, the silvery water gurgling in the pond, a night owl hooting from somewhere high atop a tree, the mellow croaking of a bullfrog. The plaintive sounds reminded her of many such nights she'd enjoyed in her family's small garden in Mayfair.

Reaching the star-gazing apparatus, Lord Brewster moved to adjust it, then turned at once to Neala.

"Would you like to be the first to look at the stars, Miss Abercorn?"

"Oh, indeed!" Neala replied with genuine enthusiasm. She stepped to the instrument and put her eye to the opening. At first she was overwhelmed by the radiant brightness, but then she began to make out something that resembled a piece of moldy cheese. "Why, it is perfectly thrilling," she said to Lord Brewster, wishing she might know more about it, but unsure of precisely what to ask. Relinquishing her place to young Lady Tentrees, she ventured shyly, "I-I should like to learn all about the planets and stars, sir. P-Perhaps you might teach me."

The elderly gentleman guffawed. "Don't know a damn thing about 'em, Miss Abercorn. Can't see much use for planetary knowledge, myself."

"Oh." Neala lowered her gaze. "One wonders why you would have a telescope at all, my lord?"

"Cards, Miss Abercorn. Won the blasted thing on a bet, though I can't think now why I wanted it." He returned to the instrument again to adjust the height for Mr. McGill, who was just stepping up to look. "Expect you'd like a look, too, wouldn't you, Winterton?"

Lord Winterton had been standing quietly to one side. Neala felt certain he had been watching her, but she couldn't think why. When he stepped up to the apparatus, she hurried to put a vast distance between herself and that gentleman. Still, she distinctly heard the remark Lord Winterton made to Lord Brewster as he bent his dark head over the instrument.

"Plenty of merits to a knowledge of astronomy, Brewster."

Neala ached to ask Lord Winterton the questions that burned in her mind, but, of course, she did not. She hung back, watching first one, then another of the guests peer through the instrument. Soon, Lord Brewster stepped to her side again. "Would you care to take a stroll among the roses, Miss Abercorn."

The alarmed look she turned on him prompted him to add, "The moon is quite full. I assure you we shall be in plain sight of everyone." A gesture drew her attention to the well-lit paths of the garden that the party had just walked through.

A nervous smile wavered across Neala's face. "Then I-I suppose it would be quite proper." The gentleman had never asked her to do such an intimate thing before, did it mean that he was about to . . . to? Feeling the palms of her hands grow clammy, Neala swallowed hard.

Before setting out, she flung a nervous gaze over her shoulder toward Lord Winterton, but he again had his eye pressed to the tube. She could hear his deep voice explaining some wonder or other to an enthralled Helene and little Mrs. McGill. Neala longed to join the ladies in order to hear what the knowledgeable man was saying.

Instead, she made a valiant effort to fix a smile upon her face and allow Lord Brewster to escort her again into the garden. They walked quite a distance in complete silence, Neala aware of his heavy footfalls crunching loudly on the gravel beneath them. Her own half-boots made a considerably lesser noise. Vaguely, she was aware of similar sounds about them. Perhaps others of the party were also strolling along one or another of the many garden paths.

Upon reaching the center clearing, the rotund gentleman stopped near the fish pond and turned to face Neala. After what seemed an interminable moment, he began to speak. "Miss Abercorn, I have come to care for you, deeply—"

"Is the water deep here?"

Both Neala's and Lord Brewster's heads whirled about.

"I say, doesn't look so very deep!" Lord Winterton marched to the rim of the pond and gazed with abject interest into the sparkling depths. " 'Course I expect that sort of thing can be deceiving, eh, Brewster? Much like the distance of the planets when viewed through a telescope. Quite an interesting phenomena, wouldn't you say, Miss Abercorn?"

Neala was far too surprised to utter a word, but as it turned out, she didn't have to.

Quack! Quack! Quack!

"I say, I believe the little fellow recognizes me!"

Neala could not suppress a giggle as the tiny ducklet Winterton had rescued two days ago paddled straight up to where he stood peering into the dark blue water.

Quack! Quack! Its tiny orange bill worked feverishly.

Reaching into the pocket of his coat, Lord Winterton withdrew a biscuit and promptly crumbled it onto the water. "There now, you've had your dinner," he said, dusting the crumbs from his hands and turning once again to his stunned audience, the round-eyed Neala and a bristling Lord Brewster. Winterton grinned. "I admit I have fed the little fellow on occasion."

"Harrumph," Lord Brewster grumbled. "If you don't mind, Winterton, Miss Abercorn and I were just—"

"Studying the stars from this angle?" Lord Winterton cocked his head to gaze with renewed interest at the sky. "As I said before, I find heavenly bodies quite fascinating." He turned a disarming smile on Neala. "Take Miss Abercorn, for instance, she looks quite heavenly by moonlight, wouldn't you agree, Brewster?"

His face a thunder cloud, Lord Brewster looked from Winterton to Neala and back again. " 'Course, she does! Haven't you something better to do this evening, Winterton? Something . . . *inside?*"

Folding his arms across his chest, Winterton shrugged. "It was your idea to venture into the garden tonight, Brewster. And I quite agree, far too lovely a night to spend indoors, wouldn't you say, Miss Abercorn?"

Her eyes round, Neala managed a slight nod.

"Shall we stroll about the pond?" Winterton suggested brightly.

"Miss Abercorn and I *were* strolling about the pond."

"Splendid! Then you shan't mind if I fall in with you?"

Lord Brewster gave the taller gentleman a look that said he wouldn't mind if Winterton fell in somewhere, so long as it wasn't in with them.

The trio walked a few steps in silence. Finding herself between them again, Neala felt especially uncomfortable this time. Why had Lord Winterton been so insistent upon joining them? A few steps more and she became aware of a crunching sound, as if someone were chewing. Glancing upward, she saw that Lord Winterton was munching on a biscuit.

"Lemon. Quite good. Would you care for one, Miss Abercorn."

Neala tentatively shook her head. "No, thank you, sir."

"Well, I should like one!"

"Of course, you would, old man. Precisely why I brought along plenty. Enough to feed the little wadling there, and whoever else might come along. Here you are." He handed Brewster a plump, round biscuit.

The gentleman popped the whole thing into his mouth at once, chewed it loudly and swallowed. And, then . . . he coughed. And coughed. And coughed again.

Winterton reached to slap his friend on the back but it was no use. The elderly gentleman was already in the throes of one of his uncontrollable coughing fits.

Neala became concerned. "Perhaps I could get something for you, my lord?"

"Good idea, Miss Abercorn." Winterton said. "Fetch a glass of water for us, if you please."

"No . . . *cough* . . . won't do . . . need—"

"Perhaps you'd best toddle along inside then, Brewster."

The red-faced Brewster nodded thickly and hurried off toward the terrace, the wracking sounds from his throat having not diminished a whit.

Neala and Lord Winterton watched 'til the gentleman reached the terrace and disappeared safely through the double doors.

Shaking his dark head slowly from side to side, Winterton murmured, "Shouldn't have eaten the biscuit."

Neala glanced up. "One would think you had given it to him of a purpose," she said, her tone a trifle cross.

Lord Winterton made no reply, but in the glow of moonlight, Neala saw one dark brow lift, then she felt his warm hand lightly touch her back and with the veriest hint of pressure, he urged her forward. "Shall we continue, Miss Abercorn?"

She hesitated, unsure exactly what she ought to do. "Perhaps we should wait for—"

"We shan't venture from sight, Miss Abercorn."

They strolled the entire circumference of the pond in silence. Upon reaching and then passing up the exact same spot where Lord Brewster had abandoned them, Winterton said, "I believe we have covered this ground before. May I suggest we explore a side path?"

Neala glanced anxiously toward the house. "But, what if—"

Winterton stopped dead in his tracks. "May I point out that, as bright as the night is, our good friend Brewster will not experience the least difficulty in catching up to us, Miss Abercorn."

Neala gazed over the garden. Long rays of silvery moonlight flooded every nook and cranny. Except for the path lined with poplars. There, shadows that were quite long and dark fell across the gravel. Elsewhere the roses and hedgebushes had been trimmed close on waist high. Tangled honeysuckle vines clumped along the ground, climbing an occasional trellis or post. Beyond the garden, she could easily make out the shadowy forms of those still on the lawn, milling about the telescope.

"Well, I-I . . . suppose it would be . . ."

"Of course, it would be!" He took her arm and promptly led her to the path lined with populars. Overhead, the dark branches swayed soundlessly against a star sprinkled sky.

After a few steps, Neala said, "I-I do hope Lord Brewster has recovered by now."

"I rather expect he has, Miss Abercorn. For the moment, at least."

Neala turned a quizzical gaze upward. "What do you mean, sir?"

Winterton shrugged. "We all have to pop off sometime. Brewster is not getting any younger, you know. Shouldn't worry though, you will make a lovely widow."

Neala blanched. *Widow?*

"Don't mean to alarm you, my dear. Brewster has a few good years left. Of course, if you were to marry a younger man . . ."

Neala's lips tightened. "You know very well that I have no choice in the matter. Lord Brewster is . . . my only suitor."

Winterton did not reply at once, but when he did, his voice had taken on a certain raspy quality. "Can you be certain of that, Miss Abercorn?"

When Neala said nothing, he continued on in the same vein. "You are a very attractive young lady, Miss Abercorn."

Neala stopped cold. "I do not like in the least what you are doing, Lord Winterton."

Winterton paused and turned to face her. In the dim moonlight, she thought his dark gaze seemed unusually intent. "What *am* I doing, Miss Abercorn?"

Neala fought for control. On the one hand, she wished to smack his face for making sport of her, on the other hand, she . . . well, the thought crossed her mind to . . . *oh!* if she weren't so angry, she would . . .

Without a word, Lord Winterton moved a step closer to her. She felt his hand slip round her waist, and the pressure of that warm clasp on her back urged her closer to him, then even closer. When they were standing toe to toe, and his eyes fixed on her mouth, she knew that he meant to . . .

Trying to ignore the tingling shivers that quivered through her, Neala parted her lips to protest, but instead, the gentleman lowered his head and lightly, *ever* so lightly, brushed her mouth with his.

"Oh-h-h," she murmured, a low moan escaping her.

Winterton's other arm slipped 'round her back to cradle her head. Neala's eyes floated shut as again, his lips nestled onto hers. The pressing and kneading of his moist mouth against hers sent waves of exquisite pleasure rippling through her. It was simply heavenly.

When his lips moved to caress her cheeks, her hair, she sank into him, breathing, "Oh-h, sir, you . . . you mustn't . . ."

"Mustn't what, Miss Abercorn?" he whispered, his warm breath fanning her ear. "Mustn't this?" His arms tightened about her. She felt him spread his long legs apart and with a firm hand, mold her slight form firmly against his.

Neala's breath was coming in fits and starts, but the feel of her soft breasts being crushed to his hard chest caused a pulsing knot of longing to take shape in her stomach. "Oh-h, sir, I . . . I don't feel at all like myself. I'm clearly not at all well," she gasped.

"On the contrary, Miss Abercorn," his voice was hoarse, "you feel . . . magical."

Magical! Neala's eyes sprang open. What was he doing? Exerting a hard push against the gentleman's equally hard chest, she managed to wrest free. Without a word, she lifted her skirts and fled from him, running as fast as she could toward the pool of bright light that streamed from the open terrace doors. Scampering inside the house, she darted past a dazed Lord Brewster, who with goblet in hand, was mopping his brow as he tried in vain to overcome the wracking coughs that had beset him earlier.

"I say, Miss Abercorn," he began, glancing up as she scurried past him, "I've an idea it was the . . . *cough* . . . night air that caused my . . . *cough* . . . perhaps, we might talk . . . Miss Abercorn?"

Neala did not look back.

Twelve

Winterton was an abomination to all things decent. He had known, of course, or had at least strongly suspected what Lord Brewster had been about to say to Miss Abercorn before he so rudely interrupted the pair a moment ago. He hadn't meant to play the rogue . . . yes, he had. He had fully intended to spoil the intimate moment between them. He had also fully intended to kiss Miss Abercorn. Kiss her so soundly that, thereafter, she could think of no one but him.

Yes, Winterton told himself as he climbed the marble steps to the terrace and entered the drawing room once again, he was a scoundrel, a contemptible reprobate. But . . . he grinned slyly, he was a happy one.

Upstairs in her bedchamber, Neala threw herself onto the bed. How could she have behaved in so shameful a fashion? How could she have allowed Lord Winterton to kiss her? Tears streamed down her cheeks as both hands flew to cover her face. She should never, *never!* have come to the houseparty. Lilibet should have been here instead of her. Oh, what had she done? Diana was right about Lord Winterton. He was a wastrel, a wretch of the first order. And she had trusted him! But—suddenly, a flash of anger replaced her mortification and served to dry up her tears—she would not let that rake ruin her chances with Lord Brewster, *she wouldn't!*

Sniffing noisily, she sat up on the bed. Perhaps the wedding spell had weakened a bit over the years, or perhaps it had never encountered so difficult a subject as Lord Winterton, but what-

ever the case, the spell did not appear to be working as swiftly
as it ought, consequently the only course left open for Neala
was to marry Lord Brewster. At once! And she would not let
Winterton's reprehensible conduct stand in the way.

Wiping away the remains of her tears, she sprang to her feet.
She would return downstairs, search out Lord Winterton and
insist that he cease flirting with her for now and forever!

Neala marched boldly to the drawing room, but upon reaching the doorway, she paused, needing a moment to gather additional courage while she cast about for the imposing figure
of Lord Winterton. She spotted him leaning casually against the
chimneypiece, sipping his port and looking for all the world as
if nothing were amiss. Diana and Lord Edward were seated
nearby and the three appeared to be engaged in light conversation. Neala could hear the low strains of Winterton's voice and
Diana's high trill of laughter.

Absently, she noted the positions of everyone else in the
room. Helene was performing a melancholy tune on the pianoforte. Close at hand, Lord Tentrees wore a look of studied disinterest on his face. Seated on a nearby sofa, Mr. McGill was
leafing through a newspaper, while next to him, Mrs. McGill
was listening raptly to Helene's music. Melinda and Harry were
no where to be seen, no doubt, having already excused themselves, as was their custom each evening, to adjourn to the nurs-
ery to tuck in the children. Neala couldn't help noticing that
Lord Brewster was also absent from the room. She fervently
hoped he had recovered from his coughing spell and was now,
perhaps, having a smoke in the study, or maybe he had stepped
to the terrace. Thinking about Lord Brewster served to refresh
her anger with Lord Winterton.

Her eyes narrowed as she made straight for the gentleman
leaning against the mantelpiece. When he glanced up and saw
her, she noticed that his face lit up measurably. Her lips tightened. No doubt, the wastrel was refining on the bawdy interlude
that had just occurred between the two of them a moment ago
in the garden.

Giving only the veriest greeting to Diana and Lord Edward, Neala turned to address Lord Winterton, the friendly smile on his face only agitating her further. "I desire a private word with you, my lord."

"Why, I would be delighted, Miss Abercorn." Winterton set his glass aside and reached for her arm as if to escort her . . . somewhere. He gazed toward the double doors that gave on to the terrace. "Shall we take a stroll on the terrace, Miss Abercorn? Or, perhaps . . . the garden?"

Appalled, Neala pulled her arms swiftly to her sides and glared up at him with a look of loathing. True, she had not determined exactly *where* she might speak with the gentleman, but neither of his suggestions were the least bit appropriate.

Suddenly Diana's voice cut in. "Edward and I have decided to take a turn about the garden." She rose to her feet and leveled a speaking look at Neala. "You and Winterton may sit here, if you like." She indicated the chairs she and Edward had just vacated.

"Thank you, Diana," Neala said, her head held aloft. "Here will suit nicely." She flung a triumphant look at Lord Winterton as she took a seat. Without a word of protest, he followed her lead.

When Diana and Lord Edward had safely disappeared through the double doors, Neala cleared her throat. She hoped the courage that had brought her this far would continue to sustain her. Her throat felt uncommonly tight, but nonetheless, with her singleness of purpose in mind, she fully expected to encounter no difficulty in carrying on as planned. Drawing in another deep breath, she began, "I had thought better of you, my lord."

"Better of me, Miss Abercorn?" His voice was low, to the point of being seductive. "Are you saying that my kiss was not to your liking?"

Neala's eyes widened. "That is not what I am saying at all, my lord, I am saying that—"

"That you enjoyed it and would like another?"

Oh! The man was insufferable!

"Permit me to say, Miss Abercorn, that this is hardly the place." He had leaned even nearer to her, in fact, when Neala turned to glare at him, she found him close on to whispering in her ear!

Aghast, she jerked away. "You will keep your distance, sir!" She was so angry now, her voice had begun to shake. "What I mean to say, sir, is that I had thought you a more honorable man, far too honorable to force your attentions on a young lady."

Winterton said nothing for the moment. Then, in a tone far different from the teasing one he had been using with her, he said, "I humbly beg your forgiveness, Miss Abercorn. It was not my intent to force my attentions upon you. On the contrary, I had thought that—"

"Your intentions have been quite plain to me all along, sir," she interrupted, her tone full of rage.

He seemed surprised. "Have they, Miss Abercorn?"

She turned to gaze full at him, her brown eyes icy. "Indeed, they have been. And, thanks to the unprincipled manner in which you conducted yourself in the garden, sir, I am now—" she looked away, her voice quaking with emotion "—soiled goods."

Fortunately, Neala did not see the smile that curved Winterton's lips, nor the twinkle that sprang to his eye. "Well, I would hardly say that, Miss Abercorn. But, if you have come to ask me to do the honorable thing by you, I shall."

"Shall what, sir?" she mouthed, barely able to speak she was so overset.

"Why, I shall marry you, of course."

"Oh!" Anger flared again in her breast. Springing to her feet, she glared down upon him. "You are being exceedingly irritating, my lord!"

Laughing aloud, Winterton sprang also to his feet. "Why, Miss Abercorn, I detect a certain spirit in you that until now, I hadn't the least notion existed!"

She folded her arms across her middle, the toe of her boot tapping silently on the carpet. "Well, I do have spirit. But for the most part, I endeavor to keep it hidden."

Winterton seemed to be enjoying himself immensely. "I can't think why you'd want to do that, Miss Abercorn. I find it a most charming trait indeed. Coupled with your innate sweetness and purity of thought, spirit makes for a striking contrast. I am finding you more and more to my liking, Miss Abercorn."

"Oh!" In despair, Neala threw her hands up and perched once again on the edge of the chair. That she had sat down again prompted Winterton to do likewise. When next she began to speak, her tone was once more tight and controlled. "Lord Winterton, I insist that you cease this frivolous talk at once. I am quite aware that you are merely amusing yourself at my expense and I do not find that an attractive quality in you."

"Ah, I see. But, aside from that, you do find me attractive. Is that correct, Miss Abercorn?"

She cast a withering glance at him only to find his grin a bit . . . disarming. "At the moment, I am finding you most exasperating, my lord."

Winterton's smile widened. "And what would you suggest I do to remedy that, Miss Abercorn? I have already offered to marry you."

At the mention of marriage, her nostrils flared afresh. "To begin with, sir, you can leave off your shameless flirting with me. I am aware that I am not the least in your style."

"On the contrary, Miss Abercorn, you are delightful. In fact, you are the most charming young lady I have ever had the pleasure of looking after."

Neala ignored the first part of his speech. "I am well aware, sir, that Lord Brewster specifically requested that you look out for me, but the truth of the matter is, I do not need looking after."

"And what of Lord Brewster's wishes?"

"You have done quite enough to further Lord Brewster's suit toward me," she said firmly.

"That is quite true. However, may I be quick to point ou that Lord Brewster had nothing whatever to do with what hap pened between the two of us just now in the garden."

Neala gazed at him with renewed horror. "That is precisel my point, my lord. Lord Brewster would *never*—"

"And that is precisely *my* point, Miss Abercorn. Lord Brew ster *would* never—"

"You are forgetting yourself again, sir! You are most as suredly not the gentleman I first thought you to be." Neala thrus her chin up and rose again to her feet.

Winterton promptly stood as well. "If you are uncomfortabl sitting, Miss Abercorn, may I suggest we take a turn about th room . . . or, if I may be so bold, the terrace?"

Neala's lips tightened. "You have besmirched me quit enough for one evening, my lord."

He looked as if he meant to dispute that, but allowed hi better judgement to step in and influence him otherwise.

"Do I have your word, Lord Winterton, that, in future, yo will desist from . . . from your shameless trifling with me?"

Following that question, Winterton appeared to experience a great deal of difficulty controlling his mirth. He actually turned his head, but not before Neala saw the smile that crinkled the corners of his eyes. Furious that he was now laughing at her, she swept past him without another word. With deliberate steps, she re-crossed the drawing room, only to come face to face with Lord Brewster, who had just entered from the hallway.

Neala willed a bright smile to what she knew must be a very flushed face. "I hope you have sufficiently recovered from your attack, my lord," she said, proud of the even tone she had man aged to muster.

"Yes, indeed. No need for alarm, Miss Abercorn."

"I quite enjoyed our stroll in the garden, sir." At her own mention of the garden, Neala felt the already deep color in her cheeks intensify. "I-I mean, the telescope," she added. "I quite enjoyed looking through it."

"You said that earlier, Miss Abercorn."

"Oh. Well, then . . ." She seemed already to have exhausted her pool of interesting comments to direct to the aging gentleman. "Well, then, good night, my lord."

"Sleep well, Miss Abercorn."

Feeling nervousness again overtake her, Neala hastened toward the stairs and made as quickly as possible for the safe haven of her own bedchamber. Once there, she hurriedly undressed and climbed into bed. Without a doubt, this evening had turned into the worst nightmare of her entire life.

Or . . . had it?

Much, much later into the night, she was awakened by a *swooshing* sound, followed by receding footfalls in the hallway. It was not until morning that she discovered the cause for the nocturnal disturbance.

A note had been slipped beneath her door. Rubbing sleep from her eyes, Neala bent to pick up the folded sheet of paper. Making for the ray of light that seeped between the heavy silken draperies, she unfurled the missive and began to read.

My dear Miss Abercorn,

   In spite of the flippancy of my words last evening, I deeply regret my impropriety with you in the garden. Please believe that it was not my intent to take liberties, nor to cause you any degree of shame. You are a beautiful young woman, and though you may think my actions speak otherwise, I hold you in the highest regard.

   It is with great humility, that I beg your forgiveness for my bold and most despicable behavior of last evening.

   Your most faithful servant,

                                        Winterton

Reading his words, nay, almost hearing the deep timbre of his mellow voice as if he were actually whispering the words in her ear, Neala melted. In truth, she had not wanted to stay angry with the gentleman. How would it look if, throughout the rest of their lives, she remained cool and aloof to her own brother-in-law? And, worse, that she was unable to explain the reason for that aloofness? For, of course, she would never reveal to another living soul what had happened between them. And despite his . . . odd behavior of last evening, Winterton, she felt certain, was too much the gentleman to ever tell anyone either. To do so would cast them both in a bad light.

Therefore, even if Lord Winterton had not slipped a note beneath her door, Neala had already decided that she would forgive the gentleman. It was the only way.

Feeling vastly relieved that the unpleasant business was now behind her, Neala dressed carefully, choosing one of her favorite morning gowns, a pretty cream and melón stripe muslin, with cream embroidery edging the sleeves and hem. After dismissing the little maid who came every morning to help her dress, she brushed her own brown curls til they shone, dreamily recalling the compliment Winterton had paid her as they sat beneath the tree on the picnic: that her shiny hair was far too pretty to cover with a bonnet.

But, realizing with a start that she was being silly again, she cut herself up roundly. Still, she had to admit that Lord Winterton was responsible for quite a number of delicious memories in her life, not the least of which was . . . no, she would not think again on the singular moment that had occurred between them last evening in the garden, though it above all else stood out in her mind like a brilliant diamond in an otherwise empty jewel case.

With a reluctant sigh, she put aside her hairbrush, and at the same time, endeavored to drive away any lingering images of Lord Winterton from her mind. Today, she would seek the gentleman out one last time in order to thank him for the letter of apology and that would mark the end of their association. That is, until he wed Lilibet.

Upon reaching the dining hall a bit later, she found every last member of the houseparty, except Lord Winterton, already seated 'round the large mahogany table in the center of the room. Listening to their idle morning chatter, it soon became apparent that not a single one of them had the least notion where the illustrious war hero had got off to.

Lord Winterton, it appeared, had simply vanished in the night!

Thirteen

By tea time, speculation about the whereabouts of Lord Winterton had escalated to such a pitch that everyone had a theory.

"For my part," Harry insisted, "I believe he had important military business to attend to."

"Quite likely," agreed Mr. McGill, helping himself to another thin slice of cake, then depositing a slice on his wife's plate. "Though, I was under the impression that Winterton was no longer a military man."

"Military, pah!" Lord Brewster sputtered. "It's a woman. No doubt, the rake has a new ladybird sequestered away in the country somewhere."

Hearing that, Neala felt herself color, but she said nothing.

"Winterton does appear to get on well with the fairer sex," Lord Tentrees observed dryly.

"Lord Winterton is a very knowledgeable man," chirped little Mrs. McGill, seemingly quite pleased with herself for having thought of something to contribute to the conversation. So pleased, in fact, that she completely lost sight of the fact that, at the moment, she was also drinking tea. The amber liquid dribbled right out of her cup and pooled in a puddle in her lap. "Oh . . . my . . ." She scrambled at once to her feet, and in the doing tripped over Lord Edward's long leg which lay most carelessly in her path. Without preamble, Mrs. McGill plunged headlong toward Lord Edward.

"Dash it all to blazes!" he exclaimed, trying to dodge out of the way of the teetering woman, both his arms flailing about to keep his own tea cup steady and to not overturn the contents of his plate. "Why must I always be the one to suffer when Mrs. McGill spills her liquid?"

Already on his feet, Mr. McGill began to valiantly dab at his wife's wet front with a towel he had secured from somewhere, or perhaps had brought it with him in the off-chance something of this nature would occur.

"There now," he said, trying to sooth his flustered little wife. "I appear to have sopped up most of it, my dear."

"I beg to differ, sir," Lord Edward mumbled, "my trousers have sopped up most of it."

"Oh, do be still, Edward," Lady Diana said crossly, trying to look around her irritated husband-to-be to her brother, who was seated across from her, "we were discussing Winterton. Are you quite certain he said nothing to you, Harry?"

Harry shrugged. "Not that I can recall."

Diana appeared to be deep in thought. At length, she directed a pointed gaze at Neala. "I daresay, you were the last to speak with him, Neala. Perhaps you should tell us what the two of you were discussing last evening."

All eyes focused on Neala and she felt her cheeks begin to burn with fire. Her eyelids fluttering, she cast about for something plausible to say. "I . . . we . . ."

"Miss Abercorn does spend an inordinate amount of time in the gentleman's company," Lord Edward put in, his tone equally as cross as Diana's had been a moment ago.

"What has that to say to anything?" demanded Lady Tentrees. "Mrs. McGill is correct in saying that Lord Winterton is a very knowledgeable man. I have found the gentleman to be an excellent conversationalist. As apparently Miss Abercorn has."

"Well, Neala," Diana persisted, "what were the two of you discussing?"

Neala squirmed afresh. It was unthinkable that she would divulge the delicate nature of their conversation last evening!

"I say, Miss Abercorn," Harry put in, "if some harm has

befallen Winterton, it would help matters considerably if we had some inkling as to the gentleman's whereabouts."

Still, Neala said nothing.

"Miss Abercorn?" Lord Brewster said, his tone more a command than a question.

Neala felt all eyes on her. She drew in a long breath. "We . . . our conversation was of a . . . a personal nature. If the gentleman had mentioned something to me of his plans, I assure you, I would have said as much quite a long time ago."

"But, Neala, he must have said something," Diana insisted.

"The gentleman does single you out frequently," Lord Edward repeated, his tone accusing.

Neala's frightened gaze flitted to Lord Brewster. Though his brows had drawn together, the gentleman said nothing. Neala's shoulders lifted in a helpless gesture. "I am sorry, he did not reveal a word to me."

"Well," Diana concluded, her lips pressed tightly together, "I suppose we have nothing for it but to carry on. I do hope the wastrel returns in time for the party."

"As do I," Melinda put in. "If he does not, I fear we shall have quite a number of disappointed guests on our hands."

"What say?" Lord Tentrees asked, an odd note in his tone.

"The guests," Diana told him. "Many are coming only in the hopes of meeting Lord Winterton. My friend Mrs. Chetwith remarked upon it. Emma said that talk in the countryside is all about Winterton."

"I see," Lord Tentrees mumbled. "The gentleman has had an illustrious military career, still I had no idea that word of his accomplishments had spread so far afield."

"Oh, quite," Harry said, then added simply, "Winterton is a hero."

Harry's comment summed it up aptly for Neala.

Try as she might, for the entire rest of that evening and on into the following day, she could not stop thinking about Lord Winterton. She worried that perhaps her angry outburst had contributed in some way to his disappearance. But, surely that was not the case, for that would elevate her importance in the gentleman's eye to something beyond . . . well, mere friendship. Still, she fretted over what his absence could mean. Why had he simply vanished without a clue?

That next day, Neala learned that following an intense interrogation, a groom had come forward to divulge that in the dead of that infamous night, Lord Winterton had roused the fellow from a deep slumber with instructions to ready his horse. Winterton had then tossed the sleepy groom a gold coin to insure that he would crawl back into his bed and tell no one the direction Winterton headed. It was only upon threat of dismissal that the quaking young man revealed the truth to his employer. Lord Winterton had lit out cross-country, as if making for Gloucester, the boy said.

Immediately after that, the gentlemen got up a party to go and search for the missing Winterton, but it was to no avail. When they returned late that evening with no news and no Winterton, a pall seemed to settle about the group.

To Neala, it seemed the men turned rather quickly to other pursuits. Harry and Lord Brewster spent considerable time shut up in the study with their bailiff. Lord Tentrees and Mr. McGill discovered a mutual interest in the game of cribbage, and before long had got up a tournament of sorts, challenging whomever they could to play one or the other, so they could then play the winner and thereby determine a champion. Edward and Diana spent most of their time in one another's company.

When the other ladies were not discussing Lord Winterton in hushed tones, they dispersed and sought out amusements of their own. Neala offered both of her new books to Helene, who thereafter was seen curled up on a corner of the sofa, or in a chair on the terrace, reading. Later in the evening, she and Neala would then discuss their favorite parts. Melinda spent most of her days with the children. And Mrs. McGill, well, no one could say for certain what Mrs. McGill did to occupy herself. She seemed to sleep a great deal, between breakfast and luncheon, and then again, between luncheon and tea.

The only noteworthy thing that happened in the next three days was that Lord Brewster did get around to offering for Neala, and she accepted. After that which, she couldn't help noticing, the gentleman paid even less attention to her.

Neala didn't mind. She enjoyed wandering about the estate on her own, she even felt at liberty to resume her passion for riding. Every afternoon, she took to spending long hours in the saddle. Riding with the wind brought back pleasant memories for her, of those times when she was small and she and Papa would ride together. During those fretful times when Papa did not return home for days at a time, Neala used to pretend that it was she who came galloping to his rescue and, thrilled to find him again, she would bring him home.

Though Neala would never admit it herself, during her long rides now, part of her mind was always trained on the possibility of finding Lord Winterton. She couldn't bear the thought that some harm may have befallen the gentleman. One day, she abandoned the well-trodden road and set out cross-country, perhaps the same as he had done, and got almost as far as Gloucester before she turned back, stopping on the return trip at a queer little inn at the juncture of three roads where she procured a mug of ale for herself and some cool water for her horse.

Each afternoon when she returned to the house, hope brimmed fresh within her that she would find Lord Winterton there, grinning, teasing the ladies in the same engaging manner he always did.

But, it was not to be.

On the third morning of his disappearance, the entire group assembled once again in the dining hall for breakfast. Conversation was unusually thin as they ate their meal. Neala glanced up as the butler entered the room and thrust a silver salver, containing a single letter, beneath Harry's nose. After thanking the gentleman, Harry broke open the seal, and Neala watched as Harry's eyes absently scanned the page, then he leapt to his feet, his countenance pale.

"It's from Winterton! He's been shot. We leave at once!"

Fourteen

In moments, the gentlemen were gone, leaving the ladies once again to their own devices. Speculation among them ran rife.

Carrying their second cups of chocolate into a small sitting room across from the dining hall, they spoke quietly to one another of their fears.

"It's a certainty that Winterton's injury is serious," Diana said solemnly, brushing away the droplet of moisture that glistened in her eyes.

Neala felt her chin begin to tremble. Her heart had been in her throat since Harry's announcement at table. She had not felt quite so frightened for anyone since the night word reached them of Papa's accident. What would she do if Winterton's injury also proved fatal? "W-Why do you say that, Diana?" she breathed.

"Because Trench has never in his life asked for help."

"It's true," Helene put in. "At least, that is what the newspapers say. Major Lambert always performed his duties with valor, and never once did he summon help, nor apparently," she added with admiration, "did he need it."

Neala knew it was true, She had read and re-read the many accounts of Lord Winterton's brilliant career, to the point that she could quote vast portions of them from memory. "No matter the circumstances, or the risk to himself," said the *Times*, "Major Lambert could always be counted upon to carry out the most treacherous feats with the utmost bravery and precision." "Never a more fearless soldier in battle," reported the *Morning Chronicle,* "Major Lambert is a giant among men."

Neala's eyes squeezed shut and from the deepest part of her soul, she offered up a silent prayer. Please, let him live.

"Trench may be a libertine," Diana went on airily, "but he is also a gentleman and it would be a tragic loss to lose so fine a man in a senseless highway robbery."

"Are we sure it was highwaymen?" Helene asked.

"We are sure of nothing," Melinda said matter-of-factly.

"Well, if it were highwaymen, Winterton must have been unarmed," Helene replied.

"Even if he were not," Neala spoke up, "Lord Winterton would never shoot first."

"That is quite true," Diana said, "he would not."

The others solemnly nodded their agreement.

"I do hope the highwaymen are not still lurking about," Mrs. McGill said in a shrill voice, "I should hate to lose Mr. McGill. Do you suppose they are lying in wait?"

"I shouldn't think so, at least, not while it is daylight," Melinda said. "Besides Harry was not certain it was highwaymen. Winterton merely said in his note that he had been shot."

At that, Neala was aware of a sharp pang ripping through her stomach. Winterton must live! He must!

"At the very least," Melinda went on, a somewhat chagrined look on her face, "we shall now have the gentleman present with us at the *soiree* tomorrow night."

A thin ripple of laughter followed.

"That is, if he is well enough to attend," Diana added.

"Perhaps we should ready an apartment for him on the ground floor," Neala suggested. "If the wound is to a limb, he may be unable to climb the stairs to his own chamber."

"That is quite a good idea, Neala," Melinda said. She rose at once to make the idea reality.

The other ladies lingered a while over their chocolate, but soon afterward, in an effort to stay busy while they waited, Neala and Diana decided to inspect the menu for tomorrow night's supper. Helene and Mrs. McGill offered to help arrange the vast armloads of flowers that the servants had brought in from the gardens and which needed to be put into water at once.

In the Grand Hall on the ground floor, where the *affaire* was to be held, workers were busy rehanging the burgundy silk draperies that had been removed yesterday to be dusted. A small army of housemaids were on their knees polishing the parquet floor to shine. After discussing the supper menu with Cook, Diana enlisted Neala's help in overseeing the decorations, which consisted mainly of wrapping wine-colored ribbons 'round the bannister railings, and telling the servants where to position the huge garlands of flowers in the enormous room.

Soon after luncheon, having heard nothing from the gentlemen, the ladies again anxiously assembled in the drawing room. They had no sooner settled down to visit when the clatter of horses hooves on the drive and the distinctive rumble of a carriage approaching told them the men had returned.

As one, the five women scampered to the hall in time to see a footman fling wide the double doors and Harry burst inside, his face a picture of concern.

"This way, gentlemen!"

Four servants entered the marble-tiled hall carrying a makeshift stretcher upon which lay a sleeping Lord Winterton.

"Oh!" Neala's hands flew to her mouth. She had never seen a wounded person before and lying so very still on the stretcher, Lord Winterton looked as if . . . as if he were . . . she could not finish the sentence. His handsome face was streaked with dirt and his cheeks were unshaven. His coat and trousers were rumpled and soiled, his top boots, splotched with mud. He was wearing clean linen, but the shirt did not look to be one of his own, it was far too coarse and plain. Yet, it was the sight of the gentleman's waistcoat that alarmed Neala the most. The left side of the tattered garment was now deeply stained with blood, and worse, she could plainly see the gaping hole, quite near the gentleman's heart, where the bullet must have entered his body.

For a moment, Neala thought she might faint. She had not

expected to feel so wrenching a pull toward the wounded man. The sensation was staggering. It was as if the two of them were inexplicably linked, as if his pain and suffering were her own. Struggling to regain her composure, she decided the strange phenomena must be due to the powerful force of the wedding spell. In some unseen way, Lord Winterton was already a part of her family, therefore they *were* connected.

"Will he . . . recover?" she gasped, hardly able to drag her eyes from his prone body in order to look at Harry, who was standing quite near her.

"Hard to say." Harry's jaws ground together.

Neala clamped a hand over her mouth to keep from crying out.

Melinda had directed the footmen to carry the stretcher to the chamber on the ground floor that had been readied for Winterton. They did so, and because there appeared nothing further for Neala or the rest of them to do, they reluctantly turned again to re-enter the drawing room. Once there, the ladies began to ply the gentlemen with anxious questions.

"Was it, indeed, highwaymen who shot him?"

"When did it happen?"

"Were the robbers apprehended?"

"Was Lord Winterton traveling alone?"

"Were others in his party injured?"

"Where did you find him?"

"Has his condition worsened?"

And finally, "Will he live?"

Neala was still anxious for a definitive answer to that last question.

"We found him quite near here, actually," Harry said, reaching for the glass of port a servant had poured for him.

"Apparently the incident took place soon after Winterton left us that night," Lord Tentrees said.

"A tenant farmer and his wife found both the gentlemen, that is, Winterton and the fellow travelling with him, lying in the exact same spot on the ground where they fell." This from Mr.

McGill, who, in customary fashion, had taken a seat on the sofa beside Mrs. McGill.

"We'd have reached him sooner," Lord Brewster added, picking up the narrative, "but we went by way of Ross to fetch Doctor Morgan."

"Once we located the farm house, and the doctor examined him," Tentrees said, sounding as if, for once, he was genuinely interested in what was happening, "he couldn't find the bullet."

"Couldn't find it?" Diana asked, her blue eyes wide. "Do you suppose Winterton removed the bullet himself?"

"He may have." Harry shrugged. "Knowing Winterton, I'd say it was damned likely."

Neala could hardly fathom the like. "But, what of the other gentleman?" she asked. "Is he . . . ?"

Lord Edward shook his head. "The farmer said the unfortunate man was found dead where he lay."

"Oh-h-h!" All the ladies breathed, horror in their eyes and their voices.

"No idea who the gentleman was," Harry added. "The tenant who rescued Winterton . . ." he glanced quickly at the ladies, as if to determine if he were broaching a subject far too delicate for their ears, ". . . disposed of the body," he finished softly.

Apparently not the least offput by her brother's coarse talk, Diana asked, "Was the gentleman carrying nothing on his person that would lend a clue to his identity?"

Harry shook his head. "Nothing."

"All rather strange, actually," Lord Tentrees remarked.

"Farmer's wife doesn't speak," said McGill.

"Not a word?" Diana marveled.

"Mute," Brewster said. "Or rather, it seemed that way."

"I have heard of the family," Harry put in. *"Emigrées."*

"Perhaps the woman does not speak English," Neala ventured.

"Perhaps." Harry nodded. "In any event, Winterton is saved."

"Lord Winterton was very lucky," Helene murmured.

"We have been frightfully worried for him, you know," Mrs. McGill said. Mr. McGill reached absently to pat his wife's plump hand. "I am certain he will recover, my dear."

Neala clung fervently to that hope, as well.

Silence reigned for a length as they each mulled over the extraordinary event. Then Neala began, "I feel quite sad for the other gentleman. His family must be every bit as worried about him as we have been about poor Winterton."

"Poor Winterton! What's this?"

At that, all heads whirled 'round and a collective gasp escaped every person seated in the room. Lord Winterton was standing in the doorway, or rather leaning heavily against the doorjamb, looking quite a frazzle in his rumpled clothes, his dark hair ruffled and his face as white as death.

Both Harry and Lord Brewster jumped to their feet.

"My God, man!" Harry shouted. "You are in no condition to be up and about!"

A lopsided grin split Winterton's prickly face. "Merely trying to ascertain where I am, gentlemen. Awoke to find myself in a strange apartment—wondered where the devil you had taken me." He grinned boyishly. "Excuse me, ladies."

As he was speaking, they had all scurried to crowd around him.

Lord Brewster reached him first. "Set to!" he said, reaching at once to drape one of Winterton's long arms about his rounded shoulders and with a tug, attempted to spin the much taller man about. "Give a hand, Harry!"

Harry positioned himself at Winterton's other side, but was meeting with little to no success in lifting, or removing the stubborn Winterton from the spot where he stood.

"Could do with a glass of port, gentleman," Winterton said thickly, his dark eyes suddenly seeming to lose focus.

"McGill! Fetch the decanter," Harry ordered. "And you," he turned to Winterton, "are off to bed!"

* * *

Following dinner that evening, everyone drifted again into the drawing room, where a far more alert Lord Winterton was waiting to greet them.

Neala was vastly relieved to find the handsome gentleman looking much more the thing tonight. He was now dressed in his usual fashion, an impeccably tailored coat of navy blue superfine and skin-tight beige trousers. Lounging on a sofa, a number of pillows had been placed at his back. One supported his left arm, which she noted, he seemed to favor. His shirt lay open at the neck and peeking from beneath it, she could see the top part of the wide white bandage that had been wrapped tightly about his shoulder and chest.

"Well, well," began Lord Brewster, "I daresay, you seem quite improved, Winterton."

The entire group stood clustered around him. Displaying quite a charming smile, Lord Winterton said, "Excuse me for not rising, ladies. Took a bit of doing to get me this far. If I am to pop up and down all evening—"

"Indeed you shall not!" Lady Diana exclaimed. "You must conserve your strength. We have been frightfully worried!"

Suddenly, everyone was talking at once.

"How do you feel, sir?"

"Do you require anything?"

"Tell us about the ordeal!"

"What really happened?"

"Was it highwaymen?"

And on and on. Winterton fended off the questions as best he could, trying to make light of what had, indeed, been a very dangerous situation. Since, he wasn't at liberty to tell the truth, which was that his late night assignation with Lady Renfrow's contact in the country, and the two French spies he was to have rendezvoused with, had gone vastly awry, with the result that the unfortunate gentleman from London had been killed and Winterton had barely escaped with his life. Therefore, he let his friends believe that he had, indeed, been set upon by a gang of thieves, who both robbed and shot he and the other gentleman, then left them both for dead.

Though he tried his best to make light of it, for Winterton, the entire ghastly experience had been a sobering one. To the point that Winterton knew he was now a changed man. No longer did he mean to throw caution to the wind. Never again would he rush headlong into danger, or take foolish risks with his life. Lying on the cold hard ground that night, not knowing if he would live or die, and then again in the bare loft of the farmer's cottage, he had done some hard thinking. During those lucid moments when his mind was not swimming dizzily in and out of consciousness, he had reached a decision.

That he wanted what every man wanted. A wife to love, a family of his own, and a home. And the most sobering fact to Winterton was that he had already met the woman he wanted to spend the rest of his life with. But, judging from the manner in which Miss Abercorn had reacted to his kiss that night in the garden, he fully expected to encounter a bit of difficulty in convincing her that his feelings for her were sincere.

"Is it true, sir—" he warmed now to the sweet sound of Miss Abercorn's voice "—that you removed the bullet yourself?"

Winterton laughed with some degree of abandon. "I am not a surgeon, Miss Abercorn."

"But the bullet was not to be found!" Lord Tentrees maintained, his curiosity regarding the oddity still fully aroused.

"I expect it was the farmer's wife who removed it," Winterton said evenly, his only recollection of that hazy time, was that upon awakening and finding himself lying on a bed of hay in a drafty loft, he knew the slug was gone. His breathing had come easier then, and though the pain was still near to unbearable, he knew that he would live.

One day, as he lay fighting for breath in the cottager's loft, he thought he actually caught a glimpse of Miss Abercorn through the cloudy windowpane at his side. She was riding like the wind, a bonnet with a green plume bouncing down her back. He had tried to call to her, but no words came. When next he drifted awake, he looked again, but the vivid image had vanished. Still, throughout those long dark hours, it was the memory of Miss Abercorn's sweet face and the recollection of her gentle ways that sustained him.

A small pause in the questioning had ensued in which everyone seemed again to be mulling over the catastrophy. At length, Melinda said, "Perhaps we should leave off asking the gentleman questions now. We are likely to overtire him."

"I think one of us should sit with him," Diana said, already moving to drag up a chair. "I shall take a turn."

Lord Edward seemed to take umbrage at that. "Well, then, I shall stay as well."

"Perhaps we should let Winterton decide who shall sit with him," Melinda said.

Winterton spent less than half a second considering. "Miss Abercorn's presence is quite soothing," he replied at once.

He couldn't help noting the sharp look that Lady Diana flashed at the gentle Miss Abercorn as Diana vacated the chair she had just pulled up. Winterton shrugged. He had been asked to make a choice and he had obliged. No longer would he skirt the issue. As far as he was concerned, Miss Abercorn was fair game and Lord Brewster be damned. The man could either do his own courting or risk losing the young lady he had chosen to be his bride.

Apparently satisfied that Winterton would be well looked after, the rest of the party drifted to other parts of the spacious room. Lady Tentrees moved to the pianoforte and began to play, while her husband and Mr. McGill picked up the game of cribbage they had abandoned earlier. Harry and Lord Brewster toddled off to the terrace for a smoke, and Diana and Lord Edward took seats together on a sofa, rather a bit too close to Winterton, he thought, but did not comment upon it. Instead he turned his attention to Miss Abercorn, who was already seated primly before him in the straight-backed chair, her small hands folded neatly in her lap. With her so very near, Winterton already felt better.

Yet, for the moment, he could think of nothing to say. The fact that he was here with her seemed a miracle.

At length, it was she who broke the stillness. "Do you require anything, my lord?"

He wanted to tell her that his only requirement now was to draw her close, to look deeply into her eyes, to . . . Instead, he said, "Your company is quite sufficient, for the moment, Miss Abercorn."

She did not look at him.

"Did you find my note of apology?" he asked quietly.

He saw the rush of color that flooded her cheeks. "Let us not speak of that, sir," she murmured.

"But I wish to speak of it, Miss Abercorn." Of a purpose he kept his voice low, so that they would not be overheard. "I need to know that you have forgiven me."

The warm brown eyes she lifted to his filled him with fresh hope. "An apology was not necessary, my lord. I had already forgiven you."

He smiled. "You are very kind, Miss Abercorn." He searched her face, wishing to ascertain her true feelings for him. "I think you are the kindest person I have ever known."

For the space of a second, their eyes locked, then she said, "And you are the bravest man I have ever known, sir." Then, appearing to grow flustered, she looked down. "I was . . . quite frightened for you. I have never felt quite so frightened," she added, her voice almost a whisper.

"Nor have I, Miss Abercorn."

With surprise, she gazed full at him. "You, sir?"

He nodded.

"But, I had thought you far too courageous to ever feel afraid, my lord."

Winterton paused, then looked past her. "Courage, Miss Abercorn, is not the absence of fear. It is rather the ability in the face of it to carry on, to somehow master the feeling and to go on as if fear did not exist."

"Is . . . that how you managed so very brilliantly on the battlefield?"

"Precisely how. That and the fact that, on the battlefield, it was my duty to go on, to do whatever it took to protect my country, and the lives of those that had been entrusted to me."

Miss Abercorn seemed deep in thought. Presently, she said, "You are very courageous, my lord."

Winterton looked away. "Not so courageous as you may think, Miss Abercorn." His voice had grown raspy. "There is one thing I have not yet had the courage to do."

Her face was a question. "What is that, my lord?"

He lifted a smoldering gaze to hers. "To speak my true feelings to you, Miss Abercorn."

She said nothing for what seemed an interminable length. "Your . . . true feelings, sir?"

Winterton nodded slowly, but suddenly, a sharp pain rent his side and he winced.

He heard the small gasp of alarm that escaped her lips. "Is the pain so very great, my lord?"

A moment ago, he had also seen the veil of mistrust that had dropped to shield her eyes. That she was remembering his impudence in the garden was quite clear. It told him that now was not the time to tell her how he felt. Before pressing his suit upon the young lady, he must first regain her trust. He felt a wave of fresh fear grip him. Could he manage to do that before it was too late?

"Yes, Miss Abercorn," he gasped, "the pain is very great."

Instantly, she was on her feet. "Perhaps Lord Brewster, or Harry, will know what to do. I shall only be a moment."

With that, she was gone.

Winterton sank again into the cushions. He was not a brave man. Despite the fact that he had spent half his life in the army tramping across the roughest terrain known to man; despite the fact that he had managed to stay alive during the most brutal battles thus far in the war, it was laughable to think he could not summon the courage to tell one petite young lady of the deep love in his heart. He damned himself.

Yet . . . he would not give up. With considerable effort, he squared his shoulders. He would not let fear get the better of him this time either. This time the prize was far too great, and the price of failure far too loathsome to contemplate. No matter the cost to his friendship with Brewster, no matter the cost to his own pride if she refused him, it was only fair that Miss Abercorn know of his deep feelings for her, and be allowed to make her own choice between the two men who cared for her.

At that moment, he spotted Brewster advancing toward him. "Miss Abercorn said you might need a dose of laudanum, Winterton. Doctor Morgan left plenty, you've only to say the word."

Winterton drew in a long breath. "Perhaps a bit later."

Brewster parked his large frame in the chair. "You seem to have rallied since dinner. I shall credit that to Miss Abercorn." He smiled proudly.

Winterton swallowed another sharp stab of the pain in his shoulder. "I feel considerably stronger now," he lied.

"Splendid! Though, I daresay, you suddenly look a trifle pale." Brewster leaned forward in the chair. "I shall sit with you a spell, in case the pain worsens and you require assistance."

Winterton thanked him. "You have been a good friend to me, Brewster."

"Think nothing of it, my boy."

Winterton was trying to.

"By the by," Brewster puffed out his chest, "Miss Abercorn was receptive to my suit. Mustn't tell her I said anything. I had meant to make the announcement of our betrothal tomorrow night at the gathering, but she is dead set against it. Said it wouldn't do to steal your thunder. She is quite thoughtful that way."

Miss Abercorn had accepted his suit! Winterton could barely breathe, let alone speak. "Yes . . . Miss Abercorn is quite . . . thoughtful."

Brewster beamed, his short arms folded across his pudgy middle. "She's a good 'un."

"Good 'un?"

"Endearment term her mother uses. Diana, too. Means she kes a care for other people's feelings. Can also mean that she biddable. Quite an agreeable quality in a wife, wouldn't you y, Winterton." Brewster's grin widened, if that were possible. Across from him, Winterton flinched.

"I'm a lucky man, Winterton!"

Winterton nodded heavily. Suddenly, he was more aware than ver of the raging pain that threatened to engulf his heart. "I . . . believe I will have that laudanum, Brewster."

As Brewster rose to summon a servant, Winterton let his head ll back to the cushions. Drawing a ragged breath, he told imself it would take far more than laudanum to deaden the ain that was burning out of control inside him.

Fifteen

In his own chamber, Winterton eagerly gulped the spoonf
of laudanum the servant handed him.

"Leave the bottle, please," he said tightly, shrugging ginger
out of his coat, trying not to disturb his aching shoulder. "I m
require more in the night."

"As you wish, sir."

The servant set the nearly full bottle of medicine on the tab
beside his lordship's bed and after helping him to disrobe, le
the room. Winterton climbed into bed.

And waited. But, sleep did not come.

It could not come, he realized, while his thoughts were
such turmoil.

Damme! Once again, he was faced with a dilemma simil
to the one he had faced those many years ago in Londo
whether to follow his own code of honor or bow to the de
desires of his heart.

Fifteen years ago, he had had to choose between duty ar
his own willfulness when the parents of the young lady he ha
dishonored—by committing so dastardly a deed as spending
few unchaperoned moments in her presence—had demande
that he salvage the girl's reputation by marrying her. He ha
flatly refused, had told himself that by fleeing London he w
doing the honorable thing, he was saving the girl from bein
legshackled to a man who did not love her and he was protectir
his own family from further embarrassment by disappearir
from their lives forever. Neither course had been desirable

'interton, and many a day since, he had wondered if losing
e family he loved had been worth the sacrifice he made.

Damn! He reached for the bottle of laudanum again, un-
rked the cap and swallowed another sip.

Suddenly it struck him that during the past fifteen years while
e served in the military, repeatedly risking his life for his coun-
y, perhaps he had in actuality been daring Providence to punish
m, nay, to *kill* him, for the crime he had committed those
any years ago. But, his sentence had not been death, instead
e had survived many a bloody battle in the war and, three days
;o, death had passed him by again. Only to bring him face to
ce with a problem similar to the one life had handed him
hen he was a mere youth of seventeen. This one compounded
the fact that Miss Abercorn had already accepted Lord Brew-
er's offer of marriage.

Winterton sighed heavily.

Duty told him now that he should keep silent about his feel-
gs for the young lady, that he should step aside . . . defer to
rewster's claim, as it were. But, the wrenching tug in his heart
illed him in the exact opposite direction.

As indecision warred, within him, he absently reached again
r the bottle of laudanum. The sip he swallowed this time more
osely resembled a long draught. Recorking the bottle, he won-
ered if he had the courage now to pit himself once again
gainst the rigid dictates of society? To do so would mean that
e must watch the only woman he had ever loved—for he *did*
ve Miss Abercorn—marry another man, a man she did not
re for, and who, Winterton was certain, did not care for her.

While lying in the loft in the farmer's cottage, not knowing
he should ever see Miss Abercorn again or not, he had decided
at if he did see her again, he would apprise her of his feelings
id thereby give her the opportunity to decide for herself whom
ie wished to marry. But, that was before he knew that she had
ready accepted Brewster's offer. Winterton stewed; and
ached for the bottle again. And tipped it up again. *Damme.*
he most Brewster and Miss Abercorn could expect from their

union was a modicum of companionship for Brewster in h
mature years, and for Miss Abercorn, financial security for he
self and her family.

Which, could very well be the reason Miss Abercorn ha
accepted Brewster's suit in the first place. It was commo
knowledge that her family was sadly dipped, therefore, t
Brewster fortune was nothing to scoff at. But, Winterton cou
easily provide for her, as well. Perhaps not on as grand a sca
as Brewster, but certainly more than was considered adequat

Still holding the bottle, he uncorked the lid once again a
let another stream of the drugging elixir drain down his thro.
The more he thought about it, the greater the tug in his hea
became. The feeling that he *must* approach Miss Abercorn w
now near to compulsion. Never had he felt so certain of anythir
in his life. As ridiculous as it might sound, even to him, it w
as if he were *destined* to spend the rest of his life with the youn
lady. To be silent about his feelings for her was ludicrous. Du
demanded that he tell her. Otherwise, he would be sentencir
the only woman he had ever loved to a grim future filled wi
a lifetime of dismal days and . . . well, he grinned crookedl
equally dismal nights. He couldn't stomach that. He loved Mi
Abercorn far too much to see her unhappy, and that she wou
be unhappy wed to Brewster was a certainty.

Drawing in a deep breath, he began to feel a bit better.

But, a moment later, realizing he was still no closer to slee
than he had been an hour ago, he reached for the brown bott
once again. Holding it up before his eyes, he could see th
there was very little liquid left in it.

When he set the bottle down again, there was even less in

That the betrothal between Miss Abercorn and Lord Brewst
had not yet been formally announced worked in his favor. Nev
that Miss Abercorn had cried off at this stage would not ro
the *ton* to nearly the same degree that it would later, after t
announcement had appeared in the newspapers. News of th
sort, Winterton knew quite well, would vie for *on-dit* of t
season. Not that being involved in a so-called scandal concern

him—nor, he strongly suspected, would it concern Miss Abercorn. Though she was all that was considered proper, beneath that shy, quiet exterior, he believed she was cut from much the same cloth as he.

His thoughts slowed for a moment and at last, he felt a hot spot begin in his belly and spread upward throughout his body. The laudanum was taking effect. The white-hot feel of it reminded him of the hidden spirit and fire he had recently discovered within Miss Abercorn. *Damn.* She intrigued him more than any woman he had ever met. She was also the most enchanting, the most delicate, and had the sweetest disposition he had ever known. He *must* have her for his bride. *He must!*

Devil take it! He *would* have her!

Having reached so agreeable a decision, Winterton relaxed a bit more and let the effects of the drug reach upwards to his brain. To the point that he felt rather dizzy, but compared to the disquieting pain he'd felt a moment ago . . . or was it an hour ago? He wasn't entirely sure, though he was certain that the way he felt now was near to . . . pleasant. In fact, he felt *so* pleasant, he decided now would be a splendid time to speak with Miss Abercorn.

He swung his long legs to the floor and tried to stand. Not a good idea. Slumping back onto the bed, he decided it might be better to sleep a bit, then he'd speak with Miss Abercorn. Yes, then he'd speak with lovely . . . sweet . . . charming Miss Abercorn.

His dark head hit the pillow and his eyelids fluttered shut. *Ah, sleep. Delicious restorative sleep.*

"It is close on tea time," Lady Diana fretted. "If Winterton does not awaken soon, he shall miss the party altogether."

This morning, the Brewster household had awakened to cloudy skies and a high wind. Before luncheon, the restless houseguests had assembled in the drawing room, issuing collective sighs every time they heard thunder rumbling overhead and a fresh pelting of raindrops spatter the window panes and terrace. Confined to the house for the entire day, most everyone now felt at loose ends.

"At this juncture," Lord Brewster announced importantly, moving to stoke the low-burning fire, which due to a definite draft in the room had been lit this morning, "sleep is the best medicine for him. Doctor Morgan said as much, after looking in on him earlier."

"I say," Mr. McGill glanced up from the game of solitaire he was playing, "did the doctor believe Winterton to be now on the mend?"

Brewster nodded. "Seemed to. Mentioned more than once that he had turned the corner. The gentleman was resting easy. Indeed, resting easy."

"So, was Trench awake when the doctor came?" Diana asked, her tone beginning to sound a trifle irritable.

"He was for a time," her father replied. "That is, he seemed aware that the wound was being re-dressed. He smiled rather pleasantly and soon fell again to sleep."

Diana groaned. "He has been asleep all day!"

Seated on one of several comfortable sofas gathered near the hearth, Neala digested the latest news regarding Lord Winterton. So anxious was she to ascertain for herself how the gentleman fared, it was all she could do to sit still. If such behavior would not be construed as the outside of enough, she would spring to her feet and run to the gentleman's bedchamber to look in on him herself. Instead, she asked quietly, "Will the doctor be coming again today?"

At the sound of her voice, Lord Brewster glanced her way. "I think not, Miss Abercorn. Dr. Morgan seemed to feel that rest and being in the company of his friends was sufficient medicine for Winterton now. You are kind to be so solicitous of him, my dear. I daresay, I observed the wound myself and it did not look nearly so inflamed. Not nearly so."

At that, Neala breathed a small sigh of relief, though the feeling of anxiety that had beset her last evening when she sat with Lord Winterton and watched the intense look of pain on his face did not leave her altogether.

"I wonder if perhaps we shouldn't awaken him," Melinda began afresh, casting an anxious glance toward the drawing room door, where only yesterday, Winterton had put in a surprise appearance, propping himself up weakly against the doorjamb. "In spite of the inclement weather, I rather expect some of our overnight guests will be arriving soon. Many are coming only in the hope of seeing Winterton, you know."

"I say?" Lord Tentrees muttered with mild interest, a lifted brow registering his surprise.

"Oh, indeed," Melinda went on. "The townfolk who have been invited are all a-twitter to see him. To say nothing of the extra help we put on for tonight and tomorrow."

"Cook said several of the women we approached, refused to oblige unless they were *guaranteed* a glimpse of him," Lady Diana added.

"Most extraordinary," Tentrees mumbled, rising to his feet and moving to stand in front of the double doors to stare at the rain-splattered terrace.

"I expect to locals who don't often get up to London," Harry said, "seeing Winterton is on a footing with sighting Prinny."

"To some, it is even better," said little Mrs. McGill, who until now, had been listening raptly to the discussion. "For me, meeting him was quite extraordinary."

Neala silently agreed. Meeting Lord Winterton was certainly the most exciting thing that had ever happened to her. Even to speak with the corpulent Prince paled by comparison.

" 'T'would be quite frightful," Mrs. McGill added, "if the gentleman slept completely through our lovely party!"

"I do hope the rain lets up soon," Helene murmured, glancing up from the book she was reading.

"As do I," her husband said.

"Well, I shouldn't think a bit of rain will deter too many from coming," Neala put in, hoping to lift everyone's spirits a bit.

"I wasn't thinking of the party guests," Lord Tentrees said

irritably as he skirted past Neala's chair. She paid the elderly gentleman no heed. Lord Tentrees was generally a down-pin and today he seemed especially out of curl. During the past two weeks that they had all been closeted here together, Neala had more than once marveled over the fact that Helene could abide her unpleasant husband and still remain as cheerful as she was. She knew that once she and Lord Brewster were wed, the two couples would very likely spend a good deal of time together. Neala was not looking forward to that.

Still she turned a sympathetic gaze on Helene. Her brown head was bent over the second volume of *The Mysteries of Ferney Castle*. Apparently feeling Neala's eyes on her, Helene looked up and smiled, whereupon Neala asked if she had yet reached an especially intriguing part in the book.

"No." Helene shook her head. "I have not yet read that far—" she flipped over several pages "—though I rather expect I shall come upon it before too very long. The mystery is quite exciting," she added, her hazel eyes wide.

"I had a jolly time unraveling it," Neala agreed, smiling.

Overhearing the girls' conversation, Lady Diana turned toward them. "Perhaps I might borrow the book when you are done with it, Helene. I like sorting out a mystery as much as the next person, though I am not nearly so proficient at it as Neala."

Neala warmed to the compliment. She knew it had angered Diana last evening when Lord Winterton singled her out to sit with him, but, since learning that Neala had accepted her father's offer of marriage, Diana's nature had, for the most part, returned to its former sweetness. "I shall leave both books with you when I return to London, Diana," Neala said.

"That will not be necessary, Nealie dear. Before too very long," Diana lowered her voice, "all your books will be readily available to me in Father's library."

Neala blushed. "Oh, of course. I quite forgot."

Diana reached to squeeze Neala's hand. "You have made me so very happy, Nealie, dear. Unlike, Winterton," she added beneath her breath.

* * *

Preparing for the *soiree* that evening in her bedchamber, Neala tried to push aside her lingering fears for Lord Winterton's well being. He had not joined them for tea, nor for the early supper they had just partaken of. She so hoped his pain had let up and that his absence did not mean that he had taken a turn for the worse.

She had thought about him so frequently the past several days. As well as worrying about his safety and wondering where he had got off to, vivid memories of his kiss in the garden had beset her at the oddest moments. The most intrusive being, the exact second she had agreed to wed Lord Brewster! She knew her cheeks must have flamed a scarlet red then, but, she suspected that if Lord Brewster noticed, he had put it down to simple shyness on her part.

Though, that same night Lord Brewster had spoken rather eloquently of his feelings for her, Neala couldn't help noticing a certain lack of—she felt her cheeks begin to burn again with fire now—perhaps the word she sought was passion, in the gentleman's pronouncements of love for her. Judging from his kiss, she suspected Lord Winterton was brim full of . . . passion.

She blushed at the shameful thought.

Reaching for her hairbrush, she began to furiously brush a shine to her curls, at the same time wishing she could as easily brush thoughts of Lord Winterton and his searing kiss from her mind. She had had as equally a difficult time today ignoring the peculiar comment the gentleman had made to her last evening, about not having the courage to tell her of his true feelings for her. What had he meant by that? And, would he broach the subject again with her tonight?

Less than an hour later, Neala, wearing a pale pink satin gown, and Lady Diana, in ice blue silk, entered the gaily decorated ballroom of Brewster Hall. Threading their way among

the guests, Neala was struck not only by the glittering chande-
liers and elegant furnishings, but by the fact that the grand hall
itself was larger than the entire apartment she shared with her
family in London.

Enjoying the pleasant scents that assailed her—the ladies'
sweet perfumes, the pomades and musky colognes the gentlemen wore, the fragrance of fresh flowers and the enticing smells
of deliciously prepared foods—Neala knew that not only would
her Mama be pleased to learn that she had agreed to wed Lord
Brewster, she would also be a-tremor to know that once again
the means to entertain the *ton* in so lavish a fashion would be
at her fingertips.

Neala fervently wished her decision to wed Diana's father
could make her feel half so happy. But, the truth was, it simply
did not. Strolling beside Diana, she willed a bright smile to her
face as Diana greeted this guest and that one, on occasion in-
troducing Neala if she was not already acquainted with the lady
or gentleman. Presently, Lord Edward joined them and the three
positioned themselves on the fringe of the dancefloor to watch
the couples gathering in the center of the room for a quadrille.

Standing beside Neala, Diana exhaled a loud sigh. "I do so
wish Father would waken Winterton," she said.

"I shouldn't be surprised if he were already awake," Neala
replied. When the orchestra plunged into the music, she leaned
closer to speak directly into Diana's ear. "One wonders how he
could not be, considering the noise. His apartment is only just
down the corridor." A long gaze flitted that direction.

"Well, perhaps, he is," Diana muttered.

Just then, Mr. McGill approached them. "Have any of you
seen Mrs. McGill?" His brows were drawn together with concern.

Lord Edward's mouth formed a straight line. "Dear God, no!
And if I do see her, I declare I shall run the opposite direction!
I am wearing a new suit of clothes tonight and I do not want
either my coat or trousers soiled."

Neala smothered a smile. "I am sorry, Mr. McGill, none of us has seen your wife this evening."

"I have seen her," Diana said absently. "In fact, there she is now, speaking with Lady Hamilton and . . . old Mrs. Burton from the village, and . . . now, she is approaching Mrs. Banniton." A bit of interest had crept into Diana's tone. "Unlike the rest of us, Mrs. McGill seems in quite a frame tonight."

"Ah, yes," Mr. McGill muttered, glancing that direction, "so she is, well then, I shan't bother. I am off to play a round of cards. Would you care to join me, Edward?"

Lord Edward glanced at Diana, then with a small shrug, declined the offer. "I rather expect Diana would prefer I stay with her. She very much likes to dance, you know."

Diana managed somewhat of a smile. "You are quite correct, Edward, dear. The musicians are to play a waltz next and I should very much enjoy that." She turned to Neala. "You and Father have not yet danced this evening, Neala."

"Your father is in the game room," Neala said.

Registering a look of mild reproach, Diana lowered her voice. "I do hope that when you and Father are married, Nealie dear, you will refer to him as 'my husband,' or by his Christian name, which is Nigel."

Neala turned a look of horror on her friend. She could *never* refer to Lord Brewster as Nigel! It would be like calling Papa, Richard. She had opened her mouth to say as much when Edward whisked Diana to the dancefloor for the forthcoming waltz. Through the clearing left by the pair, she also caught a glimpse of Mrs. McGill. At the moment, the little woman was leaving the ballroom with several ladies close on her heels. That struck Neala as a bit odd. She had never known Mrs. McGill to be so gregarious. Just then, she spotted Emma Chetwith across the room, and putting thoughts of Mrs. McGill aside, hastened toward Emma.

Before reaching Emma, however, Harry approached Neala and asked her to stand up with him. She enjoyed both the dance and the exchanging of pleasantries with Harry throughout it.

As he escorted her again to the sidelines, he said, "Father mentioned to me that you had accepted his offer of marriage, Miss Abercorn. May I say that I am very pleased, indeed."

Feeling color rise to her cheeks, Neala lowered her lashes. "Thank you, sir."

"Well, here we are."

Now that the dance was done, Harry seemed to experience some difficulty in thinking of anything further to say to Neala. She supposed in that respect he was very like his father. In spite of the fact that she and Lord Brewster were soon to become man and wife, they still rarely spoke to one another.

At length, Lord Edward and Diana joined them and Harry made haste to excuse himself.

"Has Winterton come down yet?" Diana asked Neala.

Neala shook her head. "I haven't seen him." But, at that moment, she did see Mrs. McGill, again—this time returning to the room with four different ladies close on her heels. All four of the women wore wide smiles and seemed to be chattering quite animatedly among themselves. Neala watched the first four ladies approach yet another cluster of women, who seemed quite eager to hear what the first group had to say. Enthralled, Neala watched the drama unfold. She had never seen such gesturing, patting of flushed cheeks, and rolling of eyes. Why, the women seemed near to swooning!

A moment later, she watched Mrs. McGill break away from the group, this time leading another quartet of ladies toward the corridor. Near the long tables set up with food, a pair of servant girls stepped forward and after exchanging a few words with Mrs. McGill, they joined the party!

Neala could not refrain from commenting on this pecularity to Diana, who had just returned to the sidelines with Edward. "Have you noticed our Mrs. McGill behaving rather oddly this evening?"

Diana shrugged. "No more so than usual."

"If you ask me," Lord Edward put in, "Mrs. McGill always behaves a bit oddly."

"But, just look there, Diana. She is taking a group of ladies into the corridor, and there are two servants following them."

"Must have spilled something," Edward muttered dryly. "Glad I wasn't underfoot. Would you care for some punch, Diana?"

Diana sighed. "I suppose so. It would be something to do."

When Diana and Edward had once again departed, Neala decided to edge closer to the corridor. She would solve the McGill mystery yet! Sure enough, in less than a quarter hour, she saw Mrs. McGill return again to the ballroom and once more, every last women with her wore rapturous expressions and were again chattering excitedly amongst themselves. Neala's brows drew together as she watched Mrs. McGill busily approach another circle of women, only this time, Emma Chetwith was among them. In moments, all of the women, except Emma, scurried off behind Mrs. McGill.

Neala scurried toward Emma.

"Emma—" Neala's eyes were wide "—I simply must know what Mrs. McGill asked of you a moment ago."

Emma shrugged. "She asked if I had met him."

"Met who?"

"Why, Lord Winterton, of course."

"Lord Winterton?" Neala flung a bewildered gaze toward the corridor. "Is he awake then, and receiving in the drawing room, perhaps?"

"Mrs. McGill did not say where he was."

"Perhaps we should follow them," Neala said suddenly.

"Follow who?"

"Mrs. McGill."

Emma turned a stunned look on Neala. "Whyever for, Neala? You have met Winterton. As I recall," she grinned slyly, "he singled you out quite openly at the picnic. Has he recovered from his accident?"

Lost in thought, Neala did not answer the question. "Something is amiss, Emma."

"What are you talking about, Neala? You are acting quite peculiar."

"Not nearly so peculiar as Mrs. McGill. Come, we are going to follow her."

Emma rolled her eyes. "Have you gone daft?"

Neala picked up the long folds of her skirt. "Are you coming?"

Emma shrugged and apparently decided there was nothing for it but to do as Neala wished. The two set off.

Entering the hallway outside the ballroom, they hurried up the lengthy corridor that led to the drawing room at the front of the house.

"Do you know where she went?" Emma asked.

Neala shook her head.

"Then, how will we—"

"We shall listen."

"For what?"

"I'm not sure," Neala replied.

Emma rolled her eyes again, yet when the two of them rounded the next corner, it was she who said, "There, I see Mrs. Wentworth, from the village. She seems in a great hurry, perhaps she will lead us to Mrs. McGill."

A few feet further and Neala and Emma spotted the rather large group of women knotted together outside a closed doorway.

Neala couldn't believe it. "Why, they appear to be headed for Lord Winterton's bedchamber," she marveled. Then, her eyes widened as she and Emma watched the five or six women tiptoe single-file into the room. Neala gasped. "They are *entering* Lord Winterton's bedchamber!"

"How can you be certain it is his, there are so many rooms . . ." Emma paused, seeming to grow a bit confused in the huge house.

"I am sure because we readied this chamber for him two days ago! Oh, Emma, what shall we do?"

Emma turned palms upward. "Wait a bit, I expect, and if they do not come out soon . . . go in after them."

Neala put a hand to her mouth. "Oh, but, we couldn't!"

"I am a vicar's wife, Neala. I visit the ill quite often. Perhaps Lord Winterton has taken a turn for the worse." Her brows drew together as she pondered the situation. "Still, I can't think why it would take five women to . . . yet, on the other hand, if Lord Winterton is well enough to receive them, he is well enough to receive us."

Panic swept through Neala, but she had no time to refine upon it, for in mere moments, the ladies who had tiptoed into the gentleman's bedchamber streamed back out again. It was Emma who headed straight for Mrs. McGill.

"Oh, there you are, my dear! You have decided you would like to see him, after all?"

"Mrs. McGill, what are you—?" Emma began.

"Sh-h-h, mustn't make a ruckus. This way!"

Close on Emma's heels, Neala was too stunned to speak. Without taking a moment to consider what she was doing, she followed Mrs. McGill and Emma straight into the gentleman's bedchamber!

Sixteen

Lord Winterton's makeshift bedchamber was not the least grand, the furnishings were sparse, the floor uncarpeted. Inside the small room, the air was heavy with masculine scents—leather, musk, the faint odor of medicine. A single candle flickered on the mantelpiece, and in the dim light, Neala could plainly see the tall gentleman lying on his back on the rumpled bed, one bare arm flung above the pillow over his dark head. A light coverlet rested just above the gentleman's waistline and Neala resisted the urge to pull it up and over his bare chest, sublimely naked except for the wide muslin bandage wrapped tightly about it, going up and over the wounded left shoulder.

She forced her eyes upward to his face, where the gentleman's handsome features were relaxed in deep slumber, his dark lashes fanned out over his cheeks, the planes and angles of which were darkly stubbled with new growth. His deep, even breathing was a decided contrast to Neala's fitful gasps.

"Mrs. McGill . . ." she began, keeping her voice as low as she could, considering her agitation, "have you been bringing ladies in here all evening to . . . to *see* him?"

Mrs. McGill nodded vigorously. "Indeed, and I daresay, they have all quite enjoyed it. We've no disappointed guests now!" she concluded proudly.

"But, Mrs. McGill," Neala whispered, "did you not consider the impropriety of it?"

"We have been ever so quiet," she replied, her voice beginning to quake a bit, telling Neala the little woman was beginning to feel as frightened as she. "No one was aware we have been coming—" she sniffed, now close on to tears "—least of all the gentleman. As you can see, he has not stirred. Have I done something wrong? Must you tell my husband?"

Emma slipped an arm around the little woman's plump shoulders. "There, there, Mrs. McGill. No harm done." She turned a smile on the pink-cheeked lady. "At least, we know he isn't dead."

"Oh, Emma!" Neala cried, a bit louder than she intended.

From the bed, Lord Winterton gave a little snort, much as if he were clearing his throat. In horror, the three ladies watched as the gentleman licked his lips, swallowed, then fell silent again.

Mrs. McGill turned an accusing look on Neala. "I daresay, not a one of us disturbed him so."

"All the more reason we should leave at once!" Neala whispered back.

"But, there are others who wish to see him," Mrs. McGill protested.

Neala turned a horrified look on her. "I cannot allow it!"

"But, I have promised! There are only six or seven more and then I shall be done!"

"Emma—*stop her!*" Neala whispered. "She mustn't bring a single other lady into this room. It isn't seemly!"

Emma considered. "Well, I don't know, Neala. Sounds as if there's already been quite a parade through here. What's a paltry six or seven more? Would be a shame to disappoint them."

"Emma!"

Emma shrugged. "I admit I was quite anxious to meet him." She glanced again at the bed. "He looks so very peaceful. Perhaps there is no harm in it."

Neala glanced back at the gentleman lying sound asleep on the bed. He did look peaceful and . . . she gulped . . . quite alluring in his natural state. An unsettling stir began in the pit of her stomach. A small gloved hand fluttered to her breast as if to still it. It was quite easy to see why the ladies who had beheld him thusly had been swept into throes of blissful rapture

"It does not appear he shall be coming to the party," Emma added matter-of-factly. "We may as well let the rest of the ladies . . . see him."

Neala considered. "Well, I . . . I . . . suppose it would be all right. But, do *hurry!*"

Neala elected to wait while both Emma and Mrs. McGill hastened from the room. Biting her lower lip to keep from making a sound, she continued to stare at the sleeping gentleman. Her heart was pounding so loudly in her ears, she feared the sound of it alone would awaken him.

The interminable wait for Mrs. McGill seemed to drag on forever. At long last, Neala heard the muffled cacophony of sounds that signaled their approach—the excited trill of giggles, feathery whispers, and the shuffle of hurried footfalls in the corridor. So frightened she could barely breathe, Neala put a finger to her lips as the round-eyed women filed, one by one, into the darkened chamber.

Making space for them to stand around the bed, Neala moved silently to the foot, not taking her eyes for an instant off the still figure lying prone upon it.

"Just look at him!" whispered the lady standing next to her.

"He is far more handsome than I imagined," said her friend.

"Infinitely so!"

"Why, I have never seen a more handsome man!"

"Nor, I!" agreed another, a bit too forcefully.

"Sh-h-h!" this from Neala. They would awaken him for sure!

Just then, Mrs. McGill, who was hovering near the head of the bed, near the night stand, whirled round to lead the ladies from the room, but in the doing, a plump arm sallied to the table beside her and tipped over an empty brown bottle that stood upon it. The bottle clattered to the bare floor and shattered to a million pieces.

"Oh!" a collective gasp escaped the ladies.

On the bed, Lord Winterton's eyelids sprang open. Then with a start, his large body lunged forward.

"What the—?"

In a colorful blur of silks and satins and ribbons, the frightened ladies all scampered from the room. At the end of the line, Neala attempted to fall in with them, but the gentleman sitting upright on the bed was far too quick for her. One arm reached out and strong fingers encircled her slim wrist, preventing her escape.

"Oh!" Neala cried. "Please, sir, let me go!" Giving a fresh tug, she was startled to discover she had actually wrested free of the gentleman's somewhat less than fierce hold on her arm!

In an instant, she was safely out the door and flying down the corridor.

"May I say, Miss Abercorn," Lord Winterton leaned close to the young lady's ear so as not to be overheard, "I have never been awakened in so extraordinary a fashion."

Lord Winterton's lips twitched as he watched Miss Abercorn's long lashes drop and her smooth cheeks turn a deep scarlet. The pair of them, with Lady Diana to Lord Winterton's other side, were standing before the ornate mantelpiece at one end of the spacious ballroom, where, during the last full hour, nearly every last man and woman in the room—a few of the women faintly recognizable to Winterton—had been duly presented to him.

After being awakened from his inordinately long nap, it had taken Winterton less than a quarter hour to wash, shave, don formal attire and make a belated appearance in the Grand Hall. So hasty had been his toilette, in fact, he feared the complicated twist he had attempted with his neckcloth, something he had watched Rigas perform again and again with relative ease, and when done, declare it a bang-up Mathematical, may have ended up a few numbers short. However, Winterton mused, thus far, no one had commented upon the peculiar knot of his cravat, so perhaps all the sums were there and accounted for. He fairly itched now to be done with the formalities of being the Brewster guest of honor so that he might confront the charming Miss Abercorn about the unusual episode in his bedchamber.

She looked a picture tonight in a pale pink satin gown with a matching plume in her hair. The soft cloud of it smelled sweetly of lilacs, a scent which Winterton found especially pleasant. Every time she turned her head, he felt dizzy from the sensation. Desiring one more delicious breath of it, he leaned close to her ear again. "I daresay there is an acceptable explanation, is there not?"

Not really expecting an answer from the mortified Miss Abercorn, he watched with amusement as the young lady's lips tightened and her small bosom rose and fell with each agitated breath she drew. He knew his persistence in the matter was making her extremely uncomfortable, but, he couldn't help it, the event was simply too delicious to let pass.

"What are you two whispering about?" Lady Diana demanded, leaning around to glare at the both of them. When nothing by way of an answer was forthcoming, from either, she directed a gaze up at Winterton. "I should like a moment to speak with you, Trench," she said sweetly, "alone, if you don't mind."

His fleeting gaze darted from one lady to the other, then settled with resignation on Diana. "As you wish, my dear. We appear to be almost done here."

"Indeed, I believe all the guests have met you now."

"Some more than once," Winterton murmured, then grinned when he felt, rather than saw, Miss Abercorn's discomfort.

Diana moved to stand in front of them. "Do you mind terribly if we desert you now, Neala?"

"We shan't be overlong, Miss Abercorn," Winterton said then in a tone that sounded quite severe, added, "There is something of some import that I must discuss with you this evening."

All jocosity aside, it was indeed true that he must speak with Miss Abercorn tonight. And, since he had slept the entire day

and half the night away, he had precious little time left in which
to do so. He had one final engagement to keep tonight, the
culmination of which should signal the end of the elusive
French spy's activities, or perhaps even the end of the French
spy.

Thinking on the above matter, Winterton barely noticed
where Lady Diana was headed until they both stepped onto
terrace. The area was well-lit. A nearly full moon hung high in
the night sky, and every few feet or so, shafts of brilliant light
from the ballroom windows fell in pools to the cool stone floor.
Along the ancient balustrade, concrete urns sat at intervals, each
filled to the brim with lacy greenery and cut dog roses, their
sweet fragrance almost sticky on the humid night air. Walking
the length of the terrace, he and Lady Diana passed a number
of other guests who, anxious for a breath of fresh air, had pulled
their chairs and even a few small settees, from the stuffy con-
fines of the ballroom to the rain-freshened air out-of-doors.

Other couples were simply strolling up and down, a few of
them venturing down the steps and on into the garden. Winterton vividly recalled the last time he had ventured into the garden. A crooked grin split his features. Abruptly, he realized that
the garden was precisely the destination Lady Diana had in
mind.

Near the steep marble steps, Winterton hesitated. "Not at all
certain I could manage the return climb, my dear," he said, by
way of sabotaging her plan. It was imperative he cut this inter-
view short, he had far more pressing matters to attend to tonight.

"Oh, of course, you cannot. How thoughtless of me. Well—"
she seemed a bit flustered, then she brightened, "Oh, I know
the perfect spot where we may speak undisturbed! This way!"

She turned and headed for a rather darkened section of the
terrace, beyond both the grand hall and the shadowy area outside the drawing room. "Father often comes here to smoke,"
she said, leading Winterton straight for a small settee tucked in
a far corner. She sat down, patting the place beside her, her
bright blue eyes gazing up at Winterton expectantly.

"I cannot wait a second longer to tell you what is in my heart, Trench."

"Hmmm." He sat down, being careful not to sit too close to her, yet mildly curious as to what she had to say.

She wasted no time getting to it. "I have decided to cry off my engagement to Edward. It isn't that I do not love him, I do, it's just that—" she turned to gaze up at Winterton "—I love you more."

Stunned, Winterton opened his mouth to protest, but she held up a silencing hand.

"Please, Trench, hear me out. You know I have loved you since I was a little girl. However, I did not realize how very much until these past few days. I have been quite distraught with worry over you, first when we had no notion what had happened to you, then again after Harry brought you home. Oh—" she turned to him again, tears beginning to brim in her eyes "—I love you *so* much, Trench! And, I . . . I want to be your wife."

There was an awkward pause, during which Winterton groped for something to say.

Diana did not wait for a reply. "You *must* love me, too, Trench. Else, why have you never married?"

Having still not thought of the proper way to say "no" without unduly damaging the girl's feelings, Winterton remained silent.

"You *do* love me, don't you, Trench?"

A direct question was another matter. Winterton inhaled deeply. He was accustomed to women throwing themselves at his head, though, most did not suggest so permanent an arrangement as marriage. Something a bit less binding was more generally the norm.

"Can you not say *something,* Trench?"

"Well, I . . . I admit, I do care for you, Diana, but—"

"Oh, I *knew* it! *Oh, Trench, I—*" she moved as if to throw her arms about his neck.

A gloved hand forestalled her. "Diana, please. What I mean to say, is that I care for you like a baby sister."

Diana giggled. "Oh, Trench, I can be so much more than a baby sister to you. Why, after we are married . . . you shall not be disappointed, I promise."

"No, Diana." Winterton shook his head. "I cannot marry you."

"Oh, but, Trench—" she grasped for his arm again.

Abruptly, he stood, the suddenness of the movement catching her quite off-guard and making it quite easy for Winterton to extricate himself from her grasp. "Come, Diana. I shall escort you back to the ballroom." He had to take her inside at once. Time was running out and he must speak with Miss Abercorn before he left Brewster Hall that night.

"But, I don't want to go inside," Diana pouted. She gazed up at him, the large tears in her eyes now trickling down her cheeks. "I want you to say that you will marry me."

"I cannot marry you, Diana."

"But, why not? Is there—have you agreed to wed Lady Renfrow? She is quite *old*, Trench. Why, she must be at least six-and-twenty."

"I have agreed to wed no one, my dear. Now, be a good girl and come along. Edward will be quite atwitter wondering where you and I have got off to. To say nothing of what he would say if he knew that you had just proposed to me."

"I no longer wish to marry Edward."

Winterton put out a hand. "You do not wish to marry me either."

"But, indeed, I do, Trench!"

"We shall say no more about this, Diana." He opened his hand to her. "Come, now."

Sniffing, she settled small gloved fingers around his palm and reluctantly stood. "Oh, very well. If you refuse to marry me, then I suppose I shall have no choice but to marry Edward. At least, he is biddable."

"Ah, yes." Winterton nodded. "Biddable. I collect your father found that same quality admirable in Miss Abercorn."

"Well, at least Father is getting to wed whom he pleases."

A dark brow lifted. Not if Winterton had anything to say about it.

The two barely spoke to one another on the return trip to the ballroom. Near the arched doorway, Winterton paused.

"I would be exceedingly grateful if you would tell Miss Abercorn that I wish to speak with her." He glanced about, spotted an empty stone bench, quite conspicuous, bathed as it was in a pool of bright light—very possibly the reason it was unoccupied. "I shall wait for her . . . there." A nod indicated the stone settee.

"Oh!" Diana stamped her foot. "You are always asking for Neala! You wish to speak with Neala. You wish Neala to sit with you! One would think you are in love with Neala!" Flinging a final look of outrage at him, she turned to do his bidding.

Winterton took a seat on the cold marble bench. Presently, he spotted Miss Abercorn making her way to the terrace. Fixing a warm gaze on her, he stood, his eyes taking in every delicious inch of her delicate form. Amazing how the very sight of her was like a tonic to him, she was as pure and fresh as sunshine on a rainy day.

"You asked to see me, sir," she murmured, lifting rather frightened brown eyes to meet his.

Winterton reached to take her arm and began to guide her away from the ballroom door. That she did not protest pleased him, although he suspected the cause for her biddableness now was due more to guilt than to the fact that she wished to be with him. He had very little time left in which to spend with her, so in an effort to put her at ease, he said, "You needn't worry, Miss Abercorn, I do not mean to chastise you for lurking about my bedchamber earlier this evening."

She shot him a look. "I was not *lurking,* sir."

His lips twitched. "It certainly seemed that way. However, if you had stayed a bit longer . . ."

"Sir!"

He laughed aloud. "You may leave off with the explanation, Miss Abercorn. We haven't the time for that now."

He hastened toward the exact same spot where Lady Diana had just taken him and mentally thanked her for showing it to him. Once there, however, thinking that it might alarm the young lady, he did not guide Miss Abercorn to the obscure settee, instead he stopped near a set of stone steps that led to another part of the grounds.

"I haven't much time left this evening, Miss Abercorn, and there are a number of topics I mean to address with you."

Neala thought Lord Winterton's tone sounded unusually ominous, but considering her fear of reprisal over the bedchamber incident, she was grateful for small favors. "I am listening," she said.

In the semi-darkness, she saw his answering smile and a ripple of pleasure surged through her. "That is another thing I quite like about you, Miss Abercorn. You are attentive, and most intelligent, I might add. Too many women are quite flighty, to the point of being bird-witted. At any rate—" he reached into a breast pocket, withdrew a folded piece of paper and handed it to her. "I wanted to give you this. Keep it for me, and if I do not return tonight, take it to Lord Sidmouth at the admiralty office in London."

Growing alarmed, Neala glanced down at the paper in her hand.

"You've no need to know what it says, Miss Abercorn. You wouldn't understand it anyhow. Suffice to say, that it has to do with the . . . war effort. Once this is in the proper hands, both the meaning and the action to be taken, will become quite clear."

"But, sir, why do you say, *if* you do not return tonight? You cannot mean that you are—"

"Indeed, I do mean that, Miss Abercorn. I must be off presently, and while it is not likely this time, the possibility always exists that I shall . . . not return."

Neala sucked in her breath. "But, sir—"

"Do not fear for my safety, Miss Abercorn. If I do not return this evening, it may not signal the worst. It may mean that I have gone up to London."

Neala leveled a look at him. "I insist that you tell me at once what this is about. I cannot harbor another day, or week, of not knowing what . . ." she hesitated, fearful of saying too much.

He smiled down at her. "I quite understand, my dear. I should feel the exact same way about you." He drew a breath. "Very well. I haven't the time to go into great detail, but, suffice to say, that I was not beset upon by highwaymen the other evening. The man who shot me and killed the gentleman with me was a . . . Frenchman. I was to have met him, gained his confidence and reported my findings to the authorities. The trouble was, the Frenchie recognized me and pulled his pistol without allowing either of us to speak. There were times in the Peninsula, Miss Abercorn, when I worked closely with Colquoun Grant. Perhaps you have heard of him?"

Neala's eyes were large. "Indeed, sir. I have read a great deal about him. He is a very famous spy-catcher."

"That is correct, Miss Abercorn. He is the best."

"He cannot be better than you."

Winterton smiled.

"What of the other fellow? The one who was killed?"

"He was a traitor to England. A new recruit of Lady Renfrow's. On his first assignment. Unfortunately for him, he was judged guilty by association with me, and executed."

"What has Lady Renfrow to do with this?"

"Ah, yes. I have not yet explained her part in this ugly business, have I?"

Neala shook her head, and listened with interest as Lord Winterton explained how his suspicions about Lady Renfrow grew from the chance sighting of the war office clerk and the Bow Street Foot Patrolman whilest he and Miss Abercorn were on their way to the Green Park.

"I did not wish to involve you in this dangerous business, but I feel I must take you into my confidence now."

"I am glad you told me, sir." And she was, though she fervently wished she could prevent the gentleman from going anywhere tonight. "I cannot help but fear for your safety, sir."

"The authorities will be with me. On the day I sent the note to Harry, alerting him to my whereabouts, I sent one also to the magistrate, telling him of the meeting that was scheduled to take place this evening, at midnight."

"But, it is close on midnight, now, my lord."

"Indeed. The meeting will be held not far from here at an odd little inn situated at the juncture of three roads."

"I am acquainted with the inn! I paused there one day."

Winterton's brows drew together. "What could have taken you so far afield, Miss Abercorn?"

"I had been riding."

"Ah, riding . . ." he murmured. "Well, in any case, my presence this evening is required simply to point out the culprit's identity. I will take no part in the capture."

Neala digested that. "I do wish Harry, or someone else, could go in your place."

"Only I have seen the man. There is very little danger, my dear."

Neala looked down at the note in her hand. "If there is very little danger, why have you entrusted this to my care?"

Perhaps at her show of astuteness, he grinned. "That information is too valuable to fall into the wrong hands, Miss Abercorn. And, I trust you implicitly.

Neala gazed up at him. "I trust you, as well, my lord."

His voice grew raspy. "Do you, Miss Abercorn?"

Neala nodded.

He swallowed. "I've something further to say to you tonight, Miss Abercorn."

Her breath in her throat, Neala waited.

"I love you, and I want you to be my wife."

Neala stared at him as if, of a sudden, he had sprouted two heads! "You . . . cannot mean that, sir!" He *couldn't* mean it and even if he thought he did, he did not!

"But, I do mean it," he breathed, taking a step closer to her, his dark eyes intent on her mouth.

Neala took a small step backward. "But, Lord Winterton, you cannot care for me!"

"Why ever not?" he sputtered. "I do!"

"But, I have already accepted Lord Brewster's suit! And then, there is the sp—" she bit her lip to keep from telling him all about the wedding spell "—you simply must . . ."

"Must what, Miss Abercorn? Must step aside? No, I cannot. I love you far too much to allow you to marry a man you do not love."

"But, sir, I—"

"You do not love him," he said firmly. "Your betrothal has yet to be announced. It would be perfectly acceptable for you to cry off at this point."

Neala bristled. "I cannot. I will not!"

"Not even if you love another man?"

"I . . . do not love another man." Her voice cracked a little.

"But you do not love him."

Neala thrust her chin up. "You are being impertinent, my lord."

Winterton's eyes narrowed. "I am being truthful, Miss Abercorn and I believe that you do care for me. For you to wed Lord Brewster, feeling as you do about me, would be nothing short of deceptive."

"I am deceiving no one!"

"You are, if you are leading Brewster to believe that you care for him."

"I will not discuss this further."

"Very well." Winterton squared one shoulder, the uninjured one. "Then I shall discuss it without you. I care very deeply for you, Miss Abercorn. And I refuse to let you enter into a marriage that will doom you to everlasting torment."

"Are you saying that Lord Brewster will torment me?"

"I am saying that being legshackled to a man you do not love will torment you."

Neala's nostrils flared. "Plenty of women marry gentlemen they do not . . . love greatly." For an instant, she was vividly reminded of her Mama and Papa's tumultuous union, but she thrust that unpleasant thought from her mind.

"That is quite true, Miss Abercorn, and from the outset, those loveless marriages can expect little more than to hobble along after a fashion. Is that what you want for yourself, Miss Abercorn?"

Neala was beside herself over the turn of the conversation. He could not mean what he was saying! He could not! Finally, she mouthed, "It is the most I can hope for."

Winterton fixed an intent gaze upon her. "That is not true, Miss Abercorn. You have agreed to wed Lord Brewster for reasons you do not wish to divulge to me. Is that not correct?"

Neala lowered her lashes. It was true. It was also true that Winterton would know her reasons for marrying Lord Brewster soon enough. Once he and Lilibet were wed, he could not help but be apprised of the family's woeful financial state. She fought the urge to tell him the whole truth now. In spite of the fact that she should not, that she ought not, speak so very plainly to him, Lord Winterton had a way of . . . of drawing her out, and yes, of putting her at ease, of making it easy for her to talk to him on . . . on almost any subject imaginable. No one had ever had such an effect on her. Not even Papa. And, of course, she cared for the gentleman, she cared for him *greatly,* but only as a . . . a brother-in-law. "I am marrying Lord Brewster because . . . because it is the only way," she finally said.

"The only way? The only way for what, Miss Abercorn?"

"To . . . save my family," she barely whispered.

"Ah, yes. The lottery."

Neala gazed up at him.

"With Lord Brewster, you have won the lottery."

Neala bristled. "It is not so callous as all that."

"I am merely being truthful again, Miss Abercorn."

"You are being impertinent again!"

Winterton shook his head. "No, the other evening in the garden, I was being impertinent. And later, if you recall, I very gallantly offered to marry you. Now, I am saying that I—" his voice had grown raspy again "—*wish* to marry you."

Neala clamped her hands over her ears. "I will not listen!"

Apparently close to losing his temper, Winterton grabbed her by the shoulders. "Dammit, Miss Abercorn, I love you! I have loved you from the first moment I saw you. I cannot explain it all I know is that the moment I saw you, I felt something so strong it could not be denied. And I shall deny it no longer. wish to have you for my wife! I shall have you for my wife!"

"No! No!" Neala cried, terrified of hearing more.

Still holding her by the shoulders, the angry man seemed close to shaking her, so full of fury was the smoldering look in his eyes. "Why will you not listen to me? Am I such an ogre that you cannot bear to hear me speak of love? I have never said those words to another woman in the world, Miss Abercorn I love you!"

Abruptly, he released her and without another word, turned and stalked down the steep marble steps at his side.

Stunned, Neala watched the gentleman disappear into the shadows.

From the far corner of the terrace, she did not see the thin curl of grey smoke that slowly spiraled upward and drifted off into the night.

Seventeen

Neala was far too overset to return to the party. But before seeking solace in her own bedchamber, she searched out Diana in the ballroom and pleaded a megrim. Lord Brewster was no where to be seen, so she did not have the opportunity to bid him a good night before hurrying for the stairs.

Sinking to a cushion on the window seat in her room, she rested her throbbing head against the cool window pane. She had never felt so confused in her life. Why had Lord Winterton sought her out to confide in her? He had told her so *very* much tonight, the truth about his accident, the dangerous spy opera-tion he was investigating, and the secret meeting he was set to attend tonight at the inn. Worst of all—her stomach churned with heightened anxiety—he had told her he loved her.

Reaching to rub her aching temples, she fervently wished he had *not* found the courage to tell her that. It should be Lilibet who heard those cherished words from him, not her. It was Lilibet for whom the spell had been cast. Still . . . she recalled the time Lilibet, in a fit of anger, had tossed the bewitched gown to *her* . . . no, no! It could not be! The spell was not now work-ing in *her* favor! She would not believe it. Even though Lord Winterton had been the first man she had met after that . . . *no!* She would not contemplate such a possibility. The bewitched wedding dress had not been *officially* presented to her, it had been presented to Lilibet. That Lilibet had tossed it to her did not signify in the least. Lord Winterton was meant to wed her sister and that's all there was for it.

Fleetingly, Neala collected how very unhappy her Mama and Papa had been when Mama married against the spell. She would not let that happen to Lilibet. *She wouldn't!*

With fierce determination, she forced all thoughts of Lord Winterton and his ridiculous protestations of love from her mind. She would not think on the subject ever again. Her own path in life was set and she would follow it to the letter.

She jumped to her feet and began to stroll deliberately about the room. Very likely this lovely suite would one day be hers. The apartment was quite comfortable and she would be very happy here. Being wed to Lord Brewster could not be nearly so horrid as Lord Winterton seemed to think.

Suddenly, Neala became aware of her heart pounding frightfully loud. Very well, it was true that she did not love Lord Brewster *greatly,* but she did care for him. *Didn't she?* She waited, but when it seemed that no *honest* answer was forthcoming, she decided it was quite a silly question in the first place. Instead of refining further on it, she would retire for the night. Once she fell asleep, she could not continue to think about Lord Winterton and his fantastical notions of love.

As she was slipping out of her ballgown, the folded piece of paper that Lord Winterton had given her fell from her pocket to the floor. She bent to pick it up. And, contemplated reading it. Lord Winterton hadn't specifically said she should not read it, he had merely said she would not understand it.

Curiosity getting the better of her, Neala unfolded the wrinkled sheet and moving across the room, held it beneath the lamp . . . and saw, that . . . indeed, she could not make out a single word. The entire page was not only scribbled in French, it was also written in a strange sort of . . . gibberish. Oh, the letters were recognizable; there were A's and R's, and E's, but the words made no sense whatever.

Growing inordinately curious, Neala edged on to the chair beneath the lamp and continued to study the page. Other letters she saw, written in a different hand, had been scrawled in the spaces between the original lines, almost as if . . . someone

Lord Winterton perhaps, had been trying to unscramble the message. More intrigued than ever, Neala scampered to the little writing desk in the corner for a pencil and returning to the sofa, sat down again to see if she might figure out the mysterious code.

Following the pattern set by whomever had begun to decipher the message, she quickly replaced the rest of the A's with E's, the R's with I's, and so on. On another piece of paper, she wrote down the new words made from the new letters, however, even after doing all this, the note made as little sense as the original scribblings.

She tried several ways of rearranging the words, but her efforts were to no avail. Picking up the page again, she then noticed scratchings, which could be numerals, though they were all out of order, marked at the end of each line. Using them as a guide, she rearranged every word in every line according to the numbered sequence and was delighted to discover that she could now make out a good deal of the message!

Most of it had to do with British troop movements and the number of forces and the commanding officer's names. Realizing that she was actually holding a document containing government secrets that had fallen into enemy hands, Neala's heart began to pound with excitement. Having not yet decoded the post script, she diligently set about unscrambling it. That message was a bit different from the rest, there were no numbers at the end of the lines, and the best she could manage was something about a 'Tin Tree' being at the inn.

Tin Tree.

Tentrees!

Could it mean that Lord Tentrees was also involved in the spy operation? It was then that Neala recalled the strange comment the gentleman had made earlier that afternoon as they all sat about the drawing room expressing their hope that the rain would soon let up. Lord Tentrees had said *he* was "not thinking about the guests." He was thinking about *himself,* Neala decided, that tonight *he* must brave the inclement weather on hi way to the secret meeting at the inn!

Quaking with fear, Neala quickly redressed and scampere back downstairs to the ballroom. She would find Helene an question her about the whereabouts of her husband. Neala wa certain that Lord Tentrees would not still be at the ball. H would have already left for the inn where Lord Winterton wa headed. Helene might know the reason why.

Her heart in her throat, Neala entered the ballroom, scanning the roomful of now flushed but still smiling faces for Helene.

"Neala!" It was Lady Diana, from behind her. "You are feel ing better? Father was looking for you a moment ago. I daresay he was a bit off-put that you did not bid him a good night before you retired. Neala, you really should be more considerate i regard to Father's fee—"

"Have you seen Helene?"

"Helene? Not that I recall. Why?"

"I need to ask her about a . . . a particular part in the book she is reading."

"But I thought you had read the book."

"I have, but I . . . ummm . . . I wanted to know if she agrees with me about a certain passage."

"Now?"

"Indeed, now." Neala nodded eagerly. "I was thinking abou it now. If I wait until tomorrow, I fear I shall completely forget Are you quite sure you haven't seen her?"

"Still looking for Mrs. McGill, eh?" this from Lord Edward who had just walked up, carrying two glasses of champagne one in each hand. "Pray, do not bring the woman near me; a least, until I have set these glasses down. Here you are, Diana.'

"I was looking for Helene," Neala said, "or Lord Tentrees Have you seen either of them, Edward?"

Edward took a sip from his glass, then nodded. "Though i has been quite some time ago. They both retired early. Tentrees seemed not to be feeling well."

"I see. Well, in that case, I expect I shall also retire. Good night, again."

Lady Diana cast a bewildered look at Neala, as Neala scurried again for the stairs.

Perhaps it was a trifle improper of her, but she fully intended to rap at the door to the Tentrees suite.

As it turned out, she didn't have to. Upstairs in the corridor, she came face to face with Helene.

"I was coming to sit with you, Neala," the tall girl said. "Do you mind terribly?"

"Not at all. I wished to speak with you anyhow."

"Oh." Helene brightened, though Neala thought she seemed a trifle nervous, but did not press for an explanation just yet, not wanting to question the girl until they were alone in her bedchamber.

Once there, the two took seats opposite one another on the pair of green silk sofas before the hearth. At once, Helene began to speak. "I had thought that since you were set to—" she lowered her lashes "—marry an older gentleman, Neala, that perhaps we might become better friends."

"Hmmm, that is quite a good idea," Neala said, not questioning how Helene knew of her forthcoming nuptials. Apparently Lord Brewster was telling all and sundry. He had told Winterton. Abruptly, she said, "Helene, I simply must ask you something."

Helene leaned forward. "Anything, Neala."

"It's . . . about your husband. Is he . . . does he . . . is there the possibility that he might be involved in . . . seditious activity?"

Helene looked puzzled. "I'm not certain I understand what you mean."

"I mean espionage, Helene. It is very important that you tell me the truth. Lord Winterton's life may be at stake."

"Lord Winterton?"

Neala nodded, her expression fearful.

Suddenly, Helene burst into tears. "It's true . . . it's true,

Neala! I cannot bear it any longer. I have known for some time My husband is at a meeting now. I know not where. When he left, he said he meant to . . . to finish the job. Oh, Neala, what does it mean?"

Her heart thumping wildly, Neala sprang to her feet. "It might mean that he intends to *kill* Lord Winterton!"

"Oh, Neala! What shall we do?"

There was only one thing to do. She had to go to the inn and warn Lord Winterton before it was too late. He had no idea that Lord Tentrees meant to kill him. If he saw the gentleman, he might feel a false sense of security and walk right into the trap. She had to go. If Lord Winterton were killed, it would be her fault.

"I am going to warn him."

"Do you know where they are?"

Neala nodded. "Lord Winterton told me." Already, Neala was undoing the hooks of her ballgown. "Help me, please!"

Helene was on her feet in an instant, helping Neala out of the satin gown. "You cannot go alone, Neala!"

"Will you come with me?"

Helene drew in her breath. "Oh, I couldn't. My husband would forbid it. Are you certain you must go, Neala? Perhaps, he—"

"I must warn him, Helene. I have to go."

She hurriedly changed into her riding clothes, ran down the stairs and slipped out a side door that led to the stables. Completely unprepared for the feeling of exhilaration that surged through her, she realized suddenly how very unlike herself she was behaving. Shy Neala Abercorn was never one to take action. No, she had always been content to read about daring knights and fearless heroines who against all odds managed to accomplish miraculous deeds. But, here she was, treading that thin line of danger herself in a race against time so that she might save the life of the one man she lov—that is—she felt her cheeks begin to burn—the life of a gentleman she cared deeply about.

Climbing astride her favorite mare, she dug in the heels of

her boots, urging the animal beneath her to gallop forward. Flying over the grounds, she was grateful for the brilliant light of the moon that lit her way, at least, until she entered the forest, though even there she was able to thread her way among the panorama of dark trees silhouetted against the pale sky. Once she emerged on the other side of the thicket, she and her mount flew as one across the damp meadow, Neala feeling as if she *were* the wind, racing swiftly through the night on a golden steed.

In no time, she came upon the quaint little inn, situated exactly as she remembered, and as Lord Winterton had said, at the juncture of three roads. Neala reined in her mount, electing for the moment to remain shielded behind a protective stand of gnarled old oaks. She saw a pair of lathered horses tethered in front of the inn, but the saddles and equipage looked unfamiliar. Perhaps Lord Winterton and the authorities had not yet arrived. Through the dense fog that was beginning to swirl around the lower half of the timbered building, she made out a single lamp flickering from one cloudy window pane. An ominous shiver ran up her spine. Feeling her heart suddenly begin to beat erratically, she drew in several long breaths to calm herself.

"We are not afraid," she murmured to her mare, "we are *not* afraid!"

As if understanding her words completely, the horse shook its long mane from side to side.

Neala reached absently to pat the animal's damp neck.

"We shall do as Lord Winterton said, we shall carry on in the face of fear as if fear does not exist."

Drawing in another deep breath, she straightened her shoulders and cocked an ear to listen. But, apart from a gentle chorus of night sounds—a dog barking somewhere in the distance, the wind rustling through the treetops—Neala heard nothing. After a long day of loud thunder and hard rain, the countryside had once again become peaceful and serene, the night air clean and fresh-smelling.

Not quite sure what she ought to do next, Neala decided to

venture closer to the inn. Perhaps it was Lord Winterton inside, and the spies not yet arrived. Slipping noiselessly to the ground, she led her horse across the muddy road and hurriedly tied the ribbons to a post.

Advancing up the path to the doorway of the inn, she heard the muffled sound of men's voices coming from inside, and paused to listen. Unable to discern Lord Winterton's deep baritone among them, a fresh flicker of apprehension coursed through her. Perhaps if she entered the inn from the rear, she could get a peek at the gentlemen inside. If Lord Winterton were not among them, she could scamper back outside and wait for him here.

Retracing her steps, she picked her way across the cluttered yard to the side, stepping over puddles of rain water, lifting her long skirt as she tramped through patches of high grass and around piles of assorted debris on her way around the inn. At the rear of the building, the silence seemed unusually deep, causing Neala's nerves to tighten with tension.

Glancing about, she saw that the ancient wooden door at the back of the ramshackle building was standing ajar. She thought it odd that the yard seemed so very quiet and that neither the innkeep nor the cook were anywhere about.

Slipping cautiously through the opened door, she blinked to grow accustomed to the dimness inside. A fire in an open grate had nearly gone out, leaving only red-hot embers to cast a reddish glow on the bare stone floor. Hanging from the crane over the fire was a black pot containing some sort of meat stew, Neala judged from the smell. She caught sight of a poker, a pair of fire-dogs, and a rush-light holder leaning haphazardly against the blackened front of the hearth. Nearby, an orange cat lay curled up asleep.

Neala took a small step into the room and the cat stirred, arching its back lazily, then settling down to watch her. Neala edged along a wooden table standing in the center of the room. On it was an assortment of crockery, a pitcher, an iron skillet and a stack of pewter plates. She was aware of shelves lining the wall opposite the fireplace, but it was too dark to see what was on them.

Satisfied that no one, other than the orange cat, was about, Neala scampered the rest of the way across the kitchen to the door. Tiptoeing through it, she discovered that it gave on to the hallway that led straight to the common room. Moving noiselessly to the wide opening, she hugged the rough-hewn door-jamb, and hardly daring to breathe, stole a quick peek around it.

Two large men were seated at a small table in the far corner of the deserted room. Speaking in low tones, every now and again, the men glanced toward the darkened hallway where Neala stood. The men were shabbily dressed, both looked unkempt and about neither was the look of well-bred gentility that Neala was accustomed to seeing in gentlemen of the *ton.* An icy knot of fear formed in her stomach when she spotted the pair of large ugly pistols lying on the table in front of them.

Her heart thumping wildly in her breast, she darted back to the kitchen and was halfway across the room when her boot came down upon something soft. The screeching caterwaul that suddenly pierced the stillness was so shrill that Neala also cried out.

"Oh!" She lurched forward and this time trod upon the cat's tail.

Me-ow-w-w!

Neala fell against the table, knocking over the jug that stood there. With a crash, it toppled over and a pool of glistening white milk began to form near the edge and then to drip, drip, drip onto the floor. Already hearing the thunder of footfalls in the corridor, Neala knew it would be mere seconds before she was joined in the kitchen by the two men from the common room.

Having brought nothing with which to protect herself, she grabbed the iron skillet that sat upon the table and hastened to flatten herself against the closest darkened wall.

In an instant, one of the men appeared in the room, holding

a lantern high above his head. Upon spotting the orange cat busily lapping up the spilled milk, the scowl on the man's face relaxed a bit and he knelt to pet the cat, calling in a thick French accent to his companion, " 'Es only a cat, Andre."

It was the first time Neala had clearly heard either of the men speak. This one was obviously French. Was he the very French-man who had shot Lord Winterton? An uncontrollable rage boiled white-hot within her. Without taking thought, she made a lunge for the large man whose back was toward her.

Whomp! She let the skillet fall heavily against the man's low-ered head. Without so much as a squeak, he fell unconscious to the floor, but the lantern in his hand was like a clarion call to his companion when it tumbled with a clatter to the floor beside him. Fearing fire, Neala dropped the skillet in order to right the lantern.

"Jacque!" came a shout from the corridor.

Neala's head jerked up. With fear pounding wildly in her ears, she scampered again for a shadowy place near the hearth, her fingers reaching this time to curl about the iron poker lean-ing there.

"Jacque!" the second Frenchman called as he thundered into the room. Spotting his felled companion upon the floor, he dropped to his knees beside him.

It was the unguarded moment Neala was looking for. Both hands holding the poker raised before her, she made a mad dash for the kneeling Frenchman.

He must have heard her footfalls on the stone floor, for he lifted an angry gaze to search out the intruder. At that exact instant, Neala took a wild swing at him with the poker, but the man was far too quick for her. One raised hand forestalled the blow. Hanging onto the sharp end of the metal rod, he fastened a narrowed gaze upon Neala and rose angrily to his feet. But, not looking where he was going, his next step landed smack in the middle of the milk that pooled on the floor. When his foot slid out from under him, Neala found herself once more in sole control of the poker. She didn't waste a second whacking the man across the chest and when he lurched forward, hitting him once again square across the shoulders.

She watched him sprawl limply across the body of the first man, then suddenly, the dark inn came alive with noise and confusion. Neala spun around as four men burst into the room, two from the opened back door, two more clambering through the opening to the hallway. One man carried a raised lantern, its bright light swinging to and fro as he ran.

At once, Neala recognized Lord Winterton.

And he, her.

"Miss Abercorn!" he sputtered. "What are *you* doing here!"

"Sir!" Neala was never so happy to see a familiar face in her life.

"Answer me!" he demanded. "What are you doing here?"

Neala's eyes were wild. "I—I—"

"Look here, Major," one of the men said, having discovered both the Frenchmen lying unconscious on the floor. "Looks as if the young lady has made herself useful."

Winterton gazed at the spectacle on the floor, then back at Neala, who was still holding the iron poker in one hand. "Well, I'll be damned, Miss Abercorn, did you—?" Suddenly, he threw his head back and burst out laughing. "Why, you meddlesome little—"

It was not the reaction Neala expected. "I only came to save your life!" she blurted out. Her lips tight, she flung the poker to the floor before she lost her temper entirely and walloped the laughing Lord Winterton with it.

"You'd best get your lady friend out of here, Winterton," another of the men said sternly. "These jackals are likely to come 'round any second."

Winterton moved to grasp Neala by the wrist. "Come on, you little minx, you've no business being here."

Her breasts heaving with fury, Neala tried to fling the gentleman's hand from her arm. "I can find my own way back!" she cried, struggling to sweep past him and escape through the opened back door.

"Oh, no, you don't." With his good arm, Winterton scooped her up off her feet and carried her, wriggling and protesting, back through the darkened inn and out the front door. With some assistance from his weakened left arm, he plopped her onto the back of her mare and flung the ribbons up after her.

"Tentrees!" he called into the darkness. "See that this little rapscallion makes it back to Brewster Hall unharmed! We've everything under control inside."

"Very well, sir."

Neala heard the older gentleman's disinterested reply as well as the sound of his horses hooves approaching from behind her. Still reeling with anger, she snatched up the ribbons and spun her horse about, not waiting for anyone to escort her anywhere.

Racing headlong into the night, she had never felt so furious in her life. Furthermore, she did not care a whit if she ever saw Lord Winterton's handsome face again! She had risked her life for him and all he could do was laugh! The ungrateful man could go straight to bloody hell for all she cared! She never wanted to see him again.

Eighteen

It did not surprise Neala the next day to find that Lord Winterton had not returned to Brewster Hall during the night.

Nearly all of the houseguests had slept late, including those who had been invited to stay over, in order to be on hand the following morning for Lady Diana's wedding.

"Lord Winterton has returned to London," Lord Tentrees announced after everyone had assembled in the drawing room to await luncheon, which for most was serving as the first meal of the day. "The gentleman had an important business engagement that required his immediate attention," he added dryly.

The news about Winterton was met with some curiosity but, in typical fashion, Lord Tentrees declined to enlarge upon the matter, so after several people had registered their remarks regarding the state of Lord Winterton's health and others had marveled upon his ability to travel so soon after his accident, the subject was summarily dropped.

Neala had not slept at all well the previous night. Aside from feeling intensely mortified with herself over behaving in so foolhardy a manner the previous evening, her anger with Lord Winterton was still at the boiling point. So far as she was concerned, it was a good thing for him that he wasn't there.

She determined now to put the unfortunate episode completely from mind and perhaps never to think on it again. With calculated deliberateness, she entered into a light-hearted conversation with Emma Chetwith and two other women from neighboring estates. Her plan was succeeding very well until

Helene drew her aside only moments before the entire company was to file into the dining hall for the noon meal.

"My husband and I reached an understanding last evening, Neala dear, and I have you to thank for it." Helene's smile was considerably brighter than usual. "When I confronted Robert, my husband, last night about his involvement with the—" she lowered her voice "—espionage activity, he was more than happy to take me into his confidence."

"I see," Neala murmured, pleased that Helene was feeling better but not the least anxious to discuss further anything that concerned Lord Winterton, as this most assuredly did.

Helene's eyes were sparkling. "You can imagine how thrilled I was to learn that my husband bore no ill-will toward Lord Winterton! He was quite shocked that I thought he meant to kill the gentleman. You see, Robert, has been working closely with the war minister, trying to stem a veritable flood of government documents that have been disappearing from beneath everyone's noses. Robert had not told me about the unfortunate business because he thought I would not be interested. But, of course, I am. I am quite interested in political concerns. Though, I had never told Robert that until last night." Helene smiled again. "At any rate, apparently, the riddle was solved to everyone's satisfaction last evening, and now all is well again. Thank you so much, Nealie, dear. I feel ever so much better!"

Neala managed a weak smile. "I am happy for you, Helene."

"We shall become fast friends, Neala, I am certain of it!"

At that moment, the girls were interrupted when a somewhat solemn Lord Brewster stepped up to escort Neala into the dining hall.

Seated to his left, she ate the light meal in relative silence but, near the end of it, leaned over to address the elderly gentleman. "I should like a private word with you, my lord, if you don't mind."

"A private word, eh? Very well, Miss Abercorn. I will receive you in my study this afternoon."

Once there, Neala told the still long-faced gentleman that she wished to be married as soon as possible once they had all returned to London.

"As soon as possible, Miss Abercorn?" Lord Brewster's tone lifted.

"Indeed, my lord. The sooner, the better."

"Well, then—" the gentleman's puffy face brightened, "I shall procure a special license for us post haste, if that will please you, my dear."

Neala's small smile did not quite reach her eyes. "It would please me very much, my lord."

Beaming, Lord Brewster moved as if to clasp her to him, then dismissed the idea and instead, said gently, "When we are alone together, Miss Abercorn, it would be quite proper for you to address me as Nigel. And, I shall call you Neala . . . or wife, whichever you prefer."

Neala flinched. "Neala will suit nicely."

"Neala, it is, then!" He did reach for one of her hands and squeezed it warmly between his own.

That night at dinner, Lord Brewster took the liberty of announcing their betrothal to the others. Afterward, Neala shyly smiled her way through a jubilant round of congratulations and well wishes. No one was more thrilled that Lady Diana; no one more surprised than Emma Chetwith.

"Why, Nealie, you little sly-boots! I had no idea that you and Diana's father were . . . well, are you certain it is what you want, Nealie dear?"

Lifting her chin, Neala nodded tightly.

The next morning, she carefully schooled her features into a pleasant smile in order to get through Diana and Edward's large wedding, held at Gloucester Cathedral.

The day dawned a bit overcast, but by time the huge party arrived in Gloucester, the sky had turned a brilliant blue with billowy white clouds floating lazily across it. The interior of the church was decorated with banks of sweet smelling roses that were tied with pink ribbon streamers. Diana looked radiant in the lovely white satin wedding gown that Neala and her mother had fashioned for her.

Both Neala stood alongside Diana at the altar, listening attentively as the young couple repeated their vows. Following the ceremony, an open laundau, pulled by four white horses and driven by postillions in gold and white livery with white silk hats, carried the newly wed pair to a spacious assembly room where a sumptuous wedding breakfast was served.

It was a beautiful wedding celebration. And, with the exception of Mrs. McGill spilling punch on her husband's trousers, nothing went awry. All in all, Neala was glad to have been on hand to share the joyous occasion with Diana.

"We shall do it all again for you and Father," Diana confided to Neala, only moments before the bride and groom climbed once again into the carriage and set off for an extended wedding trip to Bath.

Later that afternoon, after all the local guests had departed, Neala and the rest of the houseparty set out for London.

Upon arriving back in Town, it both pleased and surprised her that Lord Brewster insisted upon seeing her to her door and consulting at once with her mother in regard to their forthcoming wedding plans.

"We cannot publish our intent to marry until permission has been expressly granted by your mother, my dear," he said, as he and Neala made their way up the stairs to the tiny flat.

"I can assure you . . . Nigel," Neala barely whispered his name, "Mama will be pleased beyond measure when she hears our news."

Pleased beyond measure was putting it mildly.

"You have made me the happiest of mothers!" Lady Abercorn exclaimed, enfolding Neala in a crushing hug the second Lord Brewster was out of earshot. "What a good 'un, 'ye are, Nealie girl! Tell us everything that transpired while you were in the country!"

"I only want to hear about Lord Winterton," Lilibet said, pursing her lips.

Neala obliged them both, skimming lightly over the parts that involved herself and *him*.

"But, Lord Winterton's shoulder has mended by now, has it not?" Lilibet cried, upon learning that the war hero had been shot. "Oh, I can hardly wait to see him! Did he say when he meant to call, Neala? Did he?"

Neala shook her head, a part of her hoping that the gentleman would *never* call, while another part had begun to feel a bit . . . well, anxious to see him. But, of course, she was being silly. Why should she want to see him again? Still, as the days passed, and Lilibet's impatience with Lord Winterton's absence grew more pronounced, Neala found herself echoing her sister's disappointed wails every bit as loud, if only to herself.

Alone in her bedchamber at night, she tried valiantly to ignore the gnawing hunger she felt in her heart to see him again, but as the feeling deepened, it finally became impossible to ignore. Unable to sleep most nights, she paced the length of her small room, recalling again and again all that Lord Winterton had said to her during their time together in the country. Most especially she dwelt upon what he had said that last evening when he took her onto the terrace. Vividly, she recalled him saying he could "deny his feelings for her no longer."

Was she reaching that same point?

If it were true, the very thought terrified her.

Yet, deep in her heart, she finally came to realize that her feelings for Lord Winterton were stronger than anything she had ever felt before. She had never met a man like him. With him, she felt *alive*. He drew her out as no one ever had. He listened to her, sought out her ideas and opinions. And, best of all, or perhaps, worst of all, he had said he loved her. Was it true? Did he love her?

They had had such grand times together—the picnic on the River Wye, the quiet moments when they had just sat and talked. And before that, their drive to Green Park. Even the night at the opera stood out in Neala's mind as wonderfully exciting, especially now that the gentleman had told her the real reason he had been forced to abandon her that night.

Oh, she fervently hoped he was all right now, that nothing untoward had happened to him on his journey back to London.

Just thinking about the gentleman made Neala feel breathless and trembly inside. She could not stop thinking about how he had *singled* her out so many times in the country. And how he made her feel *desired*. No man, most especially not Lord Brewster, had *ever* made her feel that way. Just recalling the feel of Lord Winterton's lips on hers made Neala's cheeks burn with fire all over again.

Oh! She covered her face with both hands. How could she marry Lord Brewster feeling as she did about Lord Winterton? As the long days—and even longer nights—dragged by, the yearning she felt in her heart to see him again grew to such excruciating heights she thought she might perish from the sheer pain of it.

But, still, the gentleman did not come.

"I can't think why Lord Winterton has not come to call," Lilibet whined, for the tenth time in as many days.

"I am certain there is some plausible explanation, my dear," Lady Abercorn said, her faith in the wedding spell apparently as strong as ever. "He will come."

"Lord Brewster has not called either," Neala said, her tone a trifle defensive, "and we are set to become man and wife inside a week."

Lady Abercorn did not look up from her sewing. In the past ten days, she had hurriedly selected fabric and notions to make a new wedding gown for Neala, and something of a *trousseau.* "Your time in the country has changed you, Neala," she said pensively. "You are not nearly so shy and retiring as you used to be. Are you quite certain you have told us everything that transpired?"

Neala glanced sharply at her Mama. The three women were

scattered about the parlor that evening after supper, Grandma O'Grady having already gone to bed. "I have told you all that I can recall," Neala replied evenly. "It was not a particularly eventful visit."

"But, Lord Winterton was there! How could anything be *un*-eventful where he is concerned? Can you think of nothing else to tell me about him?"

Feeling hot color flood her cheeks, Neala sprang to her feet and began to pace before the hearth. "I have told you everything, Lilibet. Must you persist in bringing that gentleman's name up at every turn?"

Neala's lips were tight as she folded her arms across her chest and continued to pace. Only when she noticed her mama staring at her oddly, did she cease her walking up and down.

"On second thought," Lady Abercorn said, "Neala is not obliged to tell us everything. She is soon to become a married woman and as such, will have a life of her own." A pause ensued. "Did Lord Brewster indicate where the two of you will reside after you are married?"

Neala suppressed the urge to request that Mama also leave off speaking about Lord Brewster. "He . . . Nigel did not say. I expect we shall divide our time between Brewster Hall and the house here in London."

"Nigel!" Lilibet giggled.

Lady Abercorn was watching her eldest daughter closely. "Well, I am certain you shall be very happy, dear."

Neala wasn't certain of anything of the kind. If the way she felt now were any indication, she would never be happy. Not *ever!* Hastening to excuse herself for the night, she hurried to her own room again. And, found that, as usual, once she was in bed, she was unable to fall asleep.

As her wedding day drew even nearer, her frame of mind worsened. To the point that she continually felt irritable and was prickly to a fault.

"I shall be glad when you are married," Lilibet said, "you are as grouchy as an old bear!"

"The gel is eager to be with the man she loves," Grandma O'Grady remarked wisely, rocking back and forth in her chair in the parlor. "Neala's a good 'un, she is."

Neala was not a good 'un. And she hated the idea of marrying Lord Brewster. The announcement of their betrothal had at last appeared in the newspapers, the delay for that finally explained in a franked letter she received from Diana.

"Edward and I are *deliriously* happy! Hope you don't mind, Neala, but I have asked Father to wait until our return to London before deciding upon a time and place for your wedding."

When Diana finally returned to town, arrangements had subsequently been made for the ceremony to be held in the small Lady Chapel at St. Luke's church, with a reception to follow.

The wedding was set for tomorrow at noon.

Neala wondered what would happen if the bride refused to attend.

Following supper on that last evening, Grandma O'Grady retired early and Lilibet soon after.

"Well, I expect I shall also turn in," Lady Abercorn said, shaking out the garment she had been stitching a hem into. "I can think of nothing else to do before tomorrow." Gathering her sewing things, she stood up. Near the door, she turned to Neala, who had spent the entire evening curled up on one end of the sofa, pretending to read. "Don't linger too late, Neala dear."

A few steps closer to the door, Lady Abercorn paused and turned again. "Mustn't take on so, Neala. Marriage isn't all bad. I assure you, having plenty to spend during the day will more than make up for . . . whatever discomfort you experience at night."

Neala managed a wan smile. "Good night, Mama."

Nothing could make up for the way she felt now, Neala thought, turning again to her book.

When, at last, she heard the sound of Mama's bedroom door closing, she rose to her feet and wandered to the small window at the top of the room. Pulling the curtain aside, she gazed out . . . only to vividly recall another time she had stood here, watching Lord Winterton climb atop his curricle and drive haltingly away.

A sad smile crossed her face. With a heavy sigh, she returned again to the sofa and picked up her book. But, it was no use. The words merely blurred before her eyes.

She went to the window again.

The street below was deserted. The only movements she could detect were the flicker of the street lamp and wisps of fog floating low over the damp cobbles. Then, like a phantom growing out of the mist, she saw a lone carriage approach. Breathlessly, she watched it draw nearer, then clatter noisily away.

With another sigh, she returned again to the sofa and sat down, when suddenly, an odd sound caught her attention. It sounded much like a shower of raindrops pelting the window pane, but it was not raining outside. She listened, and the sound came again.

Scampering back to the window, Neala drew aside the curtain and looked out.

And could not believe what she saw.

A gentleman . . . *yes!* it was Lord Winterton! standing on the flagway below, a handful of pebbles in his palm.

"Miss Abercorn!" he called up to her.

Flinging up the sash, Neala leaned out.

"I have come to save your life!" he called, the smile on his face so bright it appeared dazzling in the dim light.

"You have . . . what?" she called back.

"Come down and I shall explain!"

Her heart pounding wildly in her breast, Neala turned to do the gentleman's bidding, then turned abruptly back to the window. "I shall just go and get my bonnet!" she called out.

Lord Winterton laughed aloud. "Forget your bonnet, you silly goose! Come down at once!"

Neala flew to the door of the flat and hurried down the darkened stairwell. Lord Winterton met her on the flagway below.

Flinging his arms about her, he lifted her off the ground and twirled her around and around. "I came as fast as I could, little one," he said, setting her down on her feet again. "Thank God, I am not too late!"

"Too late for what?"

"To make you my bride! And, I warn you, I shall not take no for an answer this time!"

"But, I cannot marry you, sir."

"Of course, you can, and you shall! My military assignment is done, and today I sold my commission. I am a free man. We shall be married at once!"

"But, I cannot marry you," Neala said again.

Lord Winterton gazed quizzically at her. "Why ever not, dear one? You love me, do you not?"

Her brown eyes round, Neala swallowed. "I—I—"

"There! I knew it!"

"I have confessed to nothing, my lord."

"You have confessed plenty! You risked your pretty neck to save my life, didn't you? And, now that I think on it, I have yet to thank you properly!" He moved as if to gather her into his arms and kiss her, but Neala thrust her chin up and pulled away from him.

"Is that why you laughed at me that night?" she demanded.

"Laughed?" Winterton threw his head back and did just that again. "What a sight you presented! Those two scallawags didn't come around for hours. For a little thing, you've a mighty blow, Miss Abercorn."

Neala cocked her head to one side. "You certainly appeared to be laughing at me," she said self-righteously. "The same as you are doing now."

"So, I am. But it is because I am so pleased to see you!" He reached again to take her by the shoulders, his dark eyes intent upon her lips. "I love you and I want to make you my bride."

"I have said I cannot marry you, Lord Winterton."

"Of course, you can. I shall obtain a special license for us and we shall be—"

"No!" Neala jerked from his grasp. "I cannot marry you!" Turning her face away, she felt her chin begin to tremble and hot tears to well up in her eyes. "I cannot marry you," she mouthed again, the truth of her words causing a lump the size of Gibraltar to form in her throat.

Tilting her chin to look at him, Lord Winterton's tone was gentle. "You are crying, my darling? Why?"

Hearing his voice so full of solicitation for her feelings brought a rush of fresh tears to Neala's eyes. She squeezed them shut in order to halt the flow of moisture that threatened to run in torrents down her cheeks.

"You do love me, do you not?" he asked gently.

Neala knew she could deny her feelings no longer. She *did* love him. *She did!* Ever so slowly, she nodded her head. "Ye-s-s, I do love you. I do."

"So," he said softly. "There it is." He moved again to gather her into his arms, but again Neala wrested away.

"No! You do not understand, I cannot marry you!"

He stared at her in total confusion. "I fail to see why you persist so strongly in refusing my offer. Is it that you believe you cannot cry off your pledge to Lord Brewster? Because, if it is, I assure you, that can be quite easily taken care of."

Neala turned a tear-stained face upward. "H-How?" She was quite interested to know how she might cry off at this late date, herself.

Winterton shrugged. "Simple. I had dinner with Brewster tonight. I thought he seemed rather glum for a gentleman about to be married. He finally confessed to me that he had overheard a certain . . . *private* conversation between you and me. Seems he was having a smoke on the terrace that night, in a far corner. Said he could not help overhearing us. He also confessed that he had begun to suspect that you and I were . . . well, so, you see, my dear. Brewster is too much the gentleman to stand in our way, especially when he knows that we care so deeply about one another." Winterton's dark head shook from side to side.

"And I *do* care for you, my dearest girl. Fact is, I have loved you from the first moment I saw you."

Neala's heart sank. So, it *was* the wedding spell. Lord Winterton had been the first man *she* had met after Lilibet had flung the bewitched wedding gown to her. Lord Winterton did not *really* love her. He had been bewitched. She could not look at him.

His dark eyes clouded. "What is it, Neala? What is the trouble now?"

A hot tear trickled down her cheek. "You do not love me, sir," she said in a small voice. "You have been . . . bewitched."

"Bewitched?" A half-smile appeared on Lord Winterton's handsome face. "You had best explain that to me, my dear."

Neala swallowed hard, then plunged in. She told Lord Winterton the entire story, not omitting a thing. She began with Grandma O'Grady's arrival and moved on to the birthday present. She told him about the wee people and the fairy dust and how Lilibet had refused to accept the bewitched wedding gown and how, in a fit of anger, she had tossed the ancient dress to Neala.

"So, you see, you do not really love me, sir; it was the wedding spell. Mama says, once the spell has been cast, it cannot fail. You have been bewitched, Lord Winterton."

Winterton was having a difficult time containing his mirth. His chest was heaving with repressed laughter and his eyes were crinkling at the corners. "I am sorry, Miss Abercorn," he said, finally letting go and roaring with laughter. He laughed 'til tears rolled down his cheeks. When he had calmed down, he managed, "That is the silliest piece of fustian I have ever heard, Miss Abercorn. But, the truth is, I *have* been bewitched, not by some silly leprechaun, but by you! You never fail to delight me, my dear!"

Though Neala tried, she could not resist his advance this time. Winterton hugged her fiercely to his chest, laughing all the while.

"I have never met so charming a young lady," he said, amusement still coloring his tone as his lips brushed the soft curls of her hair. "Even if Grandma O'Grady's wedding spell were true, it wouldn't make the slightest bit of difference to me, I would still want to marry you!"

Neala stiffened in his arms. "You would?"

She felt his strong nod against her head. "Indeed, I would. As I said in the beginning, I have never met a young lady who would risk her life to save mine. For that reason alone, I love you beyond reason. Now, will you have me?"

Neala could not believe her ears. He *did* love her! Feeling the last vestige of her resistance toward him melt away, she both smiled and nodded her assent. "Yes," she cried, "yes, I will marry you. I love you dearly, Lord Winterton."

"Trench," he corrected.

"Trench," she murmured. "But," she drew back to look up at him, "are you certain that Lord Brewster will understand?"

Winterton's dark eyes smiled down at her. "If he does not, I can always send for you to come and save my life."

"And, I would! I should come at once! Why, that night at the inn was the most exhilarating experience of my life. I confess, I have never felt so a-tremor!"

A dark brow lifted. "Never?"

Slowly lowering his head, Lord Winterton settled his sensuous mouth upon Neala's parted lips and did not release her until she had begun to tremble in his arms.

"Well, hardly ever," Neala murmured breathlessly. She sank again into his arms; certain, at last, that the man she loved with all her heart had not been bewitched by an Irish wedding spell, but that he loved her every bit as much as she loved him.

Epilogue

Notice in THE LONDON TIMES, August, 1813.

Miss Neala Abercorn, daughter of the late Sir Richard and Lady Abercorn, and Major Trench Lambert, Viscount Winterton were united in holy wedlock this day in St. Luke's Cathedral in London. The bride wore a peculiar gown of ivory silk, featuring long puffed and banded sleeves, the bodice trimmed with row upon row of antique blonde lace. The flounced skirt was dotted with sparkles, the likes of which have never been seen before, the hem was adorned with embroidered rose petals. It is believed that the unusual design of the bride's dress heralds a return to the styles of antiquity in a young lady's choice of wedding attire.

Dear Reader,

If you are like me, you also feel an overwhelming longing to experience life as it was in the romantic time-period known as the Regency. Then, a real man was a gentleman, right down to his polished Hessians, and a proper young lady still blushed when caught staring overlong at milord's broad shoulders—not to mention his thigh-hugging inexpressibles!

For me, the pull was so great I simply had to delve deeper, to learn more about the past I found so intriguing. Not even travelling to London, or visiting Brighton and Bath, was enough to satisfy me. I had to know more! From this longing grew *The Regency Plume,* a bi-monthly newsletter dedicated to accurately depicting life as it was in Regency England.

Each issue of *The Regency Plume Newsletter* is full of fascinating articles penned by your favorite Regency romance authors. If you'd like to join me and the hundreds of other Regency romance fans who experience Prinny's England via *The Regency Plume,* send a stamped, self-addressed envelope to me, Marilyn Clay, c/o *The Regency Plume,* Dept. 711-D-NW, Ardmore, Oklahoma 73401. I'll be happy to send you more information and a subscription form. I look forward to hearing from each and every one of you! In the meantime, I hope you enjoyed reading BEWITCHING LORD WINTERTON, and will look for BRIGHTON BEAUTY when it comes out next year!

Sincerely,

Marilyn Clay

ZEBRA REGENCIES ARE THE TALK OF THE TON!

A REFORMED RAKE (4499, $3.99)
by Jeanne Savery

After governess Harriet Cole helped her young charge flee to France—and the designs of a despicable suitor, more trouble soon arrived in the person of a London rake. Sir Frederick Carrington insisted on providing safe escort back to England. Harriet deemed Carrington more dangerous than any band of brigands, but secretly relished matching wits with him. But after being taken in his arms for a tender kiss, she found herself wondering—*could* a lady find love with an irresistible rogue?

A SCANDALOUS PROPOSAL (4504, $4.99)
by Teresa DesJardien

After only two weeks into the London season, Lady Pamela Premington has already received her first offer of marriage. If only it hadn't come from the *ton's* most notorious rake, Lord Marchmont. Pamela had already set her sights on the distinguished Lieutenant Penford, who had the heroism and honor that made him the ideal match. Now she had to keep from falling under the spell of the seductive Lord so she could pursue the man more worthy of her love. Or was he?

A LADY'S CHAMPION (4535, $3.99)
by Janice Bennett

Miss Daphne, art mistress of the Selwood Academy for Young Ladies, greeted the notion of ghosts haunting the academy with skepticism. However, to avoid rumors frightening off students, she found herself turning to Mr. Adrian Carstairs, sent by her uncle to be her "protector" against the "ghosts." Although, Daphne would accept no interference in her life, she *would* accept aid in exposing any spectral spirits. What she never expected was for Adrian to expose the secret wishes of her hidden heart . . .

CHARITY'S GAMBIT (4537, $3.99)
by Marcy Stewart

Charity Abercrombie reluctantly embarks on a London season in hopes of making a suitable match. However she cannot forget the mysterious Dominic Castille—and the kiss they shared—when he fell from a tree as she strolled through the woods. Charity does not know that the dark and dashing captain harbors a dangerous secret that will ensnare them both in its web—leaving Charity to risk certain ruin and losing the man she so passionately loves . . .

Available wherever paperbacks are sold, or order direct from the Publisher. Send cover price plus 50¢ per copy for mailing and handling to Penguin USA, P.O. Box 999, c/o Dept. 17109, Bergenfield, NJ 07621. Residents of New York and Tennessee must include sales tax. DO NOT SEND CASH.

Taylor—made Romance From Zebra Books

WHISPERED KISSES (3830, $4.99/5.99)
Beautiful Texas heiress Laura Leigh Webster never imagined that her biggest worry on her African safari would be the handsome Jace Elliot, her tour guide. Laura's guardian, Lord Chadwick Hamilton, warns her of Jace's dangerous past; she simply cannot resist the lure of his strong arms and the passion of his *Whispered Kisses*.

KISS OF THE NIGHT WIND (3831, $4.99/$5.99)
Carrie Sue Strover thought she was leaving trouble behind her when she deserted her brother's outlaw gang to live her life as schoolmarm Carolyn Starns. On her journey, her stagecoach was attacked and she was rescued by handsome T.J. Rogue. T.J. plots to have Carrie lead him to her brother's cohorts who murdered his family. T.J., however, soon succumbs to the beautiful runaway's charms and loving caresses.

FORTUNE'S FLAMES (3825, $4.99/$5.99)
Impatient to begin her journey back home to New Orleans, beautiful Maren James was furious when Captain Hawk delayed the voyage by searching for stowaways. Impatience gave way to uncontrollable desire once the handsome captain searched *her* cabin. He was looking for illegal passengers; what he found was wild passion with a woman he knew was unlike all those he had known before!

PASSIONS WILD AND FREE (3828, $4.99/$5.99)
After seeing her family and home destroyed by the cruel and hateful Epson gang, Randee Hollis swore revenge. She knew she found the perfect man to help her—gunslinger Marsh Logan. Not only strong and brave, Marsh had the ebony hair and light blue eyes to make Randee forget her hate and seek the love and passion that only he could give her.

Available wherever paperbacks are sold, or order direct from the Publisher. Send cover price plus 50¢ per copy for mailing and handling to Penguin USA, P.O. Box 999, c/o Dept. 17109, Bergenfield, NJ 07621. Residents of New York and Tennessee must include sales tax. DO NOT SEND CASH.